Skeleton Key

Nicki Harris

Copyright © 2023 Nicki Harris

All rights reserved.

ISBN: 9798852399106

DEDICATION

This book is wholeheartedly dedicated to my amazing Stud Hubs, who dug this seventeen-year-old manuscript out of the abyss of our attic and unceremoniously plopped it in my lap with the question : "When are you going to finish this thing?" You forced me to face my fears of failure and rejection to complete a project that meant so much to me…Now, look what you've done.
Sigh…You started a series.
Thank you for believing in me, encouraging me, pushing me, pissing me off, and for never allowing me to give up on my dreams.

I love you endlessly.

CONTENTS

Acknowledgments   i

This book contains :

An UNGODLY amount of chapters.

You're Welcome.

ACKNOWLEDGMENTS

I would like to acknowledge several people here. Firstly, Sue Anne Decker. Girl, you edited the first half of this stuff and then I filed it away. Probably because I was afraid to read your critique. But, seventeen years later, as I read through the pages to re-familiarize myself with the story I began, your notes were full of love and expertise. I'm sorry I never told you thank you. You were on point, and I was a chicken.

To my mom, who instilled in me a love for literature and writing. You always encouraged me to follow this avenue and were...and always will be... my biggest fan. Thank you for believing in me and for being the first to buy this book...And also for revealing to me the mysteries of failed uploads and sending me a detailed list of edits to make. GOD BLESS YOUR SOUL, WOMAN. You saved me a lot of embarrassment. I love you forever.

To my children and bonus children, thank you for putting up with the countless hours of "OH MY GOD! WOULD YOU PLEASE BE QUIET?!" and all of the missed time together as I hammered through the completion of this first book of many. I promise I won't be the wicked witch of the south next go'round...That's a lie. I probably will be. We all know it. Thank you for loving me and tolerating the hurricane that is your mother. You all have my heart.

Babe, I already dedicated this book to you. Don't push it. It's your fault I'm typing this.

CHAPTER ONE

Angry black clouds rolled in from the distant horizon. The breeze that had lovingly caressed ancient, craggy limbs and sent eager autumn dancers to their final resting places earlier, now buffeted those same limbs violently, threatening to tear them from their homes. A lone woman stood on the balcony of a majestic southern mansion staring out at the impending storm. Fear wrapped its icy fingers slowly and methodically around her slender throat, making it difficult to breathe. Thunder crackled and boomed, and lightning shot like an electric web through the rapidly darkening sky. The rain had not yet begun to fall, but it wouldn't be long now.

A prickle of fear invaded her body as the words ricocheted through her mind.

...No, it won't be long, now...

Her long skirts, devoid of their hoop, flapped wildly around her legs as the wind whistled and whipped across the balcony where she stood gripping the railing with white knuckles. She startled as another clap of thunder exploded and shook the house. The storm was getting closer.

...And so is he...

Urgency pulsed through her veins and the thought echoed in her mind as loudly as the thunder that was shaking her immediate world.

She allowed her gaze to linger for a moment longer on the land that she had come to love, as if trying to draw strength from it for what was to come and what she knew she must do. This had once been a happy home…a place where she had imagined her dreams becoming real…a place where she could be at peace and live happily ever after, but now…

Another loud clap of thunder jolted her out of her broken musings, and she turned and hurried inside. She must hurry. There was never enough time. She hastened to the desk across the expansive sitting room, where she had been sitting earlier, and retrieved the letter that she had just penned.

The ink was still damp on her frantically scribbled words as she hurriedly sprinkled setting sand over the drying, desperate plea. She quickly folded the paper and lifted the glass from the oil lamp on the desk. Placing a small stick of red wax into the flame, she heated it and dropped a dollop of wax onto the seam of the letter and placed her seal upon it. She kissed it and breathed a fervent, silent prayer before carefully hiding it in the secret compartment in the back of the main drawer in the desk.

Carefully and deftly, she united the lace ribbon around her elegant neck and locked the secret drawer with the delicate skeleton key that she wore on it. She closed the main drawer quickly and quietly, allowing her fingers to linger for just a moment on the smooth mahogany surface. This desk had been a wedding gift from her grandmother…But she couldn't think about that right now.

A rustling in the adjoining room startled her back to reality and she snuffed out the flame on the delicate oil lamp on the desk with a quickness. The room was instantly blanketed in weather-induced shadows and a chill crept into her spirit as she stood, silently listening. Nothing but the pounding of her heart, the whistling howl of the wind, and the creaking of the old house could be heard.

Quietly, she crept to the doorway and peered carefully around the thick, mahogany frame into the semi-darkness of the adjacent room. The massive wooden door leading to the hallway was still closed and a temporary wave of relief washed over her as she moved to the cradle nestled at the side of the massive bed in the center of the room, where she had tossed and turned the night before.

Gazing down into the cradle at the sweet, little bundle sleeping there, a lone tear escaped the lashes holding it prisoner and slid down her cheek as she retied the key and ribbon loosely around her neck. Another flash of lightning illuminated the room around her. With a quick glance over her shoulder, another fervent prayer, and a resolve to protect her newborn child, she quickly and noiselessly gathered her little one into her arms and swaddled him tightly with the blankets she had taken from her bedding.

Why must one's life begin so...?

Her heart cried out and she ached with tears yet unshed for the tiny little boy in her arms, and the father he would never know…The father that never even knew about him.

His Father… Tears threatened…*No she mustn't think of that right now…She must leave…She must leave.*

It pounded through her brain in an ever increasingly panicked cadence, with every quickened beat of her heart.

Her small, slender form moved out of the room and to the balcony where she had stood before…where she had stood so many times before, dreaming of what her life would be like. How could so much have changed?

The rain was falling in sheets, now, and she cuddled her son closer to keep the damp air from permeating his blankets. She looked down into his scrunched, little newborn face and her heart twisted anew with a combination of joy and profound grief.

Oh, how he looked like his father…

His father…

She felt the tears threaten again as she shifted her gaze from her son to the orchard of ages old pecan trees lining the entrance of the expansive southern plantation, as if to drink in their beauty and peace one last time. But peace would not be found, this day.

The afternoon sky had turned as black as night and as

she peered out across the grounds, spears of electricity illuminated the object of her terror and the reason for her desperate escape. The distance was closing between them, and he wasn't alone. Fear rose up into her throat like wretched bile and she turned her back on the life and people she had grown to love and fled.

Desperately clutching her newborn son to her breast, she raced through the sitting room and threw open the massive bedroom door, banging it loudly on the wall. She jumped with the sound. She must be quiet.

Steady, Caroline…keep your senses…

As silently and as quickly as she could, she made her way down the eerily quiet, darkened hallway to the hidden passage her husband had played in as a child. Pushing firmly on a section of the wall, Caroline felt the tension click and release and a small portion of the wall opened inwardly revealing a short narrow hallway. Lacey cobwebs decorated the dusty entrance, and the only evidence of prior human presence were the small foot prints she had left when she had entered earlier that day to light the lantern at the top of steep and narrow stairs. Throwing a look over her shoulder, she entered the secret passage and closed it carefully behind her.

Taking the lantern, down, down, down the dark stairway she fled as quickly as she could manage with her skirts and her precious cargo. As she neared the bottom of the stairs, the tiny infant began to stir.

Shhh…Oh, no…. Not now….

Caroline hung the oil lantern on a nail and softly pulled the blankets away. The dim flickering light from the lantern illuminated his tiny cherub face to find him sleeping, and she breathed a prayer of thanks and relief.

Carefully, she tucked the blanket around him again and shifted her precious bundle to one side. She used her newly freed hand to pull the ribbon loose from her neck and hang the ribbon and key on a small nail protruding from the wall, there, at the base of the narrow stairs. Pressing her ear to the wall of the secret door that would open into the large, often bustling, kitchen at the back of the house, Caroline listened for any signs of activity or movement. She must not be seen. She would not have those precious people whipped on her account. They had become her family, her spiritual leaders, her friends, and she knew that they would gladly give up their lives to protect her…And she knew that the monster chasing her would gladly take them. The thought made her shudder in fear and disgust.

Hearing no signs of life, the young mother pulled the lever on the wall, pushed, and crept silently into the kitchen. Her eyes darted around the room as she closed the wall behind her, and she moved to the back door.

The rain was falling in torrents, and she glanced down at her tiny son, snuggled deeply into the blankets that she clutched so tightly. Her resolve weakened for a moment. Suddenly, there was a commotion coming from the front parlor. In her mind's eye, Caroline could see the twisted, furious face of the man chasing her. His final words to her still seared her soul with his seething hatred for her.

Her son needed a mother. Her son…

…Needed his father…

There was a fearful shriek, and angry shout and more commotion coming closer. He would most likely go up to her room before he come down there, but she had to go *now!*

"CAROLINE!!!" An almost unhuman voice roared her name. She could hear the thundering stomps of his footfalls as he climbed the stairway to her bedroom, "WHERE IS THAT GODDAMNED WOMAN?!"

Caroline could feel the venom dripping from every syllable and she threw herself and her infant out the back door and into the downpour. She clutched her son desperately to her breast as she ran frantically toward the tree line. She prayed as she ran and she wept as she prayed, the salt of her tears mingling with the pelting rain drops assaulting her face.

The wind tore at her skirts, and the blankets that held her infant son whipped about her furiously. She squeezed him tighter and ran faster and harder into the sanctuary of the forest behind the plantation. She crashed through bushes and brambles, their briars and thorns ripping through her dress and arms while the images of her life ripped through her heart, causing her to cry out. The storm was raging all around her, pelting, soaking, barraging, punishing her for believing she was ever capable of having any kind of life without him.

…Him…

She must find sanctuary. The hounds would come when her tormentor discovered that she had fled. She trembled at the thought. She had heard the hounds more than once and seen the horrific damage they had done under the approving, watchful eye of their master. Her eyes flew to the child in her arms, who had now begun to wail.

Oh, God...What have I done?

Would the rain wash her scent away?

It mattered not. He would never let her go. He would never stop searching.

Caroline crashed into a clearing and struggled to keep her footing and balance in the boggy grass. Her skirts were rain and mud soaked and so heavy . She fought to stay upright as she pushed on in frantic resolve. The baby wailed louder as lightning popped and deafening thunder crackled and boomed overhead. She lost her balance and stumbled to her knees, barely catching herself with her free arm.

Glancing back over her shoulder, Caroline desperately forced herself onto her feet and began to struggle and stumble, again, through the thick and brackish mud. The wind was tearing at her on every side and the rainy needles pierced her skin, but in that moment all Caroline could feel was the icy fingers of dread rising like prickly fire from her toes and enveloping her entire body with involuntary tremors of terror as she heard the sloshy pounding of hooves behind and beside her.

How had they found her so quickly?

She silently cursed the moments of sentiment that had inevitably delayed her escape and led her to this moment, and now it was too late.

Had he somehow known her plans? Had he posted his men to watch her?

"YOU! WOMAN!" A strong male voice barked through the howling wind and rain.

Caroline had fallen to her knees again under the weight of her skirts. Eyes closed and head hanging in exhaustions, she heard the horses stomping and sloshing all around her, nervous from the threatening weather.

Her heart racing, exhausted, she gathered her courage and struggled to her feet, standing with her back to her captors. Desperately, she pulled her infant tightly into her chest to shield him from their eyes.

"WHAT ARE YOU DOING, WOMAN? ARE YOU DAFT?" The voice shouted over the storm.

Caroline slowly turned her head and turned to face him, clinging to her newborn son, and her panicked imagination ran wild. Another violent bolt of lightning spider-webbed overhead revealing the disfigured face of a demon. Her stricken face lost its remaining color as she stood there frozen in fear, her infant screaming wildly.

...Dear Lord...

More riders splashed through the torrential downpour to

surround her.

She clung to the screaming bundle fiercely as hail began to pelt them all and the terrifying wail of twister pierced the electric air.

Summer was in full force today, the woman and the season. The air inside Summer Dalton's SUV was almost as hot as the stagnant air outside of it.

"Good grief!" She fumed, "What is UP with this air condition?" Summer fiddled with the knobs and beat on the dash with her fist. The air condition rattled and began to blow semi-cool air.

"Better than nothing," she grunted. Summertime in South Georgia could be sweltering and this one was no exception.

The radio crackled out what sounded like a tune between the static, the rumble of the engine, and the rattle of the air condition. More than once in the past few weeks Summer had grumbled about the ancient Chevy Suburban her parents had given her when she was seventeen. It was barely hanging on then and now, six years later, it was barely crawling. But it was all that she could afford right now and, even though she hated to admit it, she was kind of attached to the old bucket of bolts. Although, with everything she had spent on repairs for this tank, she could have bought a new one by now...

Her cell phone buzzed in her back pocket, and she unbuckled and shifted to get it out of her favorite jeans. One hand on the wheel, and one hand digging in her back pocket, she swerved slightly into the other lane and then back.

"C'mon, c'mon..." Summer fussed. "Get...out...of ...there...UH!" The phone slipped out of her pocket and her hand, landing on the floorboard with a thud.

"You gotta be KIDDING! JEEZ!" She threw her free hand in the air, "Well, fine! Voicemail, it is." Agitated, Summer brushed sweaty tendrils of hair from her forehead as she sent an aggravated look at the heathen contraption vibrating in her floorboard.

"One of these days, I'm gonna have to get one of those belt thingies for that piece of crap..." She huffed and returned her eyes to the road, "Why do I even HAVE that thing anyway?"

The air condition groaned and quit working again, "Why do I still have THIS thing?!" Summer fumed and rolled her eyes as her behemoth oven rolled to a stop at the only stoplight in the little town of Watson, Georgia. Quickly, she stretched for the cell phone in the floor, trying to keep her foot on the brake.

"Come here, you..." The phone was just out of reach, so she put the truck in park and stretched further. Just about the time that she got her hands on it, the light turned green, and a horn blared behind her.

"Yeah, yeah..." she growled as she strained to sit back up and plopped the phone into the seat beside her.

A quick look in the rear view told her that Mrs. Willis, the town biddy and gossip, was the culprit. Summer faked a smile, stuck her hand out the window in a mock wave, threw the truck into gear and gassed it. A thick black cloud of ozone-killing, hair-curling exhaust enveloped the car behind her, and Summer chuckled in satisfaction as she imagined old Mrs.Willis coughing and sputtering more than the old truck that had left her that way. The radio buzzed with static, so she punched it off with an impish smirk.

"I should probably feel bad about that," she thought as she rolled down her window to let in the hot breeze, "... But... I don't."

That woman was one of the nastiest, meanest-spirited old hags that Summer had ever known. She actually, proudly called herself "Tenda"... Because she tended to everyone else's business but her own.

For as long as Summer could remember, she had felt the scorn of that mean old Mrs.Willis for reasons she could never put a finger on. Summer's dad was the pastor at First Baptist Church of Watson and had served faithfully since before she was born. Her mother was a prayer warrior in every sense of the word and led the women's ministry there. Summer had always been the 'good girl' that she was supposed to be...not the typical P.K...so she didn't really know what that old battle-axe's deal was. But Mrs. Willis had been unusually nasty lately and it was beginning to bug her.

"Oh well," Summer dismissed the thought with a shrug. "Serves her right."

But her conscience nagged at her a little. Her mom wouldn't be too happy about this little episode, even as insignificant as it was. Truth was, it was respect for her mother that kept her from really letting that old witch have it. Summer knew without thinking that, before she got back home this afternoon, Mrs. Willis would have already called Mrs. Dalton and escalated the whole thing... Poor little victim that she always was.

"Poor Mom, is more like it." Summer grunted.

"Why am I even obsessing about this?" She asked herself as she turned into the parking lot of Sunny Birch Nursing Home. "GAH! Twenty-three years old and I'm worried about Tenda calling my mom…"

She shook her head as she parked and adjusted the rear-view mirror to get a look at her reflection. Her long, honey blonde hair had stubbornly refused to stay in its French braid and, with the help of the wind, was now framing her sweaty face in a wild halo of renegade curls.

"Yikes! Okaayyy…" She chuckled, as she ran her hand over the curly rogues, "Good thing there ain't any kids or small animals 'round here… Cause I'd be terrorizing them today!" She smirked at her reflection.

Grabbing the keys out of the ignition and the phone out of the seat, Summer hopped out of the driver's seat and slammed the door shut. Her whole backside was wet with sweat as she opened the creaky back door of her truck and grabbed the basket of slightly wilting flowers out of the back seat. Sticking her nose into the pretty arrangement, she inhaled the soft sweetness of her Nanna's favorite tea roses. A soft smile crept over her face, and she thought of how her grandmother's face would light up as soon as she laid eyes on her granddaughter.

Summer walked towards the entrance of the nursing home with a happy grin, the interaction with old Mrs. Willis forgotten. Time spent with Nanna was something she had always looked forward to as a child and it was no different now. Besides Summer's dad, her grandmother was her favorite person in the world.

SKELETON KEY

CHAPTER TWO

Caroline Conner stood stoically before her would-be captors, sheltering her newborn from the torrential downpour and the hail that had begun to persecute her face and arms. The wail of the storm grew louder, and the wind tore at her slight body, whipping her skirts about her madly. A rider made his way from the back of the group and shouted orders to the others above the shrieking of the tempest. She tried to make out his face, but it was hidden by his hat and slicker and she was blinded by the rain. The horse shied, reared, and threatened to bolt as the creaking and snapping of limbs worsened and grew louder. The rider closest to her dismounted and reached for her.

"Ma'am..."

Caroline dodged and stumbled as his hand came dangerously close to her tiny son. His hand caught the blanket covering her breast as she snatched away and uncovered her tiny bundle exposing the distraught infant to the elements and the eyes of the horsemen, almost causing her to drop him.

"NO!" she shrieked, fighting to shelter her infant from the ice that was bruising her own skin. Lifting her skirts, she covered her baby once more and eyed the pack of men like a lioness. *"HE IS AN INNOCENT BABY, YOU*

FOOL!" Fire blazed in her eyes as she steadied and braced herself, *"WOULD YOU HAVE HIM DIE?!"*

The soldier, startled by the fact that a tiny child nearly rolled out of her hands, regarded the stark contrast of her smallness and the ferocity with which she guarded the baby.

"Let me pass," the wild-eyed woman demanded.

Unnerved, the soldier stared at her and then glanced back at his commanding officer for further orders.

She took a step toward the unmounted man and then turned to face the group of horsemen with a maniacal look. The men surrounding her watched her, quietly taken aback at the obviousness of her insanity. There she stood, pantaloons exposed, her skirts hoisted over her shoulders to protect a child they had not known about. Her rich honey colored hair, now a dull wet brown, had fallen from its place high upon her head and was whipping wildly about her. The eyes that burned through them with every darting glare belonged to a mad woman, not the frightened creature they had first come upon in the clearing.

"LET....ME...PASS!", she roared ferociously. Shaking with adrenaline and rage, Caroline drew herself to her full 5-foot, 3-inch height and glared up into the startled expression of the man standing before her. No, the madman that she had escaped from would NOT take her son this easily. If it was a fight he wanted, a fight he would have.

"Let me pass," Caroline seethed, "or you will live to regret it! I swear it to you on my blessed husband's grave, you will regret it, the day you were BORN!!!" She was shaking uncontrollably as she held her son to her breast with a white-knuckled death grip.

Oh, Lord…Give me strength…

The leader of this band of men sat on his horse watching the proceedings silently and, in that moment, something moved in his cold heart, and he decided that he had never seen a more beautiful woman.

"Hey there, beautiful!" Naomi Dalton beamed as she greeted her granddaughter.

Summer smiled widely as she set the basket of tea roses down on the bedside table next to her grandma, "What did they slip you and don't be stingy with it!", she joked as she kissed her grandma's cheek.

Naomi laughed, "Oh honey, you *are* beautiful. And I love you, too. Besides…" she chuckled, "You're not getting' my good stuff!"

They shared a giggle and a hug.

"Oh, Nana, I missed you…," Summer squeezed the little, round woman before she let her go.

"Well, sweetie, you were just here yesterday... And the day before... And the day before that..." Naomi ticked the days off on her fingers. "Business must be good for you to be out delivering every day?"

Naomi referred to the little flower boutique that Summer had recently borrowed money to open. Ever since Summer had been a child, she had had a love for nature and every time she had visited Naomi, she had brought a huge bundle of wildflowers. It wasn't a stretch to find her creating and sharing that same brightness as a career. What an adventure! Naomi was so proud of her!

Summer forced a smile, "As good as can be expected.", she lied.

"As good as all that, hmm?"

Her Nanna knew her too well.

"In fact,...Why aren't you there now?" Naomi asked curiously as she patted the bed next to her, beckoning her granddaughter to sit.

Summer dismissed that line of questioning with a smile as she parked herself next to the older woman, "Can't a girl decide to close her own shop for a day to spend time with her Nanna??"

Naomi peered at her intently. "*Every*day?"

Summer gave in with a discouraged huff. "Okay, fine! It's just been a really slow day and I didn't feel like dealing with non-existent clients." She lifted a hand to her forehead and pinched the center of her brows, "...Not to mention that the two weddings that I had booked cancelled. Apparently, they found a 'better deal'," she made air quotes and continued with the fakest of smiles, "...SO! I actually didn't have anything to do, anyway!"

"So, let's talk about it!" Naomi chirped.

"Nope." Summer shook her head emphatically, "I came to bring *you* some sunshine...", she tossed her head and flicked her thumb toward the roses, "not to darken your day with my issues."

Naomi smiled fondly, "Sweetheart, you *are* my sunshine..."

"Yeahhh," Summer smiled ruefully, "and I make you happyyyyyy when skies are graaayyyy, too, right?" Summer sing-songed a part of the song her grandmother sang to her when she was little.

"Yes, you do," Naomi chuckled. "And when your skies are gray, I'm here to make *you* happy...so sit down and dish it, sister." She grinned, "C'mon. Give an old woman some drama. They quit letting us watch soaps again. Betty started calling herself, 'Barbara' and swore she was being stalked."

Naomi grimaced emphatically and Summer laughed.

"Now that's what I like to see! C'mon! Let me help you, sweetie." Summer's grandmother patted her tanned and slender hand, letting her wrinkled one rest there.

"It's really nothing," Summer began as she pulled her hand free and absently tucked a golden renegade curl behind her ear, "I'm just frustrated, I guess…"

Naomi nodded understandingly.

"…Frustrated and restless.", she concluded with a sigh.

"Restless, dear?" Naomi's gentle eyes sought her granddaughter's discouraged ones.

"I don't know, Nanna. I'm just tired of everything turning to crap. It just seems like every time something seems like it might work out for me, it blows up in my face…you know?"

Summer sighed and found Naomi looking at her with understanding and concern. "I'm just ready for things to go my way for once…", she paused and looked down at her hands. "That and…I think someone may be trying to intentionally sabotage my business…"

The older woman peered at her intently and Summer could feel her gaze.

"Now what makes you think that, honey?"

"Oh, I don't know…" Summer's golden eyes snapped with sarcasm, "Could it be the empty parking lot and all of the cancelled orders?"

"Well, that just doesn't make sense, dear…" the older woman ignored her granddaughter's tone. "Who would do that? Everyone loves you, and you do wonderful work! It's just a down spell, sweetie. Things will get better…," Naomi crooned as she reached toward Summer's face to tuck that same stubborn curl back into place behind Summer's ear.

"A down spell…?" Summer scoffed, "So that's what we're calling it?"

Naomi nodded encouragingly and patted Summer's arm, "Mmhmm, that's all it is, honey."

"For two solid months?" Summer questioned skeptically. "Nanna, I appreciate the thought but, I really am beginning to think that someone in this town just doesn't like me or what I'm trying to do…Although, I don't really see how selling flowers could be a threat to anyone. My shop is literally the only one in town."

"Well, maybe you're just being out 'dealt' by your competition…?" Naomi offered hopefully.

"Nanna…" Summer raised an eyebrow, "My closest competition is forty-five minutes away…Annnnd, most of my jobs are local ones. With the price of gas and living, these days…No…" she shook her head as she continued, "It's not that."

"Hmmm…" Naomi tapped a thoughtful, wrinkled finger on her chin, "…That's a good point."

She waved a dismissive hand in the air, "Well, we'll just pray for the Lord to reveal it to you, then." Naomi flashed a bright, hopeful smile at her granddaughter.

Summer groaned inwardly. It *always* came back to this.

She sighed, loudly "Not that I think He even will, but He needs to do it pretty quick-like, if He's gonna." The young woman shot an irritated look at her grandmother. "I've got a payment due in two weeks and my sales have been a whopping zilch and zero…I'm so in the red, you might as well call me Mrs. Claus…minus the cookies." Summer's half-hearted attempt at humor was a miss.

"Now what's all this about, sweetie? 'Don't think He will'…" Naomi smiled softly, "Of *course* He will! The Lord *loves* you and He always gives guidance to those who seek Him!"

Summer sighed in frustration. She really did not want to have this conversation today. There was enough on her plate to choke on without adding the supernatural to it…or the significant lack, thereof.

"Well, to put it bluntly? I feel like God is pissed at me for something and I don't even know what I did. I pray every day and every night for Him to forgive me for…whatever it is I've done…hoping maybe, *just* maybe He'll stop picking on me, you know?"

Naomi frowned slightly, "So, you think that God is responsible for your problems at the shop?" She paused and sought Summer's golden eyes. "Honey, you know that's not how He operates, don't you?"

Summer smirked, "No. I actually don't think God has *anything* to do with my shop…or with me, for that matter, other than to remind me of how totally inadequate I really am." A small tear escaped her lashes.

"Oh, now, Summer!" Naomi's faded blue eyes begged Summer to look at her. "Have you talked to God about this at all?"

"Why?" the young woman snapped, a little harsher than she had intended. She was sick to death of this subject.

Naomi opened and closed her mouth, and Summer inhaled ruefully. The last thing she wanted to do was talk *about* Him...Let alone *to* Him.

"I'm sorry, Nanna..." She looked into Naomi's gentle eyes, sighed, and softened her tone as she continued.

"Why should I talk to God about this? So I can get a great big *nothing* in response..." Summer bit back the sarcasm she could feel rising up again. "I'm sick of bending over backwards and getting rejected every single time...by Him and everyone else." She sighed heavily, "I'm doing *my* part...It's HIM..." she jabbed a frustrated finger heavenward, "who's falling down on the job, here. He never answers anyway...So why even bother anymore."

This was not the way Summer had envisioned this visit with her grandma going. She stood up, agitated, and rubbed the palms of her hands on her thighs and looked away from the penetrating gaze of her sweet and devout grandmother.

"I see..." Naomi was quiet for a moment, taking in her granddaughter's words before she continued. "What does your dad have to say about all of this?"

"He doesn't have anything to say about it, because I haven't told him," Summer looked into Naomi's understanding eyes. "I can't tell him about any of this, Nanna…It would disappoint him so much to hear me say these things…"

Another tear slipped past its feathery guards, and she lifted her hand to brush it away before it had the chance to trace its way down her cheek. "I guess that has something to do with the way I'm feeling, too. I feel like such a disappointment to everyone lately…especially Daddy."

Naomi smiled tenderly at her, "Everyone who?"

"Well, Mama and Daddy, for starters…"

"Honey, why would you ever think this? They *love* you!"

Summer sighed loudly, "I know, I know. But Daddy has always held on to this dream that I will be in ministry with him someday, but Nanna, I just don't *feel* that, you know? I mean, how can I possibly help others find Jesus when *I* can't even find Him? Heck, I don't even know what I'm supposed to be doing with my own life," she stepped away from Naomi's bed in frustration, "No, wait…" Summer paused and half-turned, snapping her fingers in the air, "…What is it that Daddy's says?…I don't know what *I'm called* to do…or if I'm even 'called' at all!" She spun on her heel to face Naomi's compassionate gaze.

"I like who I am... He doesn't get that." She slapped the

back of one hand into the palm of the other as her voice began to escalate slightly. "...And I'm really starting to think that not everyone has a calling on their lives, actually. I'm happy with my choice of careers... Or I *would* be if I could catch a break! I don't want to be a puppet like he is." Summer knew that statement wasn't true at all, but she was riled up and she didn't care.

"Sweetie, I think he would understand... You really do need to talk about this with your father."

A slight tap on the door stopped Summer's almost tirade, "Everything OK in here?"

Jill, one of the nurses on duty, poked her head in the door.

"Why yes, honey!" Naomi beamed at the fresh-faced woman as she briefly stepped into the room, "Summer was just getting' off her soapbox..."

Summer shot a sideways glance at Naomi.

Jill chuckled, "Like father, like daughter, hmm?" She was an attractive woman in her late 30s with a fun sense of humor, and Summer had always liked her.

Naomi grinned and winked in her granddaughter's direction. Summer grimaced.

"Be sure to tell your father that I really enjoyed the service last Sunday, next time you see him." She smiled sweetly at Naomi 's pretty, flushed-face granddaughter. "It really spoke to me. OH! And tell the youth pastor I said 'Thanks'... He'll know why."

Summer gulped, nodded, and looked away. Thankfully, no one could see her heart flip flop at the mention of the church's new youth pastor. *Why could she not seem to control that feeling?? Yet another thing to add to the list of impossibilities in her life these days...*

To Naomi, Jill said, "Let me know when you are ready for your meds okay, hon? Doc said he wants to try to wean you off and get you ready to go home soon."

"WooHoo!!" The older woman lifted her arms in the air and Jill chuckled again, shaking her head as she closed the door back.

Summer eyed her grandma, "I am NOT like him..." She hissed petulantly as she poked her slender finger at her grandmother.

"Oh, pish posh, Summer. Stop acting like a child," Naomi scolded. "Your father adores you and only wants what's best for you. *Talk. To. Him...* He *will* understand."

"No, Nanna. I'm an embarrassment to him. No matter what I do in this God-forsaken town, he or Mama always end up apologizing to one of the congregation... Seeing as everyone in this town is a member of that church... GEEZ... It's like the Christian mafia or something, and... and that mean old Mrs. Willis is the Godmother!"

"Now, where did *that* come from?" Naomi chuckled and tossed a wrinkled hand into the air playfully.

"Oh, it's nothing... I just choked her out at the red light before I got here..." Summer grinned in spite of herself.

"Probably serves her right, I'd say," the older woman's face crinkled into a wide smile, "Not that it makes it right, mind you..."

"But you listen here," Naomi continued, and she held her arms out to Summer as she came to sit back on the bed beside her grandmother. Taking the young woman's hands in her own Naomi said, "You don't let that bitter old fart-blossom get to you. She's miserable and she wants everyone else to be just as miserable as she is... the old coot." Naomi scrunched her wrinkled face and Summer laughed.

"She just needs Jesus. Pray for her!" She squeezed her granddaughter's hands with a patient smile.

Summer wrinkled her nose, "I wanna to slug her..."

Naomi chuckled and nodded mischievously, "Me too!"

CHAPTER THREE

"The Lord is moving here at First Baptist, this is Missy. How can I help you?" ....Silence... "I'm sorry, Brother Robert isn't in, right now. Can I take a message for him?" ...Silence... "Yes, he has voicemail. Please hold while I transfer you..."

Pastor Jim Dalton sat in his office exhausted and frustrated. Even the sound of his young secretary's soft voice through the cracked door grated on his nerves, this afternoon. He leaned forward and rested his head in his hands. Slowly he raised his face just enough to pinch his eyebrows with his fingers. *Why did ministry have to be so hard?* He had asked the Lord this question many times over the last twenty-three years, and he never seemed to get a satisfactory answer.

To the casual onlooker, things at First Baptist of Watson were booming. The Lord was blessing, the church was growing, they were one month in their new building... Shining, happy people...But there were things that the casual onlooker would never see. And it was one of these things that had Pastor Jim in a funk this afternoon. The head of the Deacon Board had just left the office and Jim was still angry over the ultimatum that had been so heatedly laid out to him, just minutes before. He had learned a long time ago not to rehash things, but this was one replay that he just could not seem to get rid of.

"Pastor, I hate to be the bearer of bad news, but, well... the Board has been noticing some pretty disturbing things at church, here lately."

Jim sat back in the lazy-boy type office chair that his wife and daughter had surprised him with on the first day in his new office. He peered intently at the older gentleman seated across from him. His perfectly groomed hair was snow white and contrasted sharply with his tanned and leathery skin. The starched khakis and white polo that he wore were as stiff as his expression.

"What's going on, Tom?" Concern flashed across Jim's face.

"Well, we decided that there have been just too many... How can I say this..." He rolled his hand in the air searching for words.

Jim closed his eyes momentarily. He had recently caught wind of a rumor going around and he knew, without asking, where this conversation would be going... And it was not something he was looking forward to. He sighed and pulled out a legal pad and found a pen.

"That has never seemed to be a problem for you, Tom,

just spit it out. What's got the bees' nest in an uproar, this time?" He closed his eyes quickly and repented. *Lord, please help me...*

Tom Davies glared at the man sitting across the desk from him... The desk that he, himself, had donated.

"Well, I guess you're right..." He chuckled to lighten the mood and mask the depth of his irritation with this infuriating pastor.

Relaxing back into his chair, he crossed his arms and stated, "Well, we just don't like all the...er...colors... We are starting to see in the church these days, to put it politely. And the Board feels that something needs to be done about it."

Jim was incensed and grieved. His suspicion had been right on. The rumor was true. Jim stared at the older man sitting across from him. *Lord help me to love this man.*

"Just what exactly are you 'politely' implying by that, Tom?"

Tom cleared his throat, "well, a few things, actually...," he raised a forearm and a hand.

Jim nodded. It was never just one thing with this Deacon Board... He looked at Tom expectantly.

"Well, first off, we don't really like all these teenagers running around here with all these tattoos and piercings and different colored hair." He made a disgusted face and waved his hand in the air, "We decided that it's disrespectful to the Lord and to the church body to be parading around making such a spectacle of themselves like that."

He jabbed a finger at Jim to emphasize his next statement.

"In fact, Johnson Michaels said that his own grandson is trying to convince his mama to let him have blue hair... Just like that David kid he's been hanging around with." Tom's expression showed his disgust, "Just disgraceful, if you ask me. And that kid's parents don't even come to this church!"

Jim smiled with more patience than he felt, "Well, just for the record, Tom, his mother was in the congregation this past Sunday morning but keep going..." Jim nodded for him to continue as he jotted down a note on the legal pad in front of him.

"And I..., ahem, er... *We* decided that we need to limit our Youth events to the youth of the church family... I mean the families that are members and are contributing to the financial needs of the church. You know we have this fancy building to pay for..."

Jim recognized the very obvious dig and clenched his teeth. He kept his eyes on the paper in front of him, while his frustration and repulsion grew. *Lord, I need you...RIGHT NOW.*

"I'm well aware of the financial status of this ministry, Tom, and I have faith that God is able to finance what He sets in motion."

"Well, sure, Pastor. We all have faith, but we do have bills to pay ...And your salary..." Tom added the last statement pointedly.

"Would there be any other issues that we need to deal with this afternoon?" Jim ignored the jibe as he jotted some thoughts down on his legal pad. He was more than ready for this meeting to be done.

"Well, there's the issue of color in general..."

Jim's head snapped up. "What does that mean?"

"Simply, that last Sunday morning we had 250 in attendance..."

The frustrated pastor interrupted him, "Praise the Lord for that. God is blessing us, don't you think, Tom?" He knew exactly where this was headed, and it made him physically sick. How was this still a mindset?

"Well, yes. Yes, He is, Pastor, and the Board feels like we need to be careful that we don't lose that blessing by letting too many of them in here."

"Them?" Jim stared intently at the older gentleman sitting across from him, "exactly which 'them' are we discussing here, Tom?"

Tom ignored the question and pressed on.

"Did you know that only half of that number was...well...*Our* kind?" He raised his finger as if he had almost forgotten to mention a point, "Oh, and another thing. We feel like our worship services are gettin' a little bit too loud and rowdy... Mainly because of *them*. It's irreverent to get so, well... 'Happy', for lack of a better word."

"Which group of people, Tom, let's be specific." Jim wanted to hear him say the words.

"Now Pastor, don't get riled up. We're just expressing a legitimate concern, here..." Tom shifted in his seat.

That's debatable...

"Don't avoid the question." Jim pinned the deacon to his seat with the intensity of his stare.

"The Mexicans and the Blacks, if you want me to be blunt."

"And what exactly do you mean by 'getting happy'?"

"Well, all that shoutin' and hollerin' when we're trying to sing and pray! Pastor, we've got a certain way that we have always praised the Lord, and that ain't it!"

Jim clenched and unclenched his teeth, his patience gone.

The white-haired man continued, "We need to keep a close watch on things or one of them people might just start talking in tongues... and just what would we do then? Jim, we ain't Pentecostals, but we *are* getting pretty dangerously close to it, if you ask the Board..." He paused for a moment. "And, at our last meeting we discussed making sure that only certain people have keys to the church...to prevent theft, you know..."

Jim sighed. How many things could one old man find to complain about? He mentally ran a list of who had keys to the church.

"Well, Tom, only a few people do have keys. Just who are you concerned about?"

"Chad." Tom stated matter-of-factly.

He was referring to the church's new youth pastor. He had accepted the position two months prior, and Jim was so proud of how this dynamic young man had hit the ground running and had instantly begun impacting the community around them. In fact, Chad Walker was one of the reasons that so many different cultures had started being represented in their congregation. He was dynamic and his influence reached way beyond just the youth ministry. Chad had a beautiful way of relating to those that society had turned their backs on, and Jim had almost danced in the pulpit when he saw the harvest of souls the Lord was touching through this young man and his ministry.

"Tom," Jim tried to keep his voice even. This was not the first time that he had had to defend this youth pastor's out-of-the-box methods, "Chad is the youth pastor. He has more right to this facility than most. He needs access to the buildings and grounds for ministry..."

"But, Jim..." Tom interrupted, "What I'm saying is, he doesn't come up here alone and that is a liability."

"I don't see how who Chad brings up here with him is of

any concern."

"Jim," Tom leaned in for emphasis, "...it was one of them gang members... And Chad left him alone in his office while he went somewhere else. That kid coulda had a gun and robbed us blind, not to mention shot the place up. Why, he was probably planning which of the walls he wanted to spray paint!" The older gentleman's face began to redden, "It's irresponsible!"

Jim prayed for any kind of patience, for what seemed like the hundredth time, and he leaned forward, placing his elbows on the desktop, eyes blazing.

"Okay," he began, "Let me start by saying that just because someone is a different race or nationality doesn't mean that they are a part of a gang or bent upon destruction..."

"Pastor," Tom interrupted, "...all the black folks in this town are gang members or support 'em...especially those young thugs. And all the Mexicans are Cartel. They're selling drugs to our kids..." He shook his snowy head emphatically, "Can't be trusted."

*I would trust a thug any day more than...*Jim halted that line of thinking, quickly. *Sorry, Lord...*

Jim's brown eyes bored into the faded blue one staring back at him, "Have you met every African American in this town?"

"Well, no..."

"Have you met every Latino person? Have you spent any time getting to know anyone that is different than you?"

Tom's eyes narrowed. "No, I have not."

"Didn't think so." Jim prayed about how to go about dealing with this. He put his pen down on the pad and closed his eyes briefly and prayed again for wisdom, "Tom, can I ask you a question?"

"Well, sure, Pastor..."

"Do you believe the Bible?"

"Yes, I do.," he nodded once, "One hundred percent. Every blessed word."

"Do you read it?"

"Yes." Tom sat back and crossed his arms over his chest. He wasn't sure if he liked that question.

"Then could you be so kind as to tell me where the Lord makes allowances for closed mindedness and racism?"

"Just what are you getting' at, Pastor?"

"Could you tell me anywhere that it condemns someone for expressing gratitude?"

"I don't like where you're going with this comment Jim..."

"Well to tell the truth, I don't like it either, Tom. I don't like the fact that the head of my Deacon Board is sitting in my office telling me that Jesus didn't die for crazy hair kids, Mexicans, or African Americans... And that, somehow, it's improper and offensive for someone who's been delivered from deep bondage to worship the Lord freely. Don't you dare judge someone's worship until you have walked a mile in their chains."

The head of the Deacon Board opened and closed his mouth, but Jim continued.

"Another thing that really doesn't sit well with me, is that I'm being told that my youth pastor shouldn't be allowed to use this facility to minister. He's a good man and I know where his heart is...and if you and the board would spend some time with him on the streets, you would, too. I trust him completely and I stand beside him. Tom, you can't clean fish before you catch 'em and for that matter, it's not even *our* job to do the cleaning. That is something only the Lord, Himself, can do... And I intend to let Him do it."

He pointed his pen at Tom emphatically, "...and I don't like that I have someone threatening my job if I don't follow along with his opinion, like a paid employee. I appreciate the accountability that the Board offers, but I will not be intimidated out of the direction I feel the Lord is taking this church body, and," he continued pointedly, "I would caution you to seek the Lord in your own 'endeavors', Tom..."

Tom's face reddened as the meaning of the pastor's words hit their mark.

"Now, I didn't say nothing like that, and you know it!" He sputtered, "You're putting words in my mouth! We ain't racist, we just don't want 'em in our church. Those hooligans don't have respect for nothing, and I won't have 'em messing up what our hard-earned money has gone to build. We have a right to decide who can be a part of this!"

Jim kept his voice even and impossibly calm, "Tom, this church was built to be a hospital to hurting souls... Not a trophy or a social club for society's acceptable and the beautiful ones. It was meant to be *used* and as long as the Lord has me leading this flock, I will be obedient to Him and follow His leading... And by-God this church will be used."

Tom stood to his feet in challenge, "That may not be as long as you think, *Pastor*." Bitter poison dripped from the title as it left the older man's lips. "Let's not forget that we have the trump card..."

Jim looked up at him from the desk incredulously. *Lord Jesus, please help me to be a shepherd to this man.*

He remained in his seat and looked up into Tom's glaring, anger-distorted face, "Here again, I ask, are you spending time in the word?"

"I'm getting' tired of you implying that I ain't living a Christian life, now!" Tom's voice escalated as he slammed his hand down on the desktop. Jim could see Missy look nervously towards the office door.

"Now, Tom, I never said that. I'm not accusing you of

anything. I'm simply wondering how you can make statements and demands like this, that are in direct contradiction to the word of God." Jim thanked the Lord that he was able to speak calmly to this man, although his emotions were in an uproar.

"You show me in there where it says that I'm wrong and I'll kiss you on the lips!" He shouted jabbing his finger at Jim.

Jim heard the ding of the bell over the front door and silently prayed that Missy would close the office door. The Lord was definitely moving this afternoon, because immediately she tiptoed to the door and closed it quietly.

Jim exhaled softly. *Thank you.*

"All right, if you want, but kissing's not really necessary." Jim turned to the bookshelf behind him, stood and found the King James on the third shelf. He normally liked the NIV, but the older members of his congregation had ideas about the accuracy of it. He knew that if he was to make a point to this man, it would have to be in King James.

Tom eyed this obstinate preacher man suspiciously, "Don't you think your Bible should be closer to you, Pastor? Kinda dusty on that shelf, ain't it?" He sneered sarcastically, "And you're asking *me* if I'm doing *my* reading..."

Jim smiled as he returned to his seat, opened the Bible to Matthew 25:31, and began reading.

SKELETON KEY

CHAPTER FOUR

Summer looked up with disappointment as another nurse entered Naomi's little room.

"Hey, Summer!" Rita smiled brightly at the pretty, young woman sitting on her patient's bed. Naomi was one of the lucky ones. Very few of the patients in this rehabilitation clinic had as much support and care as Naomi did. Yep, she was pretty blessed.

"Time for your bath!" She beamed at her patient.

"Hey, Rita," Summer returned the smile. Rita was so nice. She was definitely moving in her calling…If only Summer could find that niche, "Is that my cue?"

"…Unless you wanna help…?" Rita smiled mischievously as she waggled a towel.

Summer giggled and grimaced, "Nope! I'm good!"

Naomi chuckled as Summer popped up off the bed, "I concur. You're having enough of a day without adding this wrinkled old prune to it."

Summer laughed and kissed her cheek, "Thanks, Nanna! You're a gem."

The sun blazed unforgivingly outside of Sunny Birch. Summer stood inside the building at the exit, dreading the trip home. She lingered a minute longer and relished the cool, sterile cleanliness of the hallway before she exited the building. Reluctantly, she pushed open the door and walked into the suffocating humidity of the southern summer. Instantly sweating, the young woman headed for the four-wheeled oven awaiting her in the parking lot. As she was unlocking the door, Summer noticed the window on the passenger side was still down. She shook her head and laughed at herself. How smart was it to lock all the doors and leave the window down? Oh well, someone would actually be doing her a favor to take this hulking behemoth off her hands.

The rusty handle protested loudly as she snatched it upward and pried open the heavy, creaking door. Climbing up into the driver's seat, she slammed the door shut and checked her phone as she turned the keys in the ignition. The truck rumbled to life with a groan and Summer patted the dash affectionately.

"That's my girl…"

Glancing at her cell phone she saw that she had a missed call and a new voicemail. Rolling down the window, she flipped open the phone and pressed send. Summer put the truck into gear as she waited for the prompt to enter her password. She really needed to upgrade her phone, but money was too tight. Summer quickly typed in her code as she approached the exit of the small parking lot and waited to pull out into traffic.

"You have one new voicemail..." the automated voice told her, "Message received July 30th, at 2:30pm..."

"Yes..." A female voice came across the line, "This is Julie Whatley with the law offices of Morgan & Morgan. I'm trying to reach Summer Dalton in reference to a personal business matter. Please place a return call to 404-336-5142 at your earliest convenience. Thank you and have a nice day."

Summer frowned as she found the number in her caller ID and pressed send. That was strange...A few more cars sped by, and she pulled out onto the rural highway as the phone on the opposite end began to ring.

"Morgan, Morgan & Associates, how may I direct your call?"

Crap! She forgot the lady's name!

"Um, I'm Summer Dalton. I'm returning a call...?"

"Hold, please."

Summer sweated as she waited for whoever to pick up the line. The air blowing in the open window was hotter than the air inside the truck. *I've really got to do something about this air condition...* She put the phone on her shoulder and held it there with her cheek, while she pounded the dash. There was no response from the stubborn air conditioner this time. The phone slipped off of her shoulder and she just managed to catch it before it hit the seat. She quickly rubbed the earpiece on her jeans to wipe off the sweat and held it back up to her ear.

"Oh well, I'm almost home anyway..." She thought, resigning herself to the heat.

"Miss Dalton?" A smooth, masculine voice interrupted her frustration.

"Yes!"

"Miss Dalton, this is Chris Morgan. I'm afraid I'm calling with some unfortunate news that you are most likely already aware of..."

Summer strained to hear the voice over the roar of the engine and the wind from the windows. She wanted to roll it up, but heat stroke was not her idea of a good time.

"Okay..."

"Miss Dalton, I'm contacting you in reference to your late grandfather's will."

Woah, wait a minute.

"Wait a sec...my *late* grandfather?" Summer stuttered.

"Yes...Your recently deceased grandfather?"

Summer gulped and gasped for air. An instant wave of nausea swept over her. Her Paw-Paw...The man who had taught her to love and work the land. The man who had shown her how to bait her own hook...The man who had spent countless hours sharing stories and lessons from his life with her... She had just talked to him two days ago...He had been fine...

"Miss Dalton?"

"Ahem..." She choked back tears, "I'm sorry...um, ahem, this is just a shock."

"I understand. I'm sorry. I assumed you would have already known. I apologize for being the bearer of bad news."

"No, it's OK...... How did he..." She couldn't make herself say it, "I mean...... How did it happen?"

She thought she heard the rattle of papers, "I believe it was natural causes. He died in his sleep."

That was sort of a relief. At least he wasn't in pain...

"Is this the only reason you called me?"

"No, ma'am. Our law firm handled all of your grandfather's affairs and it seemed that he left his entire estate to you. Now if we could set up a time to go over..."

"Estate?" Summer interrupted. Her mind was reeling. Were they talking about the same man, here? Her Paw-Paw was as poor as a church mouse. What on earth did he have to leave her? And why didn't he leave it to Me-Maw?

"Yes, ma'am. We can go over all of that when you come to the office."

"Wait... I don't understand..."

"Miss Dalton. There is little to understand, here." The voice sounded impatient and rushed, "Your grandfather passed away and left his entire life fortune to you, his only heir."

Summer didn't like the tone this guy was taking with her, "No, *you* don't understand, Mr.... What's your name again?...Uh...um...Moooorgan, yes that's it! Mr. Morgan. My grandfather is...er...*was* a poor man, and what's more, I'm not the next in line... My *grandmother* is... And then my *mom*."

She slowed down to pull into the driveway of the small, white pastorium where she had grown up. She pulled up to the house, parked, and cut off the ignition. There was a brief silence on the other end of the line.

"Can I place you on hold for a brief moment?

"Yeah..." Summer pushed open the door and slid out of the driver's seat, grabbing the keys as she did. She slammed the door shut and trotted up the brick steps to the front door. She pulled open the screen door and unlocked the old wooden door. Pushing it open a wall of cold air hit her in the face and she breathed it in gratefully. With her free hand she pulled the keys out of the lock and closed the door back.

This Morgan guy needed to get his story straight. She

tossed the keys on the hall table and headed down the paneled hallway to her bedroom, flicked on the ceiling fan and did the Nestea plunge onto her double bed. She did a quick glance around the room. Almost done moving, thank God...

I wonder if Mom knows...She felt the tears threaten again as her mind came back to the shocking revelation that the attorney had dropped on her.

"Miss Dalton?" The smooth baritone voice returned.

"I'm here," She stared at the fan blades spinning above her outstretched body.

"I apologize for the wait. There seems to have been some kind of mix up. Let me just go over some details with you, to make sure we have the right person...Is that alright?"

Oh, thank God...Relief began to wash over her as she rolled onto her side and propped up on her elbow. They had the wrong person.

"You are Summer Denise Dalton, born April 1st, 1999?"

Summer inhaled sharply and her relief was short lived.

"Yes."

"Your father is Richard James Dalton, paternal grandparents...William and Naomi Dalton?"

Dread began to settle like lead in her stomach...*Oh no*... "Y-yes...That's correct..." She forced herself to swallow.

"Your mother was Caroline Marie Conner, maternal grandparents…the late Jarvis and Priscilla Conner?"

Wait…That's not right…? She sat up staring at herself in the mirror across from the bed.

"Um…Did you say Caroline Conner?" Confusion replaced the dread as Summer tried to wrap her mind around what was being said. Who was Caroline Conner? That wasn't her mother…Her mother's name was Barbara… "I think you've made a mistake or something. My mother's name isn't Caroline."

"Miss Dalton," The voice sounded irritated, "If you will forgive me, I am looking at a certified copy of your birth certificate. It clearly states that your biological parents are James Dalton and Caroline Conner."

Biological…

Summer dropped the phone. As the phone clattered to the floor, she didn't hear the voice on the other end call her name twice and then hang up. She didn't hear the rhythmic squeaking of the ceiling fan above her. She didn't hear anything except the words echoing through her brain, that had just brought her world and everything in it to a screeching halt.

Captain William Conner sat astride his horse, mentally gauging how much time they had before the funnel cloud would carry them all off. He glanced overhead into the evil, green clouds and barked an order to take the woman and babe to safety. This child was a complication that he had not expected.

Caroline watched in fear as more men dismounted and began to close in on her and her tiny son. The trees around them began to swirl and the sky was turning a frightening color. Her heart slammed against her chest as she realized that she was trapped. *Oh, dear Jesus, what can I do?! PLEASE!!* She searched wildly for an opening to escape through, but there were no openings that did not have a snorting, raring beast blocking her way.

Quickly, the circle of demons closed ranks on her and before she could react, an iron grip held her around the waist while another pried the screaming infant from her arms.

"NOOOOO!!" She screamed from the depths of her soul, kicking, and straining to reach her child. She watched in horror as her newborn son was wrapped in a slicker and given to the man barking the orders. Caroline fought wildly to break free, but to no avail. She watched him turn his horse and spur it into a gallop, away from the group of men and away from the clearing.

Caroline's heart crumbled in despair and defeat began to steal over her. She slumped in the iron-like hands of her captor. First, her beloved husband… Now, the only thing that she had left of him... Her precious son.

Rain dripped down her tormented face mingling with the tears dripping off the tip of her nose. She felt herself being lifted upwards and placed on a horse. She looked down into the sympathetic eyes of the man hoisting her into place and, suddenly, she knew what she had to do.

She sat in the saddle waiting for just the right moment, and as he reached for the saddle horn to mount behind her, Caroline kicked him in the chest. She snatched the reins and spurred the horse forward. The force of her kick coupled with the startled leap of the animal knocked the astonished man on his backside, and it was just enough time for her to flee. The horse lurched forward, scattering any opposition to her escape and she broke away from the clan, racing in the direction of the man who had taken her son.

A loud clap of thunder startled her as she neared the tree line. She reined in her horse briefly to find the path he had taken, and she threw a hasty look over her shoulder. All she could see was torrential rain and flashes of light.

She strained to hear... Anything... But all she could hear was the cracking of thunder and wailing wind. The soldiers would be upon her soon.

Another boom sent her mount into a frenzy underneath her, and she struggled to control him. The beast reared and whirled around, bolting back in the direction that she had just fled from. Caroline fought for control of herself and of the terrified animal as she realized what was happening.

No, no, no, NO!

She yanked one more time with what little strength she had left, and forcefully snatched the head of her mount around. As the horse's hind end slid to a halt, his front hooves pounded the sloppy ground trying to find footing for a turn, but the ground was saturated and slick, and they both went down. Caroline hit the ground with a wet thud as the horse flailed about trying to regain footing. Free of his rider, the beast scrambled to his feet and fled toward the trees. The dazed woman struggled to her feet in the boggy clearing. Her heart propelled her forward, but the deep mud held her prisoner. She sobbed hopelessly as she fought the bog and her heavy skirts to run toward the trees where she had seen the man disappear with her son.

Suddenly, the sound of sloppy hoof beats splashed all around and past her. She stopped, weary and defeated, as she watched those same riders who had previously overtaken her, race past her ahead of the tempest... leaving her alone in the now deserted clearing, only to stare after them in utter despair and confusion. She fell to her knees sobbing.

"Oh Lord," she screamed into the wind, *"Take me, now!. Just end my suffering... I can't... I just can't... I don't know where they have taken him...Oh MY GOD! WHERE ARE YOU?!"* She struggled to stand for one final attempt... She was so weak... So tired... Blackness settled in around her and the sounds of the storm faded

as she slipped into blissful darkness.

From the edge of the tree line, Little Wolf crouched, watching. He had watched the entire scene in the secrecy of his hiding place. He felt much respect for this small woman, and he waited for the right time, for he knew who she was, and he knew what he must do. The woman fell to her knees, seeming not to notice the turn of the weather around her... His heart pricked as she screamed at the heavens in agony. Such grief. He would have to act quickly, or she would be swept away.

He stood as the woman made an effort to stand, and he leapt into action as she collapsed in a dead faint. As swiftly as a deer, Little Wolf covered the clearing and kneeled beside her. He touched the matted mess that was her hair. Compassion for this little woman overwhelmed him. He reached to scoop her up and his heart quickened. This was more serious than he had thought. He should have intervened sooner. She was lying in a pool of muddy blood.

CHAPTER FIVE

"Pastor Jim?"

There was a timid knock on his office door as Missy stuck her raven head into the office. Her amber eyes, shy and questioning, found Jim's tired ones. She was the 18-year-old granddaughter of one of the WMU directors, and she was an absolute angel.

"Yes, Missy," he felt sorry for her. Today had been rough on both of them. After Tom had left, fuming, she had fielded the torrent of phone calls from other members of the Deacon Board and had dealt with as much hateful nonsense as he had.

"Mrs. Dalton is on line one."

Jim smiled warmly, "Why didn't you just intercom me?"

"I'm still having trouble figuring out this new system…" she smiled shyly.

"You, too, huh?" Jim chuckled lightly, "Thanks. I'll get it."

She pulled her head back through the door and then poked it back in again, just as he was picking up the receiver. He looked at her.

"Is it ok if I leave a little early today? My friends are going to the creek and asked me to go." She looked hopeful, and Jim couldn't resist her sweetness.

"Sure thing, hon. I'm thinking about cutting out early, myself…" He smiled and added, "Thanks for your help today…"

A huge smile lit up her pretty face, "Sure thing! Thanks, P.J.!"

He chuckled as she popped back out of the office, and he put the receiver to his ear. P.J.…He kinda liked that. Several of the youth had started calling him that…P.J.…Pastor Jim.

"Well, hello, honey…" he drawled into the phone.

"Well, hello there, Hot Stuff! No wonder all the old ladies in the church love you!" Naomi chuckled.

"Oh, hey, Mama," he laughed, "I thought you were Barb. How's life at Sunny Birch? Seen any good soaps, lately?"

"Don't even get me started on that one…" Naomi huffed.

Jim chuckled. "So, to what do I owe this pleasure?"

"Well, son. I'm afraid it's not too pleasant." Naomi sighed.

Jim sat up in his chair. "Is everything alright?" He couldn't get down to see his mother as often as he wanted too, but he loved her dearly and the thought of anything happening to her was distressing.

"Now, now…Don't get your knickers in a twist, I'm fine. In fact, I'll be coming home soon, hopefully. It's Summer, I'm calling about."

Temporary relief washed over him, and he relaxed back into his chair. "So, what's going on with Sunny?"

"Well, son, I'm afraid your past has caught up with you and your chickens have come home to roost."

Jim was confused, "What do you mean, my 'past has caught up' with me?"

"Now honey, don't be silly," she chided impatiently.

"Ma…I really have no idea what you're talking about…" He searched his brain for a clue.

"I just got off the phone with her…" Naomi began.

"Didn't she just see you, there?" Jim interrupted.

"Jim Dalton, will you let me finish?"

"Sorry…Go ahead, Ma." He closed his eyes.

"She called me to tell me about a strange phone call that she got. It seems that her grandfather passed away."

Jim's eyes flew open, and he sat forward again. "Harvey?! When? What happened? Does Barb know?" *This day just gets better and better. I know You don't put more on us than we can bear, but Lord, this is too much…*

"Not *that* grandpa…" Naomi paused, "…Her *biological* grandpa."

Her statement was met with silence.

"Jim?"

More silence.

"Jim? Honey, are you still there?" She worried,

"Y-yes…" he whispered in shock.

"There's more…"

"What is it?" Jim could barely breathe.

"She's on her way up there, right now, and she is NOT happy. And honey…?"

"Yes, ma'am?"

"I think you need to tell her everything."

"I'm not going to lie to her, Ma." He cleared his throat.

"I know, sweetie." There was a pause, "The Lord laid you, heavy, on my heart this mornin' and I've been praying for you all day. Now I know why."

"Thanks, Mama. You have no idea how bad I need it."

"Well, I need to scoot. I just wanted to let you know…"

"Okay," Jim struggled to compose himself, "and, Mama?"

"Yes, dear?"

"Pray…Pray for all of us…"

There was silence and then a quiet sniffle, "I have been, honey…I have been."

Jim was so thankful that he had let Missy go for the afternoon, as the ding from the side door echoed through the silent office.

"Ma, I'm gonna have to go…Summer just walked in."

"Morgan, Morgan & Associates, how may I direct your call?"

"Ahem…Mr. Chris Morgan, if you please?"

"Hold, please…"

"Not for too long. I'm in a rush." A woman's voice snapped.

"Yes, ma'am."

The woman on the other end listened to the calming hold music, impatiently.

"Ma'am, Mr. Morgan is currently with another client at the moment. Would you like to hold?" The sweet voice came back over the line.

"No, I would *not*. I need to speak to Christopher *immediately*. This is an emergency!"

"Shall I interrupt his meeting?"

Shall I interrupt...Hmph! "Of course, you shall!" The woman barked into the phone, "...and quickly!"

"Yes, ma'am. Please hold."

More irritating hold music.

"This is Chris Morgan..." The voice on the other end of the phone sounded agitated.

"Well, it's about time!" The woman huffed.

Chris recognized the voice, "If you don't mind, I *am* in the middle of a very important meeting."

"Did you get in touch with the Dalton girl?" she demanded.

"Yes, I did. And you were right. She had no idea."

"Well, I told you, didn't I? She would have never known if you hadn't insisted on contacting her...Now I'm out of my inheritance and some illegitimate bastard is getting everything I worked so hard for."

Venom almost visibly oozed from the receiver.

He was losing patience with this woman, "Unfortunately for you, I have to actually do my job, if you want your claim to that inheritance to be iron clad. I *am* bound by law, lest you forget."

"Never mind that," the woman dismissed that statement, "I have a plan, but I need your help."

"I don't have time for this…"

"Oh yes, you do. You seem to have forgotten your assistance in a certain old coot's death…? And besides," she sniffed in self-satisfaction, "I can make it very worth your while."

"You have no proof, and *you* seem to have forgotten that, currently, you aren't getting a red cent from that 'old coot'."

"Maybe not yet, but I will…If you will help me."

Chris opened his mouth to protest.

"And don't give me that phooey about being bound by law. We both know that every man has his price…If it's large enough."

There was momentary silence and the line crackled slightly.

"I don't know why I am even considering this…"

"Because you, my dear, are a shrewd businessman." She chuckled in self-satisfaction.

"Whatever. I have to get back to my meeting, but I will call you later...Do not call me here, again. Do you understand?"

Hateful cackling laughter filled the line, " 'Don't call me, I'll call you', is it?"

"Do *not* call me here again, if you want my help."

The laughter died, "Done."

Click.

CHAPTER SIX

Jim felt every one of his 54 years as he lifted himself from his chair and slowly moved to the office door. Through the brain fog, he tried to form what he was going to say to his only daughter. How to begin? How could he possibly tell her what had happened so many years ago? How could he not?

He prayed as he reached for the doorknob, *"Jesus, I know this is my own doing...my own foolishness. But I also know that You promised to be with me. Help me know what to say...Please help her to forgive me...Please forgive me, Father, for allowing her to live a lie."*

He slowly opened the door and stepped out into the main office. Glancing around the room, he found it empty.

"Now, I know I'm not crazy..." He thought out loud, "I just heard that door jingle..."

Jim went to the glass door at the front of the office and peered out into the newly paved parking lot, expecting to see Summer's Chevy. About that time, a tall attractive man in his late twenties bounded up the steps with a box in his arms. Smiling at the pastor through the glass, he waited as Jim opened the door for him.

"Hey there, Pastor Jim!....Hey, whoa…Are you okay?"

Jim forced a smile brighter than he thought possible, "Fine, fine!" He lied. "Come on in!" He carefully moved out of the young man's way as he continued to hold the door open.

"Whatcha got there, Chad?"

Chad Walker was the newly appointed Youth Pastor and Jim felt truly blessed to have him on the team. He was so passionate about teens and Jim had not seen the type of love this guy was capable of, in a long time. It was refreshing to have Chad on staff, not to mention the hopes Jim had for a relationship between Summer and this vibrant young man.

"Well," Chad began, "Remember those T-shirts we talked about? The ones the Youth Council approved?" He was grinning.

Jim nodded and glanced out the door again. *Lord, please hold her off for a little longer.* The last thing he wanted or needed was for his fiery daughter to blast in, guns blazing, in front of Chad. Not many people knew about this…yet.

"They turned out AWESOME! So much better than I thought they would! I brought 'em right over for you to see."

He pulled the flaps of the box open and pulled out a black shirt with bright multicolor print on it. He held it up for Jim to see. The front of the shirt had a solid, fluorescent rainbow circle with stick legs and beneath it, in bold white letters read 'Jesus Original.' On the back it read, '1st Bapt. Watson Student Ministry', at shoulder height and under it read, 'God made people in His image. He patterned them after Himself...Gen 1:27a'

"Well? Whatcha think?" Chad was so excited.

"I think it's great, and I want to buy the first one." Jim smiled for real, this time.

"Too late, P.J." Chad grinned as he tossed Jim a size large, "I beat you to it!"

"Chad?" Jim said as he caught the shirt and finally stepped away from the door, "We need to talk about a meeting I had, earlier, with Tom Davies."

Chad's tan face lost all of its humor.

"Let me guess, they have a problem with what I'm doing..."

Jim could see the struggle on Chad's features. One thing he really respected about this young man was his purposeful transparency...and his humility.

"I'm sorry, Pastor. I know that wasn't right to say...I'm just tired." Chad's eyes spoke volumes as they found understanding in Jim's.

"You keep doing what you're doing. Just pray for them, son, and let God do the fighting back."

The door jingled again, and Jim knew without looking

who was standing there.

Chad opened his mouth to tease her, but the jibe died on his lips when he saw her swollen, tear-streaked face. She was staring at her father with uncontrolled, unveiled disgust, fury, and fiery agony. He looked from Summer to Jim and hurriedly threw the shirts back into the box. He closed the flaps and scooted around Summer and out the door. Neither daughter nor the distraught looking older man even noticed when the door jingled Chad's exist.

Chad placed the box in the truck bed of his F-150 and whispered a prayer, *"Lord, I don't know what just happened in there, but please be with both of them. Protect what You're doing here, Dad..."*

Summer slammed the door of her Suburban and stood for a moment staring at the new church building in betrayed disgust. To her, that building represented a life that never even existed. Everything, all she knew, had been one enormous lie...Actually, multiple lies. And her dad, the beloved 'pastor', was standing at the helm of the USS Falsehood. Hot tears began coursing down her cheeks for the hundredth time and she swiped at them angrily. How could he do this to her?

She glanced around the newly paved parking lot and

noticed Chad Walker's black F-150 sitting in a parking spot three spaces from her own truck. How had she managed to miss that when she pulled in? Normally, her stomach would've been misbehaving terribly at the thought of seeing the handsome young youth pastor, but today she felt nothing but betrayal. She was numb to everything else.

Everything began to make sense, now. All the missing pieces of the puzzle were laid out and her heart broke a little more with each piece that found its way in to place. No wonder there were never any pictures of her mother pregnant. No wonder her mother looked a little distant in her baby pictures. Her imagination had run wild all afternoon.

Suddenly, a thought struck her. Had her dad been at this church when all this happened? When *she* happened…What a colossal hypocrite.

Then another thought hit her. How many people knew about this? Probably this whole, God-forsaken town! The thought horrified her. It certainly would explain a lot of things…

Well, she was going to get to the bottom of this, right now, and Chad…and whoever else happened to be in there…would just have to deal with it.

She marched up to the church building and snatched open the glass door.

SKELETON KEY

Will Conner stood with his arms crossed over his chest and his back to the entrance of the rudimentary hut that his friend had led him to. He couldn't explain why, but he hadn't had a peace about returning to his home yet, even though he was so close, so he had set camp about a mile away from the house. When Little Wolf had entered his camp this morning and had informed him that the child's mother was alive, he was filled with relief for more than one reason. The child had been in his care for a day and a night, now. What was *he* to do with a newborn? All he knew was that something had to be done or the child would die. There had been consequences for the men that had abandoned the child's mother and all efforts had been made to find her, but the rain had washed away any trace of her trail. Yes, he was very relieved, indeed.

When Will and his men had happened upon her in the clearing, he had not recognized her. Pale and too thin, she did not fit the memory of the woman he had known so intimately. Recognition had slammed into him suddenly and agony had clenched his heart in a vice. Letters from his father had convinced him of how silly and foolish she was, but this was borderline insane. He had almost pitied her…almost. Nothing could have prepared him, though, for the revelation that her blankets had hidden from his sight.

Stripped of her blankets, the level of her betrayal and the

ferocity of his anger and nearly consumed him. A child. And obviously hers, judging from the way she protected the little bastard. His father had not mentioned this in his letters! Perhaps, it was to save him the pain of the magnitude of her unfaithfulness. He had been tempted to leave her and her unholy spawn there to die, but his honor would not allow it.

Since that fateful afternoon, every time he closed his eyes, Will could still see her standing in the center of that clearing, surrounded by his men. Her skirts and hair were whipping about her madly, her eyes blazing with passion that used to burn for him alone…In that moment, he fought the urge to run to her, hold her, caress her, protect her…But the blinding reality of who and what she was, and who he had become had halted him. No matter what he did, he could not get that vivid image out of his mind. It would forever be branded into his memory.

Now, he was standing mere feet away from where she lay, and he didn't have the courage to face her. Maybe if he was whole…if he wasn't a scarred monster…then he might be able to confront her, but not like this. The memory of her horrified face was a humiliation he was not willing to bear a second time.

"Will…"

His eyes snapped back to the present and looked into the eyes of the only man he had come to trust, outside of his family.

"She is improving…"

The flapped opened and a beautiful bronze woman of strong build stooped to step out of the teepee. She was stately and elegant, and her raven-colored braid fell across her shoulder as she stood. She smiled at Little Wolf and spoke to him in a language that Will had become accustomed to hearing. She turned her ebony eyes to William, and he thought he could read traces of sympathy there and it burned him deeply. She ducked back into the tent, and they could hear her sultry alto voice singing softly.

"You are a lucky man, Little Wolf."

Little Wolf smiled widely, "Yes, I know…" His eye sought the eyes of his friend. "You are a lucky man, as well…She is a fine strong woman."

Will stiffened and looked away. "I used to think so."

Saddened, Little Wolf turned and stooped, picking a blade of grass, his loose and silky black hair falling over his shoulders. He squatted and ran his fingers down the smooth length of the grass. Little Wolf pondered on how much this man had changed since he had last seen him. His heart had grown cold.

"You have a fine son. He will be strong soon now that Kalana is nursing him." He examined the piece of grass in his hands.

"He is not mine." William snapped as his own statement pierced his heart.

Little Wolf's eyes widened, and he winced inwardly. He felt compassion for his friend. How could he be so blind? Where was the faith he had spoken so passionately about less than a year ago? The faith that he had shared with Little Wolf's people...the faith that had changed many of their lives.

He changed his approach. "She cries out for you...as if you were dead." He kept his eyes on the blade of grass as he squatted there. When there was no response, he looked up into the steely blue gaze of his friend.

"She's delirious." Will paused for a moment, thinking, "Don't tell her differently...I'm dead to her now."

"She prays for her God to return you to her..."

"It doesn't matter to me, now." He turned his head.

"So, you will not see her, then?" He tossed the well inspected blade of grass aside and stood slowly seeking his companion's face.

"No...N-not like this..." His hands trembled slightly as he touched his scarred face. He turned and began walking away.

"You do not do her justice, my friend..." Little Wolf insisted.

William whirled around, "Justice?!" He laughed sarcastically, "Justice? How is it justice that my *wife* betrays me? How is justice that that I have become a...a monster?" He threw trembling hands into the air. "How is it justice that my life has practically ended and the Good God Almighty refuses to be merciful and actually end it?" Bitterness and disdain dripped from every word, "Justice, you say..." he scoffed, "The infant in that tent is not even my own. That wretched *wench* does not deserve my pity, let alone my justification..."

"But what of the God you taught me of? Does He not ask us to forgive?" Little Wolf's eyes questioned Will's resolve.

Will spat on the ground, "Do not speak to me of God. He is not mine either...Not anymore."

With that, he spun on his heel and charged to his horse. Mounting without a word or a look back, he spurred his horse a little too hard and galloped away into the woods. It was time to go home.

Kalana came and stood beside her husband, silently. She slipped her hand into his and laid her silky head on his shoulder, eyes filling with unshed tears for the pitiful woman lying in their tent and for the stubborn man running away from his happiness. Little Wolf turned his head and pressed his lips to her brow inhaling the woody, smoky scent of her. He offered up a prayer to the God he had come to trust as he watched his stubborn and blinded friend ride away.

Caroline thought her heart would pound out of her chest

as her father kissed her cheek with a tear in his eye. He whispered something about her radiance as he lowered her veil and offered her his arm. Her hand trembled as she tucked it deeply into the crook of his arm. Her father smiled widely and patted her hand as they turned toward the opening of the doors of the church.

The music began to play, and the couple slowly made their way down the small, center aisle of the quaint little southern church. At the end of the aisle, next to the altar, stood the reason for her elation. Tall and strong... Her William. How she had waited for this day to arrive! Behind her veil, her eyes drank him in. Dark curls framed the angular, tanned face and his eyes seemed to shine like silver, as they made eye contact. Suddenly, all of her nervousness dissipated, and she seemed to float the remainder of the way down the aisle.

Suddenly, her trembling hand was in his confident one and she was gazing into the consuming depths of his navy-ringed, ice blue eyes. Emotion threatened to smother her as she handed her wildflower bouquet to her sister and surrendered her now free hand to her dashing groom.

"Dust thou, Caroline Jessica Jameson," Caroline turned her eyes away from her Prince and looked at the vicar, "take this man to be thy lawfully wedded husband? To have and to hold, for better or worse, for richer or poorer, in sickness and in health, as long as ye both shall live?"

A single tear of rapture escaped as she turned her gaze

back to the man standing before her.

"I do." She whispered breathlessly.

"Dust thou, James William Connor III, take this woman to be thy lawfully wedded wife? To have and to hold, for better or worse, for richer or for poorer, in sickness and in health, as long as ye both shall live?"

The depth of her emotion and the strength of her love nearly strangled her, and her knees threatened to give way as this picturesque man smiled radiantly at her and said, "I do."

Somewhere in her distant consciousness she heard the vicar pronounce them man and wife and then...

"You may kiss your bride, William."

Heat flew from her toes to the top of her head as William leaned in close to her. She inhaled the scent of his body and waited for the precious, tender, long-awaited touch of his lips.

Nothingness... Coldness enveloped her senses and hot pain tore through her temples, but it paled in comparison to the pain in her heart... She was drifting away... The chapel faded into the darkness...

"No!......William!......I am here!......" She called out to the man fading into the fog, "Please! Don't go!!....... Please, Jesus!...I need him!......Please don't take him from me!......" Her voice faded into a whimper.

Carolyn began weeping uncontrollably and blessed

darkness overcame her senses, and she drifted back into oblivion.

Kalana turned her head toward the moaning inside the leather tent. Little Wolf released her hand as she turned to stoop back inside of the teepee. She quietly made her way to the back of the hazy room and kneeled beside the unconscious woman. She touched Carolina's sweaty brow. The skin was hot to the touch and Kalana reached for the moist cloth located in the clay water basin at the edge of Caroline's bearskin mat. Cool water trickled down her hands as she squeezed the excess moisture from the cloth and swabbed the delirious woman's feverish forehead and face.

Sympathy and compassion filled Kalana's heart as she tenderly pushed sweaty tendrils of honey-colored curls from the face of this tortured young woman.

"Poor woman…," she thought sadly, "If your stubborn man could only see…"

A rustling at the entrance caught her attention. She looked up and smiled sadly as her husband made his way to the place where she knelt tending to Caroline. He knelt beside his wife.

"How is she?" Concern was etched upon his face.

"She fevers, still…But it's not her body that is not healing…" She turned compassionate eyes to Little Wolf.

He nodded once in silent understanding. He glanced toward the center of the room where the infant lay sleeping close to the warmth of the small fire, next to his own son.

"What of the boy?"

She smiled, her straight, white teeth illuminating her bronze features as she followed her husband's gaze, "He will be fine. He is a strong child with a strong appetite…" She chuckled quietly remembering the infant's vigorous enthusiasm when she presented her own breast to nurse him.

When Kalana turned her eyes back to Little Wolf, they held a question.

"Why would he not come to her?" She asked quietly as they moved away from Caroline's pallet to sit close to the sleeping babies.

He shook his head in confusion, "I don't know. Much has changed in him."

They sat in silence for a few moments.

"He said the child is not his…" Little Wolf began.

"The child is his." Kalana cut him off with a lifted hand and looked at him with a quiet sternness. "There is no guilt or guile in this woman… Only a broken heart." She turned concerned eyes upon her patient.

The quiet man looked at her with a silent intensity, and then at Caroline.

"How can you be sure?" He asked.

"Delirium does not lie." She stated matter-of-factly. "There is no remorse...no begging for forgiveness in her delusions. There is only grief and loneliness... Her spirit is clean." She moved to check on her own infant who was beginning to stir.

"You must convince him to at least see her." She whispered over her shoulder.

Little Wolf shook his head, "I cannot force him to face his past, even if it is the very thing that would save him."

Kalana replaced the animal hide covering her child and moved close to her husband to lean upon him, "We must pray, then."

Little Wolf put his arm around her and pulled her body close to him. He relished the feel of her as he buried his face into the dark hair on her neck and breathed deeply. He tenderly placed a kiss there.

"Yes, I'm afraid that's all we can do."

CHAPTER SEVEN

Father and daughter stood staring at each other, one furious, one resigned, but both sick. Jim opened his mouth, but the words failed to come. Summer raised her hand and closed her eyes as if to say, 'I don't want to hear it.' Jim closed his mouth and swallowed. Mentally he began begging the Lord for wisdom.

When her father didn't speak, she opened her eyes and glared at him.

"You know why I'm here, right?"

He nodded.

"I suppose I have Nanna to thank for that?"

Again, he nodded, pain etched on every line in his face.

"Shoulda figured she would rat me out." She turned away from the forlorn look on her dad's face.

"Ahem…" So, his voice hadn't completely betrayed him yet… "Uh, Summer…"

"No, Dad." She whirled around to face him again and his heart twisted at the raw agony he saw there, "I want to tell you something first."

Tears began to well up in her puffy eyes and trickle

down her face, "When I found out about this today... No wait... That doesn't quite say it...",She began again, "When I got slapped in the *face* with this today, I wanted to throw up. So many things that I never understood began to make sense to me."

She was crying again, darn it!

"Like why I never fit in, why all the old folks in town would whisper about me, why your little 'Demon' Board didn't want me to teach their precious Sunday School... But there's still one missing piece for me, Dad." She hiccupped a sob against her will, "Can you please tell me why the *one* person in the world that I idolized would let me believe that I was actually something special? Some*one* special? My GOD, Dad! I'm nothing more than a *bastard*! And-and... You let me parade around here, all of my life, acting like I was the precious, perfect little pastor's daughter!" She hiccupped again, "All the while, everyone but *me* knew I wasn't!"

She started sobbing again. She mentally cursed her lack of control. This was not the bold declaration that she had imagined.

In that moment, Jim's heart officially broke.

"Summer... You *are* special. You are my daughter and I love you... I was only doing what I thought was best for..."

"I'm a *BASTARD*, Dad! The illegitimate byproduct of a one-night stand." She spat through the tears now coursing down her face, "You were doing what was best for *you*." Summer jabbed a furious finger at him.

"Summer, you don't know the whole story..." He pleaded with her.

"You're right, I don't," she sobbed, "but I should."

Jim reached out to touch her.

"No!" She snatched away from him. "Don't touch me!"

"Well, can I at least tell you what happened?" He pleaded.

"I think it's obvious what happened..." Summer scoffed as she motioned to the entirety of herself. She shook her head vehemently, "No, Dad. It's too late for that." Her words hit their mark with deadly accuracy. "What I haven't figured out, is why mom didn't kick you to the curb when you did it. You don't deserve her …

"No, I don't... She's a remarkable woman..."

"And you don't deserve this church. They trust you and you've lied to them just like you've lied to me!" Summer pointed an accusing finger at her father.

"Now, Summer, that's enough!" Jim raised his voice to the 'I'm the dad and I mean business' tone.

Summer stared at him incredulously.

"I never lied to you, and I certainly never lied to anyone in this church. I was honest about it then, and I am honest about it now. They reprimanded me and forgave me, and graciously allowed me to continue in what the Lord called me to do here. Not many church boards would have allowed that." He sought his daughter's eyes desperately.

Summer was horrified. She had said that very thing just minutes before, but she thought that she was just venting. She didn't actually think they *knew*!

"You mean every one of them *KNOWS* about this?!" She spat in horror. "All of them?! And they approve?!"

Jim didn't know how to respond to Summer's question.

She laughed in disgusted disbelief, "I can't believe it!" She shook her head as she made her way to the door. "This place makes me sick... *You* make me sick. You and your little band of hypocrites. Well, I just came to tell you that I'm through..."

Jim's eyes shot up to meet her flaming ones, "Through? What do you mean by that?"

"Just what I said, *Daddy Dear,*" Summer turned her back on him as she reached for the door handle, "I'm through being your dirty little secret... Oh wait! That's right... It's only been a secret to me... Oops!... I forgot." Summer knew she could be really nasty when she wanted to be and right now, it felt so good to punish the culprit of her humiliation.

She tossed a hateful look over her shoulder, "I'm through with you, I'm through with this town. And the God you taught me about all of my life? Yeah, well, since He's probably one of your many lies, too? I'm through with Him, too."

"Don't say that... Give up on me, Summer, but don't give up on Him..."

She started out the door and Jim trotted across the office. He reached the door as she was storming down the stairs onto the sidewalk.

"Summer! Wait!" He held the door open and shouted out into the parking lot as his distraught daughter jogged to her SUV. "Where are you going? Please be mature about this and let me explain!"

That's great, she thought, *now I'm immature...*Something deep inside of her beckoned her to listen to him, and to give him an opportunity to explain.

She squashed that immediately.

"You had your chance!" She shouted back at him. "It's my turn now."

The smell of fresh cut flowers enveloped her as she unlocked and opened the squeaky glass door of her little flower boutique on the strip in downtown Watson. The wind chimes over the door jingled as the door passed under them. The light from the flower coolers was the only light in the shop, as she locked the door behind her . The digital clock on the front counter glowed a bright green 2:30 AM as she passed by. *Wow...* She had been out in Old Man P.Q.'s field longer than she'd realized. It was where she always went to clear her head, or in this case, to run away.

Stuffing the keys into the pocket of her windbreaker, Summer made her way to the back of the darkened store after she had checked all of the coolers and done the necessary waterings and vitamin treatments for the flowers that no one seemed to want. A sad thought crossed her mind as she climbed the stairs to the apartment located over the shop. Her flowers were a lot like her... beautiful possibilities that no one seemed to care about or desire. She fished the keys back out of her pocket and found the right one, inserted it and turned the dead bolt. An impatient 'meow' greeted her as she turned the knob and pushed the door open.

"Hey there, Mow-Mow..." She crooned at the overweight Manx beating his head against her legs. Summer stooped quickly and hefted him up into her arms, burying her face into the warmth of his fat neck. His gratitude rumbled deeply in his throat and Summer smiled as she kicked the door closed with her foot. It felt good to smile...

"Well, at least *him* loves me..." She sing-songed to the blissful feline before depositing him onto the lumpy old couch that her Nanna had 'donated' to her. Mow quickly hopped down with a thud, and padded after her into the tiny kitchen watching her every move intently... Even more so as she neared the little fridge. Licking his lips, he parked himself at the microwave on the counter, staring up at her as he waited for Summer to dish up his very late supper.

Summer chuckled and stooped as she scratched his head. Mow chirped in response as she opened the fridge and pulled out a can of his food, scraped it into his dish and plopped it in the microwave.

"You know the deal, huh, big guy?" She tapped the counter absently with her fingers and waited for the ding. The obese kitty chirped again, weaving himself in and out of her legs. She scratched his flabby belly with her toes, and he flipped over on his back for more. She chuckled and obliged him.

When the ding sounded, she took the dish out of the microwave and stirred it. She placed it on the floor for him to devour and delighted purring filled the kitchen. She smiled as she padded back to the living room.

Summer had turned off her phone when she left her dad. She had needed the space to process. Turning on her phone, texts and voicemail notifications blew up her worn-out cell phone. Normally, these messages were a good thing. It meant business or pleasant conversations with her mom or Nanna, but after today's events, she didn't even want to hear any of the messages that were lurking in her voicemail, but there they were. Five messages anxiously waiting to be delivered to the person who owned this number. She quickly scrolled through the texts and deleted them all without reading them as she made her way to the couch. She sighed deeply, plopped down on the sofa, and hit the play button. She laid her head back on the lumpy pillows and waited, dreading the voices that she would hear.

She clicked the speakerphone, and the first message began, "Hey Summer. This is your mom..." Summer smiled in spite of herself... Like she wouldn't know who it was... "I just got a call from Mrs. Willis," Summer groaned. Here we go... That old biddy must have called on her cell phone as soon as it happened. "Sweetie, I know you're having a hard time financially right now, but please let your dad check your catalytic converter. Mrs. Willis said that she nearly choked to death on the fumes that came from your truck today..." Summer snickered briefly. "I told her I was sure you didn't mean to smoke her out. I hope I was right... Oh! And honey, don't forget about the WMU meeting tomorrow night. We're going to choose our secret pals and I want you to bring some arrangements as examples of good, reasonable gifts. I thought it might help your business... Okay?"

Summer sighed.

"Okay. Well, I know you hate for me to leave a book on voicemail, so call me later, okay? Love you honey!"

The message ended and Summer deleted it.

Mow waddled into the living room and hefted himself up on the couch. He laid down next to Summer's thigh and began cleaning his face and paws, purring contentedly. The sound vibrated her leg. She chuckled softly and scratched his ears, "That didn't take long, Fatty Catty..." Summer clicked on the next message.

"This message is for Summer Dalton. This is Julie Whatley with Morgan, Morgan & Associates. Please return my call, in reference to an urgent business matter. The number is..." Summer closed her eyes and pinched the center of her eyebrows. These were the messages she was dreading... "Please call at your earliest convenience."

The message ended. Summer left it in her in box and clicked on the next message from another unrecognized number with a sigh.

"Um, hey, Summer..." Summer's eyes widened, and her heart began racing involuntarily, "...This is Chad. I was, uh, AHEM...I was wondering if you would like to catch some dinner tonight..." Summer's eyes grew wide, ""Um...Okay. So, yeah. Give me a call and let me know if you want to hook up...No! Not *hook up*, hook up..." He chuckled nervously and Summer smiled, "That came out wrong...Um...get together, you know...? That kind... Ah, geez. Okay, well...Give me a shout. Bye."

The message ended.

Summer sat up on the couch and stared at the cheap curtains covering the window across from where she was sitting. Her heart threatened to jump out of its place in her ribcage. Did she hear that right? Chad Walker wanted to take her dinner? Tonight? ...*TONIGHT!*

Wait a minute...That would have been LAST night...Great. Just perfect.

"He probably thinks I'm a huge jerk." She flopped backwards onto the cushions, and she clicked on the next message from the same number, received just a few minutes later.

"Hey again. I guess you kinda need a number to call me back at, huh?" He chuckled into the phone again and Summer really liked the way it sounded... "My cell is 678-588-4563 and my home number is 478-256-8897. Oh! And you know the church number. I'll be there around 4 o'clock this afternoon. Oh, wait...Caller ID...Jeez. Okay, anyway...Hope to hear from you. I'll leave your machine alone, now." Another chuckle.

Summer felt sick. He *had* been at the church yesterday afternoon...Right when Hurricane Summer blew in with guns blazing. She put her hands over her face in embarrassment. Her mom had always chided her about her temper and thinking before she acted...So now, on top of feeling insanely guilty for how rotten she had been to her dad, she now had to deal with the colossal humiliation of showing out in front of the church's gorgeous youth pastor, whom it was apparent that she had officially ignored and snubbed.

Then a horrifying thought struck her. Had he ever even left the office? She didn't remember! She had been so angry and hurt that the only thing she saw was red...Oh,

God! What if he had been there the whole time? What if he had heard everything? She could never face him again.

Summer stared at the phone in her hand. She recognized the number on the next message as her mom's. Given the time stamp, she knew it what it was about, and she really wanted to just delete it, but she couldn't. She pressed the unheard message.

"Summer…This is Mom. I think we need to talk, honey. I know you don't want to talk to Daddy, but will you talk to me? I think I can help you understand some things. Please promise me that we can talk before you make any decisions? Please call me, honey. I love you so very much…from the moment I first saw you and held you in my arms, I have loved you. Please call me?"

The message ended.

A tear slipped down Summer's cheek. She wanted to know everything, but at the same time, she didn't. Wasn't ignorance bliss? Only…She wasn't ignorant of it anymore…She sighed as she wiped the tear away with her thumb. The last unheard message waited for her. The number looked familiar.

"Ahem…Hey, Summer." She looked at her phone as she recognized the voice. It was Chad again. "It may be none of my business, but I noticed you were pretty upset at the church and I just wanted to extend a friendly shoulder to cry on…if you need it, that is…um…or you can tell me to kick rocks…just wanted to let you know…And it may not be great timing, but if you wanted to catch dinner or lunch tomorrow, just let me know. Um…Okay…I'm gonna go now…You probably think I'm some kind of obsessed creep…" Another nervous chuckle, "Well, anyway…I hope things work out for you…Bye."

The message ended.

Despite the weight on her mind, one of the worries in her heart began to be replaced with a girlish hope. A small smile played about her lips as she laid her throbbing head back on to the cushions of the lumpy cushions and closed her eyes. She started to pray, but then remembered that she wasn't speaking to Him…So she tossed the phone onto the couch beside her and forced herself to ignore the pull on her heart and drifted off to sleep, to the soft, deep rumbles of a very satisfied and content fat-cat.

CHAPTER EIGHT

Attorney Chris Morgan checked his appearance in the private bathroom in his plush office on the tenth floor of the Johnson-Drake building. His dark curls framed his handsome face in a comely way and his thick, dark eyelashes accentuated the cobalt color of the eyes staring back at him. He liked to think of himself as a modern-day Cary Grant... The perpetual bachelor, ever dashing and mysterious. He was more than good looking, and he knew it, and he used it to his advantage whenever he could. Today would be no different. Chris smiled at his reflection revealing perfect white teeth and winked his approval. He straightened his tie, turned, and stepped back into his office.

Striding to his desk, he pressed the intercom and spoke into the machine on his desk.

"Julie?"

A young woman's sweet voice came over the speaker, "Yes, Sir?"

"Has Ms. Dalton arrived yet?" He queried.

"Not yet, Sir."

"Alert me as soon as she does."

"Certainly, Mr. Morgan." She cooed.

"Thanks, doll." Julie blushed on the other side of the wall.

He straightened and glanced around his luxurious office. From the Italian leather chairs and exquisite mahogany desk to the signature vases and oil paintings, his workspace was nothing short of elegant... But that was to be expected for the new senior partner. Chris physically swelled with pride at the sheer impossibility of his new title. Being the youngest member in the firm, at the age of 30, the journey to senior partner had been a trial from day one, and from day one, Chris had determined to work... or *con*...his way into some respect. That's where his good looks had come into play. He wasn't necessarily proud of how he had made it to this office, but to him, everything he wanted had a price and he was willing to pay it to get it.

The intercom on his desk buzzed.

"Yes?"

"Sir, Ms. Dalton has arrived and is waiting to see you."

"Send her in." He straightened and put on his most dashing smile. The objective: Love at first sight... He smiled to himself. Lust, if he was lucky.

Summer arrived in Pickinsville around ten o'clock AM full of bitterness and questions for the attorney who had contacted her. She wanted history. She wanted pictures. She wanted answers, and she was determined to get them. She had refused to speak with her father about this situation. In fact, she had refused to speak to him at all since their heated conversation two days prior. No matter how her mother had tried to convince her, she had adamantly refused. Summer didn't want *his* version. She wanted the truth. Something deep inside told her that she was being immature and irrational, but she just didn't care. Didn't she have a reason to feel this way? Wasn't she justified? She decided that yes, she did and yes, she was.

She turned down the radio to hear the GPS more clearly and followed the directions to the upscale law firm. The air conditioner was blowing frigid, and she adored her mom for letting her borrow her Camry for the two-hour road trip. Summer wasn't sure what kind of place this was, and she wanted to make a good impression. That, and she had an inkling that her bucket of bolts would have left her thumbing a ride sixty miles outside of Watson... If it even made it that far.

She followed the signs to the parking deck and found a space convenient to the elevator. Putting the car in park, she set the emergency brake and switched off the ignition. Lingering for a moment, Summer stared into oblivion as she tried to imagine what kind of implications today's meeting would hold for her life. One thing she was sure of was that she was *not* going to give those nosey people in Watson, Georgia the opportunity to judge her ever again. If that meant that she had to leave for good, then so be it.

Her pretty brow furrowed, and her heart constricted at the thought of leaving behind the little town where she had grown up... All of her family...

More pain.

"It's not your town and it's not your family anyway," a voice whispered into the depths of her soul, *"Everything you ever knew is nothing but a lie..."* Tears threatened for what seemed like the millionth time and she shook her head to clear the unwelcome thoughts.

"Stop it, Summer," she chided herself, "Get it together, girl. You can't go in there a weepin' mess..."

Checking her reflection in the rearview mirror, Summer resolved to cry it out on the way back to Watson, hoping that that concession would ease the ache in her throat. It didn't. She wasn't sure what she would do when she got back home, but one thing she knew without a doubt was that she couldn't stay. That was the only thing she had managed to decide in the last two days since she had received this colossally life changing information, but the 'hows' of it all were still fuzzy in her mind.

Laying her hand across her flat stomach, Summer didn't know if the nausea she felt was from the sausage biscuit she had wolfed down earlier, or from her frazzled nerves. Probably both. Taking a deep, cleansing breath, the former pastor's daughter pulled the handle, opened the car door, and stepped out of her mother's car and into her future. The mere thought of that scared her to death.

"Okay," she thought, "A little dramatic…Take it easy, Sunny-girl…You can do this…"

She closed the door and hit the lock button on the remote key chain. A smile played about her polished lips. The little toot that the car made signifying that the alarm was set, never failed to tickle her.

"I really need a new car..." She said aloud, "... with one of these thingies..." She smiled to herself as she hit the lock button on the remote one more time and the car horn tooted. She chuckled and dropped the keys into her purse before tucking it under her arm.

The click-click-click of her heels echoed throughout the expanse of cement and vehicles as she made her way to the elevators. Summer looked down at her stylish pumps as she walked. She hated to dress up, but when she did, she knew she was more than decent looking. Today was no exception. She had wanted to make sure that this big city lawyer didn't think he could screw around with her just because she was from the country. She was a businesswoman and, for once, in a town full of strangers who didn't know who or what she really was, she wanted the respect that she deserved.

Her honey-hazel eyes sparked with apprehension and expectation as she exited the elevator and marched into the law firm with a purpose and the beginnings of a plan.

Chris stood as Julie opened the door for the young woman he had spoken with earlier. As she gracefully stepped around his secretary and into the plush office, he was momentarily stunned by the purity of her simple loveliness. He didn't believe in God, but he was sure there was an angel floating into his office at this precise moment. Her golden hair was twisted up into a stylish curly mess on top of her head and she had the rarest colored eyes he had ever seen. Silver earrings dangled perilously close to the slender, graceful line of her neck. Her white, linen pantsuit hugged her lithe body in a most alluring and modest way, and when she smiled her hello, her glistening, pouty lips revealed perfect teeth the same white as her suit. Her tan was deep and becoming, and Chris very obviously appreciated her beauty. The resulting blush on her face was enchanting. He had spoken with her several times over the past two days, but he had had no inkling that she was this beautiful. It was *good* to be the boss. He was going to enjoy every minute of his new assignment.

A shadow passed over his face briefly as he assisted this beauty with her seat. There was one aspect of his job that was rather distasteful, given the sudden revelation of his attraction for her. But he would cross that bridge when he got there.

The young attorney stepped back behind his desk and seated himself across from a young woman he was anxious to get to know... On a more *personal* level. He put on his most dashing smile and introduced himself.

Ms. Dalton. It's so good to meet you in person. I'm Christopher Morgan, your grandfather's attorney, and the executor of his will."

Kalana smiled contentedly as her son nursed happily at her breast. To her, there was no greater joy than this new adventure of motherhood. She had been certain that, on the day of her marriage to Little Wolf, her heart would burst with all the emotion she felt, but she had never expected to experience the devotion and fierce love that she was experiencing, now, as she watched her little one heartily enjoy his dinner. Kalana glanced at the woman lying so still on the other side of the teepee and wondered how long it would be before she would nurse *her* son again.

Silently she offered up a prayer to the God that Little Wolf had introduced her to, as a sympathetic tear rolled down her cheek. How many times, since she had taken on this responsibility, had she placed herself in this woman's predicament? How many times had she fought the urge to chase that stubborn man down and make him see what a fool he was? She sighed. And how many times had she, herself, questioned the plan of her newly found God?

Closing her eyes briefly, Kalana inhaled peace and exhaled confusion. Inhaled trust, and exhaled fear. She looked down at her infant and relished the sweet plumpness of his now sleeping baby face. She lingered a moment and then pressed a soft kiss upon his downy head. Gently removing him from her breast, she wrapped him snugly in soft clothes and animal skins and laid him tenderly beside the other sleeping infant. Patting the sleeping bundle softly, she murmured a prayer over them and shifted from her knees to her feet.

A soft moan from the other side of the small room startled Kalana and she came quickly to the side of the young woman, whom a moment before, had appeared so lifeless. Picking up a cloth out of the basin of water close by, she quickly squeezed the excess water from it and dabbed her patient's head with it. The young woman's hand reached up and touched Kalana's and then her eyes fluttered open, looking directly at her. There was confusion in her golden eyes, and she opened her mouth as if to speak, but no sound escaped her.

"Shhhhh…" Kalana crooned, "Do not try to talk. Here, drink this…"

The young woman looked confused and then closed her eyes once more, but as Kalana lifted her head and presented the cup of medicine water, her patient drank it desperately.

"No, no! Not so fast…" Kalana tipped the cup back.

The young woman looked at her intently. There was a

question in her eyes. She looked from Kalana to the cup in her hand and then around the tent. When their eyes met again, she coughed and spoke in a dry, raspy whisper.

"Where am I…?"

Kalana smiled and thanked God. She touched the young woman's brow and both cheeks. There was no sign of fever! Her smile broadened, "You are with my husband and I…"

The confusion written on the other woman's face told Kalana that she could not understand her. Kalana had learned to understand English through the many nights when Little Wolf and William would sit by the fire talking, but she never learned to speak it. She stood abruptly and hurriedly left the tent to fetch Little Wolf. He would communicate for her! Kalana was excited and more than pleased. She couldn't wait to reunite a portion of the broken little family that God had placed in their lives. But deep in her heart, a part of her also hoped that this young woman was the answer to the many prayers of a lonely young squaw.

Blurry figures and suffocating warmth greeted her as Caroline struggled to open her heavy eyelids. She could hear murmurs and rustling close by. She felt so weak, as if her limbs were heavily weighted, and they stubbornly refused to obey her as she attempted to stir. The rustling on the other side of the tent ceased as Caroline's knees slowly began to raise and lower. Her brow furrowed in confusion when she felt a cool damp cloth dab her forehead, and she raised her hand and touched the hand holding the cloth. Caroline's fingers lingered there for a moment as she turned her head and tried to focus on the form kneeling beside her.

She opened her mouth to speak but her throat was dry and closed.

"Shhhhh..." She heard a voice murmur comfortingly. And then there was a string of words she couldn't understand.

The dabbing of the cloth ceased, and soon the hands that soothed her were helping to lift her head off of her mat and there was a bowl-like cup at her lips. The cool, herbed water flowed over her cracked lips into a parched mouth. She gulped greedily and the cup came away from her lips quickly. There were more soothing words that she couldn't comprehend.

Caroline opened her eyes once more and her blurry vision began to stabilize on an exotic looking woman with dark skin and hair. This woman's ebony eyes held concern and compassion as she spoke soothingly to her. Caroline's gaze slowly moved from the woman to her surroundings. First the cup of water, then the fire in the center of the room, next to the odd markings on the walls, and then back to the woman kneeling over her.

Cough, "Where am I?" She rasped.

The woman set the cup down. She pressed her hand to Caroline's brow and then to each side of her face and smiled, her white teeth illuminating her bronze features. She spoke in response and Caroline struggled to make sense of it, but she just couldn't understand it. The woman seemed to see that and abruptly stood to her feet, stepped away from Caroline, and ducked out of a small opening in what appeared to be the wall.

Too exhausted to think anymore, Caroline turned her head away from the opening. Her entire body protested the movement, and she wondered how long she'd been lying there like that. A stabbing pain in her breasts startled her as her body slowly followed her head and she rolled to her side. Dazed she touched her breasts, wincing as she did so. They were twice their normal size and as hard as rocks.

Ouch! I need to nurse the baby...

Sudden realization struck her. Her heart twisted and she cried out with the agony of it. She pushed herself into a sitting position, her head pounding with every desperate beat of her broken heart. She must find him... Struggling to her feet, Caroline stumbled haltingly toward the low opening. Leaning forward to exit was almost too much pressure for her throbbing head to bear, so she dropped to her knees onto the earthen floor and proceeded to crawl out of the tent. She had no idea where she was. She had no idea who had saved her or why. The only thing she knew was that no matter what she would find her son... Even if she died trying.

Just a few miles away, a wayward son stepped through the dimly lit decorative, mahogany doorway of his father's southern mansion... Half a man with half a heart.

As the door closed behind him, his father stepped into the hall. Recognizing the silhouette, the older gentleman touched the sleeve of the young man whose back was facing him. As the soldier turned around to face him, a gasp froze in the father's throat...

"Dear God! William!"

CHAPTER NINE

Summer stared at her reflection in the mirror of her hotel room for a last-minute perfection check. Baring her teeth, she checked for the infamous "lipstick on the teeth" syndrome. Seeing that her teeth were free of that menace, Summer nodded her approval as she began dropping different pieces of make up into her clutch and then the rest into her cosmetics bag and zipped it shut.

Her mind replayed the events of the morning and afternoon. Chris Morgan had been younger…and more attractive…than she had imagined. She blushed again as she recalled the way he had looked at her as she had stepped into his office. She recalled how he had been so very close…She had never had a man look at her that way before…Like he would die if he didn't kiss her. And so blatantly, too! She remembered how her blood pressure had skyrocketed and heat had sizzled through her veins, from her toes straight through the top of her scalp. A small smile played about her perfectly finished lips. This evening might prove to be interesting indeed.

Summer seated herself across from the much younger than expected attorney. His dark hair was curly and stylishly unruly, but it was his eyes that held her attention. Summer didn't think she had ever seen eyes so vividly blue and, maybe it was her imagination, but they seemed dangerous and mysterious.

"Oh, stop it!" Mentally, she chided herself for allowing herself to be impressed. It was *supposed* to be the other way around. She flashed a dazzling smile back at him as he introduced himself.

"Ms. Dalton! It's so good to meet you in person!" He extended his hand, "I'm Chris Morgan, your grandfather's attorney and the executor of his will."

When she took his hand, her fingers began to tingle and, when he didn't let go immediately, the tingle traveled up her arm and into her chest where her heart began to flutter infuriatingly. Carefully, Summer slid her hand out of his grasp and settled back into her chair, in a futile attempt to settle this crazy feeling inside of her. Chris noticed the effect his touch had on her, and he smiled inwardly... Just as he had hoped... This was going to be easy.

He seated himself across from her and began, "So, here we are. How are you handling all of this?" His eyes searched hers and they seemed to be filled with concern.

Summer cleared her throat, "Honestly?"

Chris nodded.

"Not very well." She stated. "As per our previous conversation, this came as a... shocking... revelation to me. I was not aware that I had a different mother than the one I know." She tried unsuccessfully to hide the raw betrayal that she still felt.

Chris nodded, "Once again, I am truly sorry for being the catalyst for that revelation..."

"Oh, it's not your fault," she interrupted, "but if you don't mind, I do have some questions regarding all of this."

"Certainly," he smiled, "What would you like to know? I'm an open book."

His smile was a winning one, she decided, as her gaze lingered on his lips. And then she wondered just what kind of open book he was... Romance... Adventure... Mystery... Danger... Maybe a little bit of all of it in one? She could feel that infernal blush creeping up her neck again. *What are you doing?! STOP IT!*

"Ms. Dalton...? You were saying that you have some questions?"

The creeping blush immediately inflamed her entire face. "Oh! Ahem! Yes!" *Good grief!* Her eyes shot to his and then down at her hands neatly folded in her lap. "Y-yes, I do..." Summer laughed nervously. This was not going well. Not like she had planned at all.

The handsome attorney chuckled deep in his throat.

Summer chanced a look at his face. He was enjoying this! *Get it together!* No matter how hot this guy was she had come to do business and, she had business to do.

Chris smiled widely and asked, "Well, what do you need to know? I have all of his records, account information, stocks, bonds, everything..." He stretched back in his chair, his hands folded behind his head casually. "Would you like to know how rich you are?"

The question snapped Summer back to reality of sorts, "How rich I am?" Brief confusion filled her eyes. She had not even thought of that... "Well, I guess so... But first I want to know about this man... My grandfather... What was he like?" She inwardly cursed the vulnerability that she felt, and knew, was written in neon across her face.

Chris took her in for a moment. Was it possible that this charming woman sitting across from him actually had not considered that an 'inheritance' meant a 'fortune'? Here she was, in his office to discuss that very thing, or so he had assumed, and she seemed only vaguely interested in the word 'rich'. He didn't know what to make of her. She was irresistibly innocent and the blush that dusted her face and chest was fascinating. Maybe she was just that good of an actress. Yes, that had to be it. He sat forward.

"Well," he began, "he was well known in the community..."

"So, he was well liked, then?"

"I said he was well known... Not well liked."

Surprised and somewhat bothered by the statement, Summer asked, "What does that mean?"

Chris quickly checked himself. Obviously, a good name meant something to this intriguing young woman. If she needed to believe that the man was decent, he could do that. But he wasn't going to lie about it either. He smiled reassuringly, "Just that he was, more or less, your typical... Ah... Hermit. He seldom went out into public."

"Oh..." Summer was thoughtful as she turned her eyes to the tasteful Venetian blinds covering the expansive window to her right. She kept her eyes there. "So, could you tell me about him? About his life?" She looked back at Chris, her eyes holding numerous questions yet unanswered. "I know nothing about him... Was he lonely? What happened to my birth mother? Do you know how I came into the picture?" Summer blushed for what seemed like the thousandth time, "...er...um...Do you know the circumstances?"

Her eyes searched his with an agonized desperation that she tried to mask. In that moment, Chris was completely intrigued and taken in. It wasn't as he had suspected at all. This woman was no actress. She genuinely wanted to know about this man, his life, and how she fit into it. So much for protecting her sacred belief... These questions, if answered honestly, would destroy the image of the old man that she was obviously trying to build.

For the first time in as long as he could remember, Chris

experienced a slight nervousness and regret for what he was preparing to say. This feeling surprised and unnerved him. He began carefully, "Yes, it's complicated, and yes." He shifted in his chair. "Being a hermit, Jarvis was definitely lonely. Especially after his wife, Priscilla, died... er... passed. I'm sorry..."

"No, no." Summer shook her head and flipped her hand, "It's okay. I'm not your garden variety female. I've never been sensitive to that kind of thing. If you would just give it to me straight, I would actually appreciate it much more."

Chris peered at her, inwardly impressed and his curiosity was growing by the minute. There was more pluck to Summer Dalton than he gave her credit for, and he was drawn to her even more. He did love a straightforward woman.

"All right then. Here it is. But I warn you, it's not a pretty story."

Summer nodded. Somehow she had known this. She took a deep breath and prepared herself to hear the history of her beginning.

Chris sighed, "Well, let me start by saying that your grandmother died of a broken heart..." He sat back again, making himself comfortable in the oversized, leather chair.

"Did you say my grandmother?" Summer was confused.

Chris nodded, "You see, she was a good woman. Well

known and well liked, here in town. She was very active in the community and in community service. She was a very devout Christian woman."

Summer noted the look of distaste that flashed across his chiseled features when he said the word 'Christian', but honestly? She felt the same way.

"... When she and Jarvis married, she had wanted children immediately. Jarvis, on the other hand, hated them. She loved him enough, though, that she conceded to his wishes and for five years they were childless. But as you know, nature sometimes deals us its own hand, so...Needless to say, when Prissy turned up pregnant, your grandfather wasn't your typical doting husband. In fact, he immediately moved her out of their bedroom and into her own room on the second floor of his mansion. He prohibited her from going out of the house because he didn't want anyone to see her in that state. He made up a lie that she was ill and kept her friends and family from even visiting her. She became a prisoner in her own home."

Summer listened intently. Chris could see no emotion on her face at all. *Curious.*

"He basically ignored her..." He continued on, "The only time she even saw him was in passing, and he shunned her then. It was as if Jarvis believed Priscilla had purposely dealt him this blow, and he refused to forgive her for it. When the time came for her to deliver, as the doctor arrived, Jarvis left. Priscilla was devastated, but she remained loyal to him. She named your mother

Caroline, after your great, great grandmother, Caroline Conner, and secretly she hoped that Jarvis would see the baby and his heart would soften towards her and to his child.

But Jarvis refused to see the child and when he would happen upon them, he would give Caroline no more than a cursory glance until one day, a business partner stopped by to deliver some paperwork. He happened to see Priscilla and Carrie (that's what Priscilla called her). Jarvis put on a stellar performance for his partner...i.e., 'the doting father' and 'loving husband'. He was a very shrewd man. He saw then, how having a family could boost his reputation and possibly increase his business. So, he began to include Priscilla and Carrie in his life more readily... But only on a surface level. In his heart, Jarvis still hated Priscilla for the intrusion of their daughter.

Chris watched Summer's face as he spoke. Still, there was nothing. And she didn't say anything, either. Most women would have commented on the man's coldness, but she said nothing. He paused for a moment.

"Shall I continue?" He asked.

Summer nodded, "Yes... Please. I need to know what kind of stock I'm from. You're already helping to answer some questions I have had about who I am. Please continue..."

Further impressed, he continued the narrative, "Years passed, and Carrie grew into a rebellious young woman."

"Understandably..." Summer stated.

Chris smiled and drank in her appearance. She was so beautiful. He realized that he was staring when she looked down at her hands and began to blush again. He just couldn't get over how charming she was... Grinning, he continued.

"As I said, Carrie was rebellious and looking for validation. Priscilla was a constant mediator between Jarvis and Carrie, and it all came to a head when Carrie turned up pregnant." He watched with interest as Summer scooted forward in her seat. "Priscilla, herself, even struggled when Carrie told her what had happened... That the father was a preacher of her precious faith." He paused for effect.

Exasperated, Summer pinned him to the chair with her golden eyes, his looks and charm no longer affecting her ... For the moment, anyway. She inhaled and exhaled, half rolling her eyes.

"Okay, You've got my attention. Would you just tell me what happened?"

Chris chuckled and put his hands in the air, "Okay, Okay..." Another maddening chuckle. Summer thought she would scream. "It seems Jarvis and Carrie had had words one evening, and Carrie left the house in a rage. I'm not sure what was said, but it was enough to give Carrie something to prove.

She packed all of her things and moved into a hotel in the city. She was drunk in the bar one night and broke down into tears. There was a man who approached her, and asked her if she needed to talk..."

"My father..." Summer suddenly felt nauseous and didn't want to hear anymore.

Chris noticed the change in her countenance. "Ms. Dalton, are you alright?" Instinctively, he reached across the desk for her hand. She allowed him to have it. His hand felt strong and confident... Something she desperately needed right now. His thumb gently caressed the back of her hand and Summer watched the motion and then she raised her eyes to meet his. As Summer looked into his eyes, Chris felt something move in his chest. "Should I stop?" he asked.

Summer didn't know if he meant the hand thing or the story, but she really didn't want either to stop. She shook her head slowly.

Their gazes locked for a few more seconds and then, to Summer's disappointment, Chris released her hand, sat back, and continued.

"Anyway, Carrie was taken in by this man's genuine concern and care for her ..."

This didn't surprise Summer. Her dad was one of the most caring guys she knew. What she wanted to know was how he could betray her mom like that?

"... She confided in him and oddly, he and her...they

seemed to have a lot in common. She offered him a drink, swearing that it would help him relax... No offense, but personally, this guy sounds a little too gullible..."

Summer frowned, "I wouldn't know. All I know is that I have never seen him drink, nor was I allowed to even *think* about doing it myself."

Chris was amused and he mentally noted the fact, "Okay then, maybe not... Anyway, at first he refused, but then, after much convincing he gave in and before long, from what I understand he was hammered."

Here it comes...

"According to Carrie's story, he was supposed to leave that night, but was too drunk to drive. So, she took him to her room and... well... to be blunt," Chris looked at her, "here you are."

Summer swallowed back the lump in her throat. This didn't change anything... Her dad was still a cheating jerk.

"So... That tells me what happened, and lets me know what kind of man Jarvis was, but it still doesn't tell me what happened to my birth mother? I would like to meet her if at all possible..."

Chris sat forward and looked into her eyes apologetically. "I'm afraid that's impossible. She died a year after you were born." He was inexplicably moved by the struggle on Summer's lovely face. "Would you like to know how, or is just that information enough?"

Summer appreciated the attorney's sensitivity to her situation. Closing her eyes and inhaling, she tried to gain control. This was so much harder than she had expected, "How did she die?"

Chris watched her intently as he continued, "When Jarvis found out that she was pregnant, he demanded that the father marry her and make an honest woman out of her. The problem was…" He sat back in his chair.

"He was already married…" She finished.

"Yes. Needless to say, that did not help Jarvis 's opinion of her at all. He insisted that she was to give the child up for adoption, but Carrie flat out refused. When she did that, he cut her out of his will and disowned her. This broke Priscilla 's heart and it was the last straw for her. Her health was already failing and when Jarvis insisted that Carrie would never return, and that Priscilla could have no contact with her, she lost the will to live and died shortly after. Jarvis didn't even allow Carrie to be at Priscilla's funeral.

Anyway, Carrie was truly alone now, and she knew that she couldn't support both of you with little more than a high school education and a low paying, dead end job. But she still bucked the idea of complete strangers raising her baby. So that's when she called your father and propositioned him. She informed him of her situation and offered you to him and his wife, with the stipulation that she would see you once a year as a distant 'aunt'. Your parents agreed and when you were born, you became Summer Dalton.

Unfortunately for Carrie, her situation never improved. A little less than a year later, drugs came into the picture and soon after she was found dead in a hotel room. Apparently an overdose."

Summer's head was reeling. What a morbid story... *But, honestly, why should it be any different. It was a perfect beginning for a bastard...* The voice in her head whispered. Chris stood when her face paled. He stepped around his desk, reached for her hand, and helped her to her feet. He felt a deep sadness and concern for this woman, and a regret for being the literal bearer of such bad news.

"That's enough information for one day, I think." He stated gently, "How about this? Our firm will put you up in a hotel for the night, and you and I can meet for dinner. Afterwards, I can take you out to the estate and show you around. You are in no condition to travel at the moment." He moved closer to her.

Dazed, Summer looked up into his eyes... He was too close. She placed her hand on his chest to push a little more of a comfortable distance between them. Chris placed his hand over hers and held her hand there relishing the feel of it. She was blushing insanely, now... This was too much... She was too vulnerable right now... She had to get some distance between them so she could think clearly.

"Y-you need to back up…I can't think with you so close…" She thought.

Chris smiled wanly and chuckled deep in his throat.

"Oh…Is this better?" He moved even closer to her. She was practically in his arms.

Summer was mortified! Had she said that out *loud?!* She wished the floor would open up and swallow her whole.

"N-no, it's n-not…" She cursed her stammering as she twisted regretfully out of his arms. "Ahem!" She straightened her suit jacket as she put a safer distance between them, and grabbed her purse out of the chair, her face flaming. She extended a stiff arm and hand to the dashing man standing in front of her, "I will accept your offer, IF…" She emphasized, "IF you agree that this relationship is strictly business and will remain that way."

Chris laughed, his cobalt eyes sparkling in amusement, and he took her extended hand, "Deal."

"Deal." Summer parroted with purpose.

"Julie will make the arrangements for you and will give you the hotel address. I will be by at 5:30 to pick you up. We'll catch an early dinner so you can have time to wander the grounds of your new estate." He said as he escorted her to the door.

"Wow…" She turned to face him pensively, "That sounds so weird…"

Chris dazzled her with multi-million-dollar grin, "You'll get used to it."

CHAPTER TEN

The line on the other end of Chad's cell phone was ringing for the fourth time.

"Hiya! You've reached Summer Dalton. I can't catch your call right now, but if you tell me who you are and how to reach you, I'll get back to you as soon as possible. If you would like to place an order, please leave the details and your contact information, or you can call the shop at 478-296-3445. Thanks, and have a great day!"

Another voice prompted Chad to leave a message after the tone.

"Um... Hey, Summer. This is Chad. Just thought I would check on you... You know... See how you're doing? Give me a call back and we can catch lunch if you like? There's something I wanted to ask you...A business question... Talk to you later, K?"

Perplexed, Chad ended the call and stared at the closed sign on the door of Summer's shop. It had been that way for three days now. Pastor Jim had said something about her leaving town, but he had hoped that she hadn't done that yet. He remembered how broken his pastor had been as he had revealed the cause of the tirade that Chad had almost witnessed. Chad had been shocked, but he had greatly respected Jim for being so painfully honest and transparent, when it could very well cost him his pastorship.

"You're an idiot..." He told himself, "Why would she stay around here?" He had hoped that she would take him up on his lunch and dinner offers before she left... Oh well...

Summer Dalton had caught his eye the very first time he had laid eyes on her. She had been outside on the blacktop at the old church, shooting hoops with some of the younger teenage boys. She had been wearing a pair of shorts that could have easily been her dad's, judging from the size of them, and a form-fitting faded, black wife beater. Her shoulder length, golden hair looked like she had attempted to tame it into a French braid, but little curls had escaped and were flying all about in an attractive, unkempt fashion.

He watched in appreciation as she maneuvered the ball like a pro, in and out of her legs and skillfully dribbled up to the net and then, in a single graceful movement, had netted the ball with ease. Her tanned face had lit up and she whooped in a most unladylike fashion, as she threw her hands up in the air in victory. She bounced back to the boys, who all chorused a moan, and they had all laughed and shared high fives.

Chad remembered the twinkle in Jim's eye when the new youth pastor had asked who the pretty, blonde basketball star was. He had had Jim's approval for a while now, but he had just never found the nerve to pursue anything more than a casual relationship with the pastor's lovely daughter... Until now... And he was suddenly wishing that he hadn't. He felt like a fool.

At twenty-six, Chad had been out of the dating scene for a long time... For the last three years, he had wanted to focus his desires on his heavenly Father. All that time, he had been praying for his future wife... Asking God to keep her, encourage her, prepare her...As Chad had gotten to know Summer more and more, and had prayed about her, he felt very strongly that the hand of God was in this... Maybe he had missed it? Obviously, he had misread her signals... *Maybe*... He frowned.

Maybe he just really *wanted* it to be God's will... Perplexed, he glanced upward into the colorful evening sky, "Dad... I don't know where she is, but I know that you can see her. Please keep her safe... And...Help me to put this behind me and focus on what you called me to do here."

Slipping his cell phone back into the holster on his belt, Chad turned and strode back to his pickup truck. He popped the handle and slid into the driver's seat. As he turned the key into the ignition, voices on the radio sang about surrender and moving forward. Chad closed his eyes and leaned his head onto the steering wheel of the truck.

"I surrender my life to you, Lord. Everything. My hopes, my dreams, my wants...Summer..." he paused for a moment... "All of it."

He raised his head and put the truck in gear, "I'm moving forward."

"So, tell me what happened, son."

Bill Connor sat across the ornate mahogany table from his recently returned son. His faded blue eyes taking in the disfigured face that used to be the cause of much female swooning. He had asked the question many times since William's return and had been answered with the same scornful silence every time.

William sat silently with deaf ears. He raised the fine, silver goblet to his lips and let the pungent sweetness of the muscadine wine invade his thinking. How long had it been since he had tasted goodness such as this... The last time had been when his father had toasted him the night before his departure for the war. His wife had been by his side...

"William!"

His silver eyes lifted to meet those of his father.

"William, you haven't said a word since you returned..." The fork clattered against the side of his plate as he put it down in exasperation.

William dropped his eyes again.

"Did you lose your voice as well as half your face?" The elder man demanded with a wry smile.

The remark hit William like a fist in the gut.

"Well, I guess it's a good thing that that no good woman of yours left you before now." He picked up his fork again and gave attention to cutting the piece of salted ham on his plate, "She woulda hollered and ran off, for sure, when she saw you like this."

He stuffed an oversized piece in his mouth as he looked up to find silver fire staring him down.

"Oh, now, William." He pointed his fork at his son casually, "You didn't expect me not to notice that half your face is blown off..." Bill set his knife down, grabbed his napkin, and wiped his mouth.

William gritted his teeth and balled his fists on the table, "I didn't expect you not to notice, what I *do* expect is not to be mocked and judged by my own pa."

"Judged? Shoot, boy! I ain't judging you. You're sitting at my table ain't you? You can't help it one of them Yanks had a good eye..."

William stood to his feet, knocking the chair backwards as he did. He glared at his father, then turned and stalked out of the room. The two young slave girls attending the table jumped as the chair hit the hardwood floors. They scurried to retrieve it and set it upright.

"William!" Bill called after him, "Best to get used to it.

You can't hide forever... And folks *will* notice." He glared at the two little girls, staring wide eyed at him.

"What are you niggers staring at?" He barked. "Get that plate cleaned up! Lazy little beasts!"

The girls, no more than eight to ten years old, jumped into action, fear driving them to complete The Master's demand as quickly and as carefully as possible. As they gathered the untouched plate and utensils of The Master's son and turned to hurry into the kitchen, the scars of brutal whippings could be seen across the dark flesh of their exposed calves.

Kalana hurried back to the teepee excitedly, tugging Little Wolf behind her. She ducked inside and instantly popped back out with a startled look on her face.

"She's gone!" She exclaimed.

"What?" Little Wolf ducked into the tent. He took a second to let his eyes readjust to the dim light and peered intently around the room. Kalana was right. The skins that had covered their patient were in a pile, but there was no sign of the young woman that had been there minutes before. Then, as if with one mind with Little Wolf, Kalana ducked back into the teepee and they both moved to the protected place where both babies had been sleeping. Little Wolf pulled back the light woven blanket covering them, to find both babies nestled snugly in their bed. Returning the blanket to its place, Kalana and Little Wolf shared a perplexed look before moving quietly back out of the teepee.

"Where could she be?" Kalana asked concern etched upon her tanned face.

"Shhh..." Little Wolf hushed her quietly, putting a finger to his lips and listened to the wood around them. In a moment, they both heard a rustling no more than fifty feet from where they stood and then quietness. Then rustling, then quiet. He smiled and pointed in the direction of the sound.

"Caroline..." His smooth, masculine voice spoke her name gently, as not to frighten her, as he carefully and stealthily made his way to the location where the rustling had stopped.

Caroline halted. Fear seized her stomach and tied it into a sound knot as she hovered over the ground on her hands and knees.

Just be still...

Her mind raced to put a face with the voice that had called her by name, but she didn't recognize it. A twig snapped ten feet behind her position and adrenaline shot through her veins. Jumping to her feet, Caroline ignored the insane pounding in her head, and bolted right into the vice like grip of a regal looking Indian man. Confusion flashed across her face. The twig had snapped behind her

… Then as she struggled to free herself, the woman from the teepee stepped out from behind a small tree.

"Let…me…GO!" She wriggled with as much strength as she had to get out of this man's arms, but his arms were like iron bars holding her prisoner. Winded, she relaxed for a moment. She felt him loosen his grip on her and Caroline tried to jerk free of his arms, but he locked her in again. A strange sound filled her ears and she strained to look at this man. He was *laughing* at her! Of all of the *nerve*!

Kalana stepped forward, cradling a small bundle, and smiled. "Husband," she touched the Little Wolf's arm, "Let her go."

Caroline glared at him, infuriated, and then turned toward the woman's voice as Little Wolf released her from his iron-like hold. Her golden eyes met Kalana's gentle, dark ones and then she stared in disbelief as Kalana extended a small, grunting bundle of blankets toward her. Caroline's breath caught in her throat as she realized what was happening. Tears welled up in her eyes and spilled down her cheeks, as she took the bundle gently from Kalana's hands and glanced from the mewing, wiggling blankets to the beautiful woman giving them to her, and then back to the blankets again. Caroline swallowed as, gingerly, she lifted the hand-woven blanket and pulled it back to reveal her very own tiny son.

"Oh!" She gasped and fell to her knees clutching the tiny baby to her breast. "Oh, thank you, Jesus!" She sobbed, covering his precious cherub face with teary kisses.

Kalana's eyes filled with compassionate tears, as she knelt beside Caroline and stroked the downy hair of the baby that she had nursed and cared for, for three days. Caroline looked up at her through speechless tears in confused gratitude. When their tearful eyes met for the second time, Kalana knew that her new Lord had answered her prayers, and she wrapped her strong arms around the young mother and infant and took them into her lonely heart.

CHAPTER ELEVEN

The view from the balcony of the Conner estate was picturesque and breathtaking. Summer could hardly believe what she saw. Was this actually hers, now? She laughed to herself and shook her head. Ages old, moss-covered pecan trees and white, wooden fence lined the gravel drive and the sweet smell of the gardenias in the flower garden directly below her, wafted gently upward on the warm summer breeze, as if to welcome their new mistress home. A sense of awe and appreciation overwhelmed her as she slid her hands along the newly painted iron railing.

"It suits you..."

Summer jumped, slightly startled. She turned and smiled serenely at the handsome attorney, "You think?" She turned her eyes back to the vista in front of her, inhaling deeply as she did.

Chris nodded, as he leaned on the thick mahogany door frame leading out to the balcony, silently appreciating the view he was taking in. For once, he wasn't lying to get what he wanted. The quiet beauty of this grand estate *did* seem to suit the quiet strength of the young woman standing before him.

"It's amazing..." She began, "More beautiful than I could have ever imagined..." Her words trailed off.

Chris moved to the railing beside her, letting his hands hang loosely over the rail as he put his weight on his elbows.

"You know, you haven't asked me about the money yet..."

He gave himself the pleasure of letting his eyes roam over her beautifully lithe body, as he waited for her response. She was delightfully casual in a white, cotton baby doll shirt, trendy ripped jeans that teased him with little peeks of the tanned legs under them, and thin silver flip flops. Her golden hair fell in loose, stylish curls down her back, and he secretly envied the breeze as it gently caressed them. A marked difference from this morning's 'all business' look, but every bit as alluring.

Summer could feel his eyes on her and she blushed infuriatingly. She looked down at her hands on the railing and smiled uncomfortably as she tucked her hair behind her ear, "To be honest, Chris... I haven't even thought about it..."

She chanced a look in his direction and was relieved to find him staring out over the landscape again.

Chris nodded. He actually believed her. "Well...?" His cobalt eyes met her golden ones. There was laughter in them.

Summer laughed, "Well, what?"

He smiled brightly, straightened, and faced her spreading his hands out in question, "Don't you want to know?"

She took him in for the hundredth time. His baby blue polo and faded jeans looked amazing on him.

"Well...?" She asked hesitantly. She wasn't actually thinking about the money...

"Thirty-five million."

His words brought her thoughts to a screeching halt. Summer choked on her own saliva. *COUGH!*,

"Wh...what?!"

Chris grinned, "Well, that's just your personal account. That doesn't include your business accounts and all of your holdings...You know stocks, bonds, properties, yadda, yadda, yadda..." He was surprised at just how much he was actually enjoying her innocence and her genuine surprise.

"How many 'yaddas' are there??" Summer sputtered, trying to wrap her mind around what he was telling her.

He grinned again as he took her hand, "A lot." He chuckled.

Summer swallowed hard. Surely that couldn't be true! He was just toying with her! The intrusive thoughts made her blood boil. *Big city lawyer going to get the best of the small-town girl, was he? No, sir.*

She pulled her hand away from him suspiciously, "Just what kind of fool do you take me for?"

Chris stared at her in utter confusion. This was definitely

not on his radar of responses. "I...don't know... what...you...mean?" He squinted his eyes slightly and cocked his head in question.

"Hmph! Sure, you don't." She accused. "Thought you would drag me out here and impress me with the beauty of this place, drop a ridiculous number on me, and I would just fall right into your arms... Right?"

Now it was Chris' turn to blush. This was new. Actually he DID hope she would fall into his arms, but she wasn't *exactly* right...All of what he had told her was the truth. She was, indeed, very wealthy.

Summer didn't miss the blush and it fueled the fire, "So I was right, then?" She demanded heatedly.

"Ahem," he began... Might as well be honest for once. This was not something he was accustomed to... "Well, I, um..."

She crossed her arms and glared at him, expectantly.

"I was actually going to suggest that you retain a different attorney at our firm..." Chris began.

Now it was Summer's turn to be confused and she searched for words.

"... because I was going to ask if you would be interested in being more than just a client..." He swallowed awkwardly as he brought his eyes up to meet Summer's stunned ones. Why did he suddenly feel like he was back in high school? What made this woman any different than any of the others?

Summer gaped at him, the wind flying right out of her sails. She opened and closed her mouth.

"Um...?" She uncrossed her arms awkwardly and tucked her hair behind her ear again, fidgeting with the wayward curl.

Chris saw his opportunity and seized it.

"Listen, Summer...I've never met anyone like you...Anyone so..." He searched for the right word, "...REAL. I can't remember the last time that someone as beautiful as you was so...genuine..."

He thinks I'm beautiful...

The heat that began at her toes slowly crept up her legs...

"Most of the women I've dated have been so superficial...Zero depth. All of them had an agenda. There's something different about you. Something... *deeper*...," he stepped closer to her, reached for her hand and took it in his as he sought out her eyes, "Something I would like to spend more time discovering..."

Summer gulped. He was so close, and that cursed heat was traveling at an alarming speed up from her legs, through her stomach that was flipping like a flapjack, and into her chest.

Looking deep into her eyes he said, "Summer, I'm trying to say that I want to be more than just your attorney..."

Summer was beside herself. Her face was on fire, not to mention the rest of her whole body! He was too close again...She couldn't think clearly...Wasn't she supposed to be mad at him?...Oh! She couldn't remember!...He was leaning in.

He's going to kiss me!

Her mind told her to stop him, but her lips didn't want to listen.

"Summer…?" he whispered.

"Hmm..?" She wasn't listening ...

"Will you?"

"Will I what?" She asked absently as he leaned in , ever closer, until his lips were brushing lightly against her quivering ones.

"Get a new attorney?"

Her mind screamed all of the reasons why she should say 'NO', but her arms said '*Yes*' as they wrapped themselves around his muscular shoulders, and her lips agreed whole heartedly as they gave in to the warmth of his tender kiss.

"I've called this town hall meeting to discuss some issues that have recently come to my attention," Pastor Jim began as he spoke to the milling congregation of the First Baptist Church of Watson, "If everyone will please take their seats, we'll get started..."

The weary pastor looked out over the congregation and, in spite of the sickness of his heart over the loss of his relationship with his daughter, he was encouraged by the faces that he saw there.

There was Cindy Matthews, recent convert, and single mother of three; Jatory Goodman, new member and an officer of the Watson City Police; across the sanctuary was Enrique and Janice Sanchez, newly married and new to the community...and there were many more like them filling the pews to take an active part in the building of their church community.

Jim looked down at his notes and opened the Bible to locate his selected passages. He prayed as he flipped the thin pages, *"Lord, you are faithful. You are good. You are my help and the Lifter of my head. You are my Strength,"* he could feel his faith rising, *"You are my Joy and my Song. You are my Wisdom. You are the Lion of Judah, and Your roar overcomes and astounds my enemies! Thank You, Father!"* Jim bounced in the pulpit. Oh, how he loved his Jesus...

He raised his eyes as the congregation began to settle and to quiet. He smiled as he looked from face to face and thanked God again for allowing him to be their shepherd. "Well, if everybody's ready, we'll get this show on the road..."

There was an "Amen!" from an anonymous voice and then a chorus of chuckles.

"Would you stand with me as we enter the Holy of Holies?... Father, we welcome You here..."

"He's there right now!" Tom Davies spat in rage.

"You're kidding me?!" The woman's voice on the other end of the line was incredulous.

"No, I'm not kidding you! He said he was going to bring the 'issue' before the church and let the church decide in a 'Town Hall' meeting."

"But the board *already* decided what to do about all of this mess! Why is he bringing it before the whole church?"

"That's what I told him, but he refused to listen! Said that the board wasn't the majority... Said that we had turned into a 'self-righteous parliament' and that if decisions that affected the church body were being made, that the church body had a right to know and be involved in the decision!" Tom was livid, "He actually invited us to be there! Can you believe that?"

"WHAT?!" The woman on the other end of the line was just as livid, "Well, did you remind him that he *does* answer to us?"

"I sure did, and he said that he answers to God Almighty, and only God Almighty."

"Humph! Well, don't you worry, Tom, when we get done with him, God almighty will be the only one who listens to *him*."

Click. The line went dead. Tom hung up the phone in his kitchen and stared at it on the wall. His blood pressure was too high, He could feel it. He walked to the bathroom and retrieved his blood pressure medication from the medicine cabinet. This preacher was going to be the death of him.

On the other side of town, a very vindictive and scorned woman related to herself, as she picked up the receiver once again that these Daltons were entirely too much trouble.

"So, what are you saying, Pastor?" The question came from Fletcher Jenkins, a young father on the second row.

"Well, there have been some concerns about security here in the new building, and it has been suggested that all doors stay locked during the week, and immediately after services." Jim answered.

"Even the sanctuary?" Asked Myrtle Fleming, an elderly second grade teacher at Watson Elementary, obviously disturbed by the thought.

Jim nodded, "Yes, all doors."

There was an uneasy stirring and murmurs of disagreement. Chad spoke up, "Pastor Jim, I can understand the other buildings and office doors, but, I know several people...," glanced back at several of the people in the congregation, "... who come into the sanctuary every day to pray and meditate." He turned his eyes back to Pastor Jim, "If we okay this, then what about those people? I mean, I'm one of them, but I have a key ..."

There was a chorus of "yeah"s and "amen"s.

"Well, that's why we're here, folks…to hash this out and make a decision that would benefit everyone."

Victor Polinsky stood to his feet slowly, "Passstor, I ham new to dees kontry, so I mebbe yam not knowing much of Amerrican culture…but seems to me, eh…dat de drrinking place…errrr…de barrrs. Dey are open all de time, yes?"

Jim smiled and nodded as the congregation turned and listened to Victor, "Eeef dees is so, den hwhy do we close de chuurch?"

The room exploded in applause as Tom Davies and two

more board members purposely made their way down the center aisle of the sanctuary. Jim saw them and he smiled at Victor, but his smile did not reach his eyes. He motioned for the room to be quiet as Victor took his seat.

"That is a very good question, Victor, and I think you have a pretty good handle on American culture, bud."

Victor smiled.

Tom and the other board members stopped at the foot of the pulpit and glared up at Jim.

Jim ignored them.

"So as a church body, what is decided about the security of our new building?" he addressed the congregation.

Dan Taylor, a new addition to the Deacon Board rose and said, "I make a motion that all doors of the church be locked during the week..." Tom Davies smiled victoriously..., "except those of the sanctuary, in light of the need for intercession and just plain getting' on your face."

The smile faded from Tom's face as he turned and pegged Dan with a glare. Dan visibly shrunk and averted his eyes.

Several voices chimed, "I second the motion!"

Infuriated, Tom glanced around at the other members of the board incredulously.

Jim looked directly at Tom and the other two men, "All

in favor, please say 'Aye'."

A loud chorus of "Aye"s followed and Jim never broke eye contact with a boiling, red faced Tom.

"All opposed, please say 'Nay'."

Tom pierced Jim with an icy stare.

"NAY!" He demanded, and the lack of echoing support caused him to hurl furious glares at every silent Deacon Board member in the room.

Jim smiled, "The 'Ayes' have it. So passed."

Fury boiled in the older man's eyes.

"No, it is NOT passed." Tom almost shouted. "Just what is going on here?" He turned an accusing stare on the stunned congregation.

"This is a Town Hall meeting, Tom, and you, as well as all of the Deacon board were invited to be here to participate," Jim answered him from the pulpit with a calmness that he didn't feel.

"I never heard of any such meeting," the elderly deacon lied.

Whispers and murmurs that had already begun, were growing louder.

"That's a falsehood, Tom Davies, and you know it!" Accused Effie Walker, wife of a deceased Board member.

Tom opened his mouth to argue, but Jim spoke first.

"Now Miss Effie, it's entirely possible that Mr. Davies didn't get the message about the meeting tonight..."

"There was never any message!" Tom accused as he turned and jabbed a finger at Jim, "and YOU are trying to sneak around and reverse the decisions of the Deacon Board by a majority vote!"

More rumblings and whispers.

"Tom, this isn't the time or the place for this..."

"Oh, I think it is the perfect place, and it is HIGH time these people knew what kind of man they were following..." He turned a red face back to the confused congregation, "Pastor Jim, why don't you tell these good people what you've been up to in your spare time ...?" A hateful smile played about his lips.

Jim prayed desperately for wisdom and strength. He knew what was coming. He had known that Tom would not take his 'rebellion' lying down. Chad seemed to sense it too, and he rose from his place on the third row and moved to take his place beside the pastor he loved and respected so much. Jim thanked the Lord for Chad and for his support. Confusion, curiosity, and unease were written on every face in the room as the two men faced them and waited for Tom to unleash the monstrous mayhem that could very well split the church.

In that moment, Jim prayed for his flock. He looked at every single face in the crowd and prayed that what they were about to hear would not turn them against God.

"People of First Baptist, there are some disturbing things that have come to light about Pastor Jim that you, as a body of believers, have a right to know…"

"Tom…," Jim covered the mic and spoke to him, eyes earnestly pleading, "Please think about what you're doing...There will be lasting effects of this on these people's lives...Please...Think about *them*?"

"You should have thought of that before you crossed me, Jim..." Tom snarled. "Been nice knowin' ya," he threw over his shoulder through clenched teeth.

He would teach this preacher, one way or another, that you just can't cross the Deacon Board, the very power of the church itself, and get away with it.

CHAPTER TWELVE

The early morning air was cool and refreshing as it rushed in the open window of the Camry, as Summer made her way back to the town she knew as home. There was so much to do. Her mind replayed everything that had happened over the last few days... So much had happened in such a short time! *New identity, new fortune, new boyfriend...* She blushed at the thought of Chris' brilliant blue eyes and how beautiful he made her feel when he let them linger over her the way he did... *New boyfriend and a new life.*

A shy smile played on her lips.

Okay, Summer! Think! Mentally she forced herself to think of something other than Chris.

Let's see... What do I need to do first?

She tapped freshly manicured nails on the steering wheel as she thought. Thanks to Chris' suggestion to pay off her loan for the flower shop, she didn't have to worry about her mortgage anymore...So all she had to do was decide whether to close it up or to hire someone to manage it.

Hire someone... Summer smiled to herself, the thought tickling her. She could have employees now and would not have to stress about how to pay them! Being rich was *so* much easier. Whoever said money couldn't solve all your problems, must not have had enough money to solve them.

But in all reality, what was the point of keeping it open when there was little-to-no business? She did need to get in touch with the owner of the building to check on purchasing it, though. According to Chris, that would be a wise investment for her.

Summer was so thankful to have his input and expertise, and she had told him so. She had absolutely no idea what to do with her inheritance and she certainly didn't want to be unwise with it.

The sound of the wind rushing in her window was so relaxing that she turned off the radio, just to listen. Summer laughed at herself. *You can take the girl out of the country, but you can't take the country out of the girl.*

In the early morning peacefulness, a still small voice spoke to her heart... *"Summer, don't lose who you are to this newfound identity...Be careful of who you trust..."*

"Ohhh, I'm not talking to You!" Summer grunted guiltily at the ceiling of the car, agitated that He had invaded this peaceful moment. She hadn't even thought about Him in three days.

"Be careful who I trust, humph! People like Daddy? Yeah. No thanks," and just as quickly as the warning had entered her mind, she dismissed it.

On the seat next to her, her new, ridiculously expensive

designer handbag started ringing. She stretched a silver bangled wrist over and, keeping an eye on the road, dug through it to retrieve her new cell phone. A delighted smile instantly lit up her tanned face when she read the caller ID.

Summer tapped the earbud in her ear with a grin. *So fancy!*

"Hey there!" She chirped happily.

"Hey, yourself, gorgeous!" Chris' velvet voice filled her ear and she blushed violently, "Just wanted to make sure you got on your way safely..."

Summer giggled coyly, "Yeah right! You just wanted to hear my voice...Tell the truth."

"Busted. You're right." They shared a chuckle, "Seriously, though, did you have any trouble checking out of the hotel?"

Summer shook her head, "Nope. It was really weird though...People were, like, sucking up to me..." She glanced out the window as she passed a state road sign indicating that there was a gas station at the next exit. Throwing a glance over her right shoulder she changed lanes and got ready to exit.

Chris chuckled, "You'll get used to that. It's called respect."

Summer was thoughtful for a moment. *Yeah... Not used to that...* "I guess you're right... It just feels weird..."

"Did you get a chance to look over that packet of information I gave you last night?"

"Which one?" Summer laughed.

Chris chuckled, "I know, right?

It was so easy to talk to him.

"The one about the employees at the estate?"

Summer smiled wanly into the phone, "Um… Just when was I supposed to look at it, Mr. Morgan?...Before...Or after the midnight cappuccino?"

"What?" He laughed playfully, "You didn't stay up all night thinking about all of this?"

"Oh, I definitely stayed awake all night, but I wasn't thinking about all of this..." Summer was shocked at her own bravado! Where had that come from?

There was a throaty chuckle on the other end of the line, "Mmm…Well, it's nice to know I wasn't the only one who couldn't sleep..."

The heated blush that was becoming all too familiar, began to invade her body again.

"Ahem…" Summer cleared her throat. She did need to be careful. Just because she was moving forward with her life didn't mean that she was giving up her morals and values. She didn't want to lead this guy...or herself...down a road that she wasn't sure she wanted to travel. They hadn't had that talk yet, but she definitely wanted it to happen soon.

Chris seemed to notice her discomfort, and it genuinely amused him. He changed the subject, "Well, when you get a chance, sweetness, could you look it over? I need to know what you want to do about it. We need to give them at least two weeks' notice to give them an opportunity to find new jobs... It's only right."

Summer flicked her blinker on and maneuvered the car off the highway and onto the exit ramp. "Why would I want to get rid of any of them?" She questioned, "They've been there forever! I can't, in good conscience, fire any of them? They were there before I was...Doesn't feel right."

She pulled up to the stop sign and looked for the gas station. Seeing it to her right, she flicked her blinker on again, turned right, pulled into the parking lot and up to the gas pump. She switched off the ignition and sat for a moment.

"You're right." He agreed, "But you also have to consider that these people were loyal to your grandfather, not to you. You need to start fresh with new people who will be loyal to YOU." *And*, he thought, *who could possibly be bought...*

"I don't agree with you, Chris. I think they would be more loyal to me knowing that I'm his granddaughter, than if I were to hire a bunch of strangers..." She opened the door of the car and stepped out. It was noisy.

Before he could answer she said, "Hey, can I call you

right back? I just pulled up at the gas station."

There was a momentary silence, "Sure."

"Okay! Talk to you later!" Oblivious to the irritation on the other end she tapped the earbud and ended the call. She reached over into the passenger seat, grabbed her debit card out of her wallet, and closed the driver door. Flipping open the gas cap cover, she unscrewed the gas cap, popped the card into the slot, pulled it out again and pushed it into the back pocket of her jeans.

Summer leaned against the warmth of the car with a happy sigh as she filled the tank with the pricey gasoline. The morning around her was already beginning to heat up and she let her thoughts wander back to the kiss that had sealed the agreement to date Chris. A satisfied smile crept over her face, and she couldn't stop it, nor did she want to.

Chris was the kind of guy young girls only dreamed about. Charming, romantic, very successful, not to mention *insanely* good looking...and he was hers! It seemed too good to be true.

*It is too good to be true...*The still, small voice spoke to her conscience again. And again, she silenced it.

But there was something...*mysterious*...about Chris.

Yes. That was the word!...Mysterious.

Summer had sensed it at their first meeting but, truth be told, it was that fact that excited her. There was an unknown, unpredictability that she had found in him, and she loved the adventure of not knowing what to expect.

"Brrrriiinng!" Her phone started ringing in the seat.

Without bothering to check the ID, she tapped the earbud in her ear and breathed a coy giggle, "Missed me that much, did you?"

"Uhh…"

Oh no! Who was this? Immediately, Summer straightened.

That definitely wasn't Chris' voice. Summer smiled sheepishly as she watched the numbers on the pump fly.

"Oh!" she laughed, "Sorry! I thought it was someone else!" Another chuckle, " This is Summer…"

"Um… Hey. This is Chad."

The warm morning air suddenly seemed too thick as Summer gulped and shut off the pump and replaced the handle, her face flaming with embarrassment.

"Oh, hey…Chad…" She suddenly remembered that she had never returned his calls and had just left town with absolutely no word... *He must think I'm such a jerk...* She tried to convince herself that guilt was the only reason it was suddenly so uncomfortable, as she replaced the gas cap and closed the cover while she waited for the receipt to print. When it did, she tore it off, stuffed it in her back pocket, and opened the car door and got in.

"What's up?" She chirped a little too loudly.

"Um…Did you get my messages?" Chad wondered who she had thought she was talking to. He didn't like the feeling that that line of thinking gave him.

Summer closed the door, stuck the keys in the ignition and cranked the car. Putting the car in gear she replied, "Uh…Yeah. Yeah, I did…Sorry I never called you back... I…uh…" The truth was that she had been in such a tizzy that she had completely forgotten about him…Until now. Hearing his voice brought back all of the topsy turvy feelings that he tended to cause in her, but now there was a battle of conscience.

"It's cool, I mean really…" he began, "So…you headed back to Watson anytime soon?" He tried to make light of it, but he didn't do a good job.

"Actually," she smiled as she reentered the flow of traffic on the interstate, "I'm on my way now." She said, trying to convince herself that she was emotionally unavailable, now.

Relief began to wash over Chad, "Oh! Ok!... Well, listen. When do you think you'll be back in town?"

Summer glanced at the digital clock on the dash, "Probably around lunch, why?"

"You wanna meet me at Ruth's?" He was referring to a mom-and-pop diner that had been in the square, he had been told, for fifty years.

Her heart leapt into her throat. Just a few days earlier, she had been 'schoolgirl' excited about a possible date with this handsome young youth pastor...But now...Chris was in the picture in a big way. How would he feel about this? *Well,* she reasoned, *as long as it's business...We're just friends, right?* She recalled the message she had received from Chad yesterday about a business question.

"Sure!" Summer overcompensated and was definitely too chipper with her response. *Why is this so awkward??*

"Really?" Chad was surprised and excited.

"Sure thing. You said you needed to talk to me about business, right?" Secretly, she wished that it wasn't just for business...*WHAT?! Stop it, Stop it, STOP it!*

His excitement faded, "Oh...Yeah..."

"Okay! Well I'll meet you there around 11:30 to 11:45, okay?"

"Sounds good!" He faked enthusiasm, "See you then."

Hanging up the phone in his office at the church, Chad leaned back in his chair and stared at the ceiling. Not that it was any of his business, but he wanted to know where Summer had been for three days, and just who it was that had she assumed was on the line. The one thing he did know was that he *wanted* to be the one that she had mistaken him for...

So very much.

The aroma of the change of season wafted in through the open windows as the sheer curtains danced a graceful ballet in the pleasant breeze. William stood silently in the doorway of the room that he had shared with his wife, unable to cross the threshold. How many times over the last four weeks had he stood in this very place, unable to move forward? Pain clinched his heart and stole his breath as his gaze traveled from memory to memory. When would he get over this? He squeezed his eyes shut and tried to forget the happiness he had known in these rooms.

A muffled thump in the inner room startled him out of his heart-wrenching reverie and he stepped across the threshold of his imaginations. He cautiously eased to the doorway that led into the sitting room attached to what used to be their bedroom and peered into the empty space. He scanned the room thoroughly and found a spilled bottle of ink on Caroline's roll top desk to be the culprit of the disturbance. The doors to the balcony were open to let in the mid-autumn breeze... Maybe the wind had knocked it over? William crossed the room and set the bottle upright again searching for something to wipe up the spill on the desktop.

Caroline's desk...

His heart twisted... The desk had been a wedding gift to her from her grandmother up North...before the war.

With a trembling hand, William slid his fingers over the smooth wooden surface of the desk. He mentally noted everything that was on the desk.

Strange...He thought, as he noticed several loose papers strewn about on the desk. Caroline was meticulously tidy...He touched them and noticed that fine setting sand was strewn all over the desk as well. His fingers lingered for a moment before he dismissed it. Obviously, someone had used the desk besides her. According to his father's letters she had been gone for quite some time before...

William halted, the memory of the passionate wild woman in the clearing blazed into his consciousness like a branding iron. Caroline had been in the clearing the day he had returned. But how could that be?

He looked over the desk again and then around the room. It looked like the rooms hadn't been cleaned in a while... Suddenly he remembered Caroline's obstinate refusal to have the slaves clean up after her...It made sense why the room...and the desk were in disorder.

His curiosity piqued, William inspected the desktop more closely and found the center drawer to be crooked and jammed...as if the person closing it was in a rush. He sat down in the dark, cherry armchair and after several unsuccessful tries, he finally jerked it open.

Surprisingly, he found it to be empty other than a quill, a small red stick of wax, and Caroline's small seal.

He closed his eyes for a moment. He could almost see

her sitting there, penning letters to family...She had missed them so much...

No! He shook his head, and slid the drawer closed, forbidding himself to think about her. It didn't matter why she had been here a month ago...Perhaps she had forgotten something...Or had come home to grovel, who knew? The fact still remained that she had left him.

Sliding the chair back, he stood and walked slowly to the open door leading out onto the large balcony. He stepped outside and stood staring across the land where he had spent so many happy years as a boy and as a young man...

Before Caroline...

Before the war...

William sighed and turned back into the quiet sitting room, trying to ignore the urge to investigate the discrepancy in his father's letters. He slowly passed the desk and stepped through the doorway into the bedroom they had shared. He dismissed the disheveled state of the bed, the absence of some of the bedding and sent a cursory glance at the cradle beside the bed on his way out.

He would never enter this room again. His wife was gone, dead to him, and life as he had known it was over. There was nothing left for him, here, in this house. There was no reason to stay and live amongst ghosts.

What's done is done.

He stepped out into the wide hallway and closed the heavy door behind him, as if to close the door on who he had been before his life had fallen apart.

A lovely aroma, teasing his empty stomach, wafted upstairs from the kitchen below. His face felt stiff and strange as a smile crept across his solemn, scarred features. He wondered if Martha was still the head cook...

He remembered sneaking down his secret passage as a boy, after he had been sent to bed with no supper, and Martha would fix him a plate and let him eat with her two sons at the kitchen table. It was something that could have gotten her beaten or sold off if his father ever found out, but she refused to let him go to bed hungry...and The Master had never found out. In the four weeks that he had been home, William had been so consumed in self-pity that he had not even thought to visit the kitchen.

Quietly, as if he had traveled back in time to his boyhood, William tiptoed to his secret passageway and opened the wall. He winced, unconsciously, as the aroma grew thicker and more tantalizing. His stomach growled loudly and he stepped into the wall, closing it behind him. Carefully, he made his way down the narrow, wooden stairs in the darkness.

Reaching the bottom, William felt the wall for the latch that would open the door into the kitchen. His fingers brushed against something soft and silken. As he felt of it, he noticed there was a weightiness to it. Sliding his hand down the length of it, he realized there was a key attached to it. The smooth ribbon fell from the nail and slipped through his fingers sending the key clattering to the floor. Quickly, he searched for the latch to open the secret door. Finding it, he pulled it and the door released, swinging open very slowly with a quiet creak.

"Laws-a-MERCY!" Came a startled cry from within the kitchen.

William grinned, recognizing the voice of the beloved cook, Martha. He bent and retrieved the ribbon and key, shoving it into his pocket before stepping into the light of the busy kitchen.

"Martha!" he grinned.

"Massah WILLIAM?" Her deep alto voice was incredulous, "What you doin' creepin' out that wall givin' me a fright?"

In two strides, William was wrapping her hefty frame in a massive bear hug.

"Ha ha! Don't act like you've never seen that before..." he laughed as he released her. Martha flashed a mischievous smile up at him, swatted at him with her towel, and William adored her.

In her fifties, she was barely five feet tall, plump as a Thanksgiving turkey, and every bit as delightful. It had been just under a year since he had graced the doors of her blessed sanctuary, and he hadn't realized how much he had missed her…and her cooking!

"Now, Massah Will," she chided playfully, "You knows I don't know NUTHIN' 'bout no secret doors in MY kitchen…"

She winked mischievously, and when she chuckled, her whole body seemed to join in the merriment, and so did William. She looked over her shoulder at the stares of a few of the new house girls.

"Whatchall a gapin' at? Git on back to yo bizness!" She barked as she shooed them with her flapping towel.

"Still scaring the help, huh?" William chuckled.

"Oh, pshh!" She slapped the air with her hand, "Dem gals ain't no good fo nuthin' but standin' 'round…bein' lazy…" Martha wiped her plump hands on her apron as she turned back to the table in the center of the room, to finish her biscuits. "Ain't no time for lazy in my kitchen!" She fussed.

Will pulled up a chair and sat beside her, watching her. He noticed that there was more gray in her hair and a few more wrinkles since he had seen her last. A thought occurred to him, "Martha?"

"Yes, chile?" She never took her eyes off of the rolling out of the dough.

"Where are Thomas and Jeff? Haven't seen them around…Then again, I haven't really looked either…" He referred to her two sons that were around William's age.

Martha's busy hands slowed. Without looking at him,

she answered in a subdued voice, "Dey's gone."

Noting the tone of her voice, Williams's eyes shot up in shock. "What do you mean they're gone? Gone out to the fields? Or...*Gone*?"

She lifted her head and sad, brown eyes looked into William's questioning ones and he knew the answer.

"But...Why? They were some of Pa's best hands?"

Martha sniffed and wiped her eyes on her apron as she returned to her task, "You been gone a long time, Massah Will...A long time...Yo Pa ain't the man he used ta be, when yo sweet ma was livin'...He done gone crazy."

Confused, William stood to his feet, "Martha. What happened to Thomas and Jeff?"

Martha looked at him for a moment and then hustled and shooed everyone but him out of the kitchen. When she was sure they were alone, she began:

"You knows I could get myself whipped for tellin' you all dis?"

William winced. He remembered vividly the lashings his father had made him witness. In fact, he had been present at the lashing of Martha's husband...The one that had ultimately taken his life.

He nodded, "Martha, I won't let that happen...Not now."

She smiled sadly, "Well, I guess it woulda been a little

more than a month ago...Couple days 'fore you came home...Missy Carrie turned up missin'."

Carrie? Caroline had turned up missing? That would mean that she had been expected to be there...

She continued, "See, The Massah came stompin' up in here demandin' and hollerin' to know where Missy Carrie was."

Martha's eyes became moist and her voice began to tremble, "I didn't know! Honest, I didn't... But even iffn I did knows, I wouldn'ta tole him...poor chile...Anyway, my boys was comin' in from the barn, checkin' dem animals...It was sho bad weather an' all...and dey heards The Massah yellin' at me and dey heards..." her voice broke, "dey heards me a cryin' and a screamin', an' they came a bustin' in and jumps on The Massah!"

Tears were freely rolling down her dark, plump face.

William was silent.

"I hollerds for 'em ta stop...Thet I was jess fine, but dey just kep on, Massah Will." A sob escaped as she wiped her face on her apron.

"The Massah had some mens with him and dey heards the ruckus and dey comes and pulls my boys off The Massah and dragged 'em out in the weather..." Martha ducked her head and buried her face in her apron, fully.

William leaned in and put his arms around the older woman.

She spoke brokenly, her words muffled by the apron, "Dey beats 'em, Massah Will! Beats 'em like dey did my Herbert!"

A wave of nausea engulfed him as he visualized the scene she was describing, and she heartbreakingly continued.

"When dey was done, my boys couldn't hardly stands up from it. The Massah dragged me out dere and says, "Martha, iffn you don't tell me where dat no good daughter-in-law of mines is, I'll kill 'em! I'll kill 'em, Martha! And it'll be on yo black head!"

William didn't want to hear the rest of the story, but he forced himself to listen as he held the only woman he had known as a mother, after his own had passed away.

"I starts a hollerin' dat I didn't know, beggin' and pleadin' with him, but he jess wouldn't listen. Said I was a lyin' negro and dat he was gonna get the truf outta me, one way or another…"

William released her from his arms and held her by the shoulders, gently, as he looked deep into her tear reddened eyes, begging her silently to tell him that what he was thinking wasn't true. "He didn't kill them…? Martha…"

Her eyes held an agony that burned him to the deepest part of his soul. Tenderly, he wrapped her in his arms and let her cry, while a smoldering hatred began to envelope his senses. *Why?* He accused God. *Why would You let this happen?*

Then another thing occurred to him: *Caroline had been running from something when he had come across her in the clearing that day.* She had fled the house. His anger, then, burned against her even more. Why would she do something like that? She had to know that there would be a price to pay...And the price had been the lives of his boyhood friends... Both of Martha's boys.

Later, alone in his room, William sat in an overstuffed armchair recalling everything Martha had said. His mind was trying to understand all of the events that had been described. The one thing that he just couldn't make sense of was Caroline's involvement in this. According to his father's letters, Caroline had moved back north shortly after William had left for the war. That would have been nine to ten months ago, now...It didn't make sense that she would travel that far to come back for something...Especially in her condition...The child she had protected so fiercely that day couldn't have been more than a few days old at the time.

He closed his eyes and pinched his eyebrows. His head was pounding and it was getting late.

"I can't think about this anymore..." he told the emptiness of his room.

Standing slowly, William stretched his stiff muscles and

stepped to the dresser. He began undressing and as he stuck his hands in his pockets to empty them, he remembered the ribbon and the key that he had found earlier. Pulling it out of his pocket, he sat on the edge of the bed and looked it over.

The ribbon was satin, soft pink, and maybe half an inch in width. The key is what held his attention, though. Where had he seen it before? Too tired to think, William laid the key on the bedside table and stretched out across the goose down mattress. Surprisingly, sleep crept over him quickly and he gave in to its sweet invitation for the first time in a month.

The sweet smell of magnolia pleased him as he stepped into the room. There were many people there but only one held his fascination. She was lovely in the soft pink, satin gown her mother had sent to her, with her golden curls piled high upon her head, exposing a long and graceful neck. William thought to himself, for the hundredth time, how lucky he was. As he approached her, she turned and smiled the intimate smile of a lover, holding the promise of love shared later. His pulse quickened in anticipation.

"William! Where have you been? I've missed you!" She grasped his hands and leaned upward to place a tender kiss on his cheek. Warmth and pride flooded his body. This beauty belonged to him.

"What's this?" He asked referring to the skeleton key fastened at her throat by a soft, lacey, pink ribbon.

She giggled musically, "It's silly, really..." She motioned for him to come close. Something he was more than delighted to do. "It's the key to the secret drawer in my desk!" She whispered and then put a finger over his lips. "I have something special in there that only you can see!"

"Oh..?" William smiled warmly as he reached for the ribbon tail to untie it.

"No!" She giggled again as she playfully slapped his hand, "Not yet!"

William sat straight up in the bed. He strained to see the key on the table in the darkness. It was Caroline's. He had seen it around her neck at her birthday party, just a week after their wedding. Why was it in the secret passageway? No one but Martha, her boys, and William knew about it...He jumped out of bed and reached for the key.

Caroline knew about it.

According to Martha, Caroline had disappeared. He knew she had been terrified and running from something...or someone...when he saw her. There had to be a reason why and maybe this key was a clue. William turned the doorknob and quietly opened the heavy door.

Silently, he made his way down the darkened hallway to the room he had closed out of his heart, earlier that day. Taking a deep breath, he turned the handle, stepped in, and closed the door quietly behind him. It was chilly in the room. The windows had never been closed and the curtains were ghostly in the crisp mid-autumn night air. The moon gave just enough light for William to find the oil lamp beside the bed and light it with the matches in the dresser drawer.

A warm glow flooded the room and William picked up the lamp and walked to the desk in the sitting room. The disarray of the desk screamed for him to find answers as he sat down in the chair, set the lamp on the desktop, and slowly opened the center drawer of the desk. Pulling it out as far as it would open, he felt the back of the drawer and slipped the key into the slot. His fingers turned the key, and he felt the secret drawer release.

Sliding his fingers into the crack, William pulled the little secret door open enough to fit his fingers into the opening. There was a piece of paper in there! He carefully pulled it out and closed both drawers, leaving the key in place. Anxiously he turned the folded paper over to find Caroline's seal embedded in a small, red, wax dot. Carefully prying it open, he began to read Caroline's words…

CHAPTER THIRTEEN

"So, what do you think?" Chad took a sip of the coffee that the waitress had just dropped off at the table.

Summer was thoughtful, "Hmmm... I guess I could do that...?" She glanced at Chad. He wasn't as striking as Chris, but he was definitely very handsome...in a different way...a wholesome, rugged, and honest way...

Wait! What did that say about Chris? Oh stop it! She chided herself mentally.

"I mean, I was thinking about hiring some help anyway...since I won't be here very much anymore." She smiled at the man across from her, trying to control her wayward thoughts.

Chad hid his disappointment at the declaration of her intent to leave permanently, behind a quick sip of coffee, "Great! Can I call her and tell her? Or would you rather do that?"

"If you would handle that for me, that would be great," Summer smiled, "I've got SO much to do to get ready for this move, it's insane! I don't know what I would do without Chris." She needed to let Chad know from the beginning that she was only interested in being his friend...at least that's what she kept telling herself.

A deep longing filled Chad's heart. She was so beautiful, and she looked so happy. He had hoped that he could be the one that would make her face light up that way.

"What time would be good for her to come by?" He played with the straw wrapper that had missed the trash pickup, just for something to do with his hands. He couldn't look at her right now, for fear of losing his resolve, and his mind.

Summer pulled her new phone out of her bag and Chad watched her slender, tanned fingers pull out a stylus and begin tapping the screen, "Um... How 'bout five?"

She looked up into Chad's deep brown eyes. Her pulse quickened and that maddening blush began to creep down her neck at the earnest attraction she saw in them, "Ahem!... Five okay for you guys?"

"Today?" he asked, oblivious to her inner struggle.

"Yeah, I'm busy pretty much every other day... packing, business issues, yadda, yadda, yadda..." She used one of Chris' sayings as she flipped-flopped her hand causing the silver bangles on her wrist to rattle pleasantly.

"Okay...I'll call her and let her know." He smiled softly at her, unknowingly causing a stirring deep within her stomach.

Maybe it was just the chili dog that she had just finished...Not likely...

"I really appreciate you doing this, Summer. It means a

lot." Summer smiled back at him and his yearning for her grew, "I mean, really. She really needs this right now."

Chad pulled the twenty out of his pocket and dropped it on the table as they both stood, "Jill really has been trying to play catch up for a while now...and well, because of her kid...she lost the job at the nursing home, and she's had trouble finding something else. Her situation is getting pretty desperate."

Summer nodded and smiled genuinely, "Anytime, Chad! I like David. He's a cool kid. A bit odd..." she chuckled, "but I can see the good in him."

Chad smiled as he opened the door for her, "I do too."

"Hey, Jill?" Chad's excited voice came over the line.

"Yes?"

"Hey! It's Chad."

Jill smiled into the phone. Chad would never know how much she appreciated how much he had done for her. Her son, David, had come so far... And all because someone had believed in him.

"Hey you! What's up?"

"Well, I've got great news!"

"Okay?"

"I think the Lord has made a way again!" The excitement in his voice was contagious.

"Well, what is it?" Jill's musical laughter filled the line.

"Summer Dalton agreed to hire you on as manager of her shop!"

Jill was speechless. Tears of gratefulness formed in her eyes and began to spill over onto her cheeks. "Praise the Lord!" she breathed, "I…I…I don't know what to say…?"

"Well, get dressed and get over there! He laughed. "She said that she can see you at five and that only gives you two hours."

"What about David?" Jill wondered out loud.

"Are you really asking that question? Drop him off by the church on your way. He can hang out with me until you get done."

"Chad, you are a lifesaver!" Excitement and hope filled her voice.

"No, ma'am!" he answered laughingly, "that would be Jesus."

Chad gave her the specifics, said his goodbye, and hung up the phone with a smile. He loved being the hands and feet of Jesus. He stood from behind the desk and walked to the door of his office. Putting his hands on the doorknob, he began to open it but stopped when he heard a hushed voice on the other side of the door. It sounded like a woman's voice and Chad didn't know why the hair on his neck stood on end. He slowly and quietly moved his hand from the doorknob as he pressed his ear to the door.

"Did you make contact?" The voice asked.

There was a pause.

"Listen," she hissed, "don't you get ticky with me! You knew what this would entail from the beginning. Now, did you make contact, yes or no?"

Another pause.

"Good! Good... Does she suspect anything?"

Short pause.

"Good. Start putting people in place to take us to the next step." A bump next door in the pastor's office made Chad jump.

"I have to go. Someone is coming! I will touch base with you later to make sure we are moving along as scheduled."

Pause.

"Don't you patronize me, boy... And don't forget who you are working for..."

Click.

Chad waited until he heard the jingle of the front door before he opened his office door. He walked across the front office and peered out the glass door. Did he know that woman? He couldn't place her, but she seemed familiar... But then, all he could see was her back. He watched as she turned the corner and disappeared around the side of the church.

Perplexed, he turned away from the door. Who was that woman talking to and what was she talking about? His gut told him that it wasn't anything he wanted to get involved in. He had enough trouble of his own these days, yet, there was something about the conversation he had overheard that disturbed his spirit in a heavy way.

Thoughtful, he knocked on the pastor's door.

"Pastor Jim?"

He could hear shuffling inside the office, but no one answered.

"Pastor Jim? You in there?"

Chad turned the knob and knocked again as he opened the office door. His mouth dropped open in astonishment as he stepped into his pastor's office. There wasn't a sign of him anywhere and his office had been ripped apart. Spray painted across one wall in red paint was "F--- You!"

Summer smiled as she entered the quaint pastorium and overheard her mother cooing at Mow-Mow.

"Anybody home?" She called.

A loud thud let Summer know that Mow must have been on the table. She chuckled at her mother's blatant disregard for the rules of the house, as she walked down the hall toward the kitchen and met her fat feline just outside the doorway. Her mom wasn't too far behind.

"Summer!" Barb smiled brightly at her daughter and wrapped her in a warm hug, while Mow proceeded to protest his lack of attention.

"Hey!" Summer inhaled the sweet smell of her mother's perfume as she returned the embrace. It was one of the few luxuries that Barb ever afforded herself. Squeezing her mom a little harder, Summer smiled at the thought of being able to pamper her mom, for a change.

Barb released her daughter and Summer stooped and scooped the oversized kitty into her arms. Placing a kiss on his wide head, she stepped into the kitchen, placed him on the floor and plopped into a chair at the table.

"How was your trip, honey?" Barb poured a cup of coffee and sat down across from her daughter. Her graying black hair was in stark contrast to the youth in her crystal green eyes. The only other evidence of her age were the gentle laugh lines that accented her eyes and her heart-shaped mouth.

"It was…Interesting…" Summer smiled as she leaned down and ran her hand down the length of Mow's soft back. He purred deeply and arched his back as she stroked him. He turned quickly and rammed his head against her hand for another rub. She smiled and indulged him.

Barb smiled down at him as she stirred sugar and creamer into her coffee, "I think he missed you…"

"Ya think?" Summer chuckled as she scratched him under his chin and then, to his great disappointment, straightened in her chair.

"So, tell me about your trip?" Barb took a sip of her coffee.

Summer looked into her mom's bright eyes and wondered what she would say. She wanted to tell her everything, but at the same time she didn't want to hurt her. She knew her mom expected her to go, take care of whatever it was she needed to take care of, and then come home…to stay. But that just wasn't what was going to happen.

"Well…," she began, "I found out some pretty crazy stuff…like…who I really am…"

Barb frowned slightly, "Honey, finding out that you have another set of family doesn't change who you are. It just gives you a clearer picture into why you *are* the way you are... But it's not an identity..."

Whatever, mom... "Anyway, I got the real story on how I came about..."

Barb looked intently at her, slightly squinting her eyes and tilting her head, "And how did that make you feel?"

Summer returned her mother's look, "Honestly?"

Barb nodded and took another sip.

Summer sighed, "Dirty... and... angry..."

Letting her gaze fall to the table, she traced the wood grain with her pointer finger. She looked up at Barb suddenly.

"How did you do it?" She asked her mom, lifting her hand and tucking a stray curl behind her ear.

Her mother sighed softly, and set her cup down as she prayed for the right words. She had wanted to have this conversation with her daughter for many years, but she had never, in a million years, thought it would be under these circumstances. She smiled tenderly at the beautiful young woman she had taken into her heart so many years ago.

"It wasn't easy..." Barb began, "I was devastated when your dad came home from that convention. He didn't even have to tell me. I could tell by looking at him that there was something wrong. In my spirit, I felt a disconnect with him, and I didn't want to believe what I was feeling." She reached across the table for her daughter's hand and Summer allowed her to take it.

"Your dad was never dishonest with me, honey. He came to me and told me what happened. That took a lot of courage..." She released Summer's hand and took her coffee cup up again and lifted it to her lips. Taking a sip, Barb swallowed slowly as she asked the Lord how to proceed.

A lot of courage?... He was just afraid he would get ratted out...

Summer kept her thoughts to herself, but down in her heart, she knew how hard it must have been for him to admit what he had done to the love of his life...knowing that she could, and had every right to leave him. Not to mention the fact that he had just taken on the pastorship at this church...That was another sour taste altogether.

"What did you do?" Summer asked.

Barb chuckled, "What do you *think* I did? I screamed at him, I cried... I even threw a few pans at him and broke some dishes perilously close to his peanut head!" She laughed and Summer couldn't help but laugh too. The image of her sweet, docile mother screaming like a banshee and slinging pots and pans at her stunned father was pretty funny.

"Did you really?!"

"Ha ha! Yes, I did!... Poor man..." She chuckled again.

"Poor man?" Summer snorted with a smile, "I say he

deserved it."

Barb smiled and shook her head, "He deserved my anger, not my tantrum..."

Summer's smile faded as the truth of what her mom had said sunk in.

"Anyway... He left for a few days... Probably fearing for his life!" Another soft chuckle, "But one night, after a few days of crying to the Lord and feeling sorry for myself, I was praying and the Lord led me to Luke, chapter eleven. I began reading the Lord's prayer and I read something in it that I had never thought about before."

She set her cup down again, "...It said, 'Forgive us our trespasses as we forgive those who trespass against us.' Well, that just messed up all of my self-pity."

Summer watched the older woman intently.

Barb continued, "That scripture basically told me that I would be forgiven *AS* I forgave your father...So if I wanted forgiveness for my own sins, then I had to forgive your father."

"I don't agree with that, Mama..." Summer argued, "That's not what that scripture means! He *cheated* on you! Even God said that you could divorce him, right?" Mow sensed his mistress' unease and heaved his massive body up, placing his paws on her thigh. Absently, she stroked his head and scratched under his chin.

"Honey, don't you think I said those same things to myself?" Barb looked deep into her daughter's eyes. She prayed earnestly for wisdom. "Yes, God's word *does* provide for infidelity, but I was reminded of several times when I had been drawn into daydreams about old boyfriends...Times when one had reached out and asked me to a lunch to catch up...I went and old feelings resurfaced...and I thought about him often."

"That is SO not even the same thing!" Summer protested.

"Oh, but it is, sweetheart. You don't know the circumstances that led your father to fall to temptation..."

"You don't mean...?"

"No, no, no..." Barb waved her hand, "I never physically cheated on your dad, but there were times, after we found out that we would never have our own children, that I wondered what my life would have been like had I married someone else..."

"The old boyfriend at lunch..." Summer said.

Barb nodded. "I thought about how many children I would have had, what I would name them... Who they would look like..." She took another sip of coffee and returned her cup to the table, "I asked myself many times if I would have married your dad if I had known that he couldn't give me the very thing I had wanted all of my life..."

Summer was confused, "...But...I'm

his...biologically...What do you mean, 'he couldn't give you what you wanted'..."

Barb smiled softly, "Summer, your dad is infertile."

"HA!" Summer could not control the outburst. *Infertile? Was she serious?!* "Um, Mom...Do you know how crazy it is for you to sit here and say this to me? Infertile?! Obviously, there was a mistake... Maybe you are infertile, but I think he proved himself more than capable...and willing, for that matter..."

Pain momentarily flashed across her mother's gentle features at the callousness of Summer's words.

"Summer, not that I have to share any of this with you...I don't need to justify anything...But test after test was done and the results were always the same. Science doesn't lie."

"Well, mom...Not to bust your bubble or anything..." Summer stopped the biting remark before it escaped her.

Barb ignored her biting sarcasm, "Summer, honey. The fact that you are *here* is a miracle. God intended for you to be here , right now, in this moment. Even though the events leading up to your creation were wrong, you were no accident..."

Summer grunted, still not convinced that it was her father who was the incapable one. "That still doesn't tell me why you didn't kick his butt to the curb...Especially when you found out that his little indiscretion was prego?"

Her mother sighed, "Summer, I couldn't judge him for acting out what I had thought about, myself...and he was inebriated...I was stone cold sober contemplating these things."

Summer opened her mouth to protest, but Barb held up a finger, "Oh, I *wanted* to judge him, but the more I turned to the Lord about it, the more I knew that I had no right to sit in the judgment seat." She stood and walked to the sink, rinsed out her cup and placed it in the top rack of the dishwasher.

"Dealing with the Deacon Board was harder than finding out about you..." The older woman turned and leaned her backside against the sink. She crossed her arms over her chest, "...To this day, I still don't agree with how they handled it or how they have puppeted your father. It makes me so angry sometimes..."

Summer was surprised by the fierceness of her mother's tone, "I've been wondering about that myself... How is it that Daddy is still the pastor? He hinted the other day that they knew about all of this?"

"Ecch!" Barb huffed and turned her head, "Yes, they know about it...and they have held it over his head for twenty-three years, now." She turned to the empty sink and picked up the washcloth that was folded across the middle of it and began to scrub the counters. Summer smiled to herself. Her mom always cleaned when she was mad.

"Anytime he does something they don't like, they

threaten him. I told him to just tell the congregation. Just go ahead and tell them. If they tell him to step down then so be it. That would be better than where we are now."

"Why didn't he tell them in the first place?"

Barb paused in her cleaning and looked at her daughter. "Because of you."

Summer didn't know what to say, "Because of me?... I don't understand?"

Barb put the cloth back on the sink and sat down in the chair closest to her daughter, "Because, honey, people are cruel. When you came into our family, if certain people in the church and community had known the truth of your beginning, they would have rejected you and no little girl deserves that kind of life."

She reached for Summer's hand and took it gently in her own, "I know you were hurt because you were never told, but honey, please believe me that he chose not to tell anyone because he didn't want you to be hurt...That man would go to jail for you..."

Deep in Summer's heart, there was a softening. It didn't change the fact that she was still hurt and angry, but it did help to know that her dad wasn't the coward that she thought he was. That what had been done, had been done with her well-being in mind.

"Did you hate her?" Summer tried unsuccessfully to fight the tears she felt welling up.

"Who, your birth mother?" Barb smiled tenderly at her daughter, "No...I was jealous of her...She was carrying *my* baby...The miracle that should have been *mine*...But I never hated her."

Summer's golden eyes searched her mother's crystal green ones. There was nothing but love and honesty there.

"You know..." Barb told her daughter, "I was jealous of her until I saw you that first time and held you in my arms..." Tears welled up in her eyes and Summer's own unshed tears threatened to spill down her cheeks, "...then I felt sorry for her. Sorry that she would never get to feel your silky soft skin, or kiss your sweet baby toes," a tear slid down her cheek, "never get to have your sloppy, wet baby kisses, or get wetter than you as you played in the bathtub for the first time...

Summer's tears fell freely down her face.

"My heart broke for her, but as soon as I held you and looked into your eyes, pressed my nose to your tiny head and inhaled your sweet baby smell, you were mine..." She reached forward and tucked a loose curl behind Summer's ear.

"You look like her, you know..."

Summer leaned into her mother's embrace, and they cried together.

"Oh, Summer, I love you so much..." She leaned back and took Summer's wet cheeks in her hands. She looked deep into her eyes, "If I had to go through all of that just to get you, it was worth it. I thank God that Jim had that affair...If he hadn't...I wouldn't have you."

CHAPTER FOURTEEN

"I don't know who may find this letter, but this correspondence is a plea for help. I am Caroline Connor, The recent widow of William J. Connor..."

William drew his eyebrows together and frowned.

"... And I have come upon some information that poses a great threat to the well-being of the people living on this estate, as well of that of myself and my son. Among many other disagreements with Bill Conner, my father-in-law, I have been a witness to two brutal murders. I don't have time to be specific, I am running for my life, but I can say that the white man, killed in cold blood, was in direct opposition to the views of Bill Connor. He was gunned down in the front hallway on his way out the door, by my father-in-law. I was coming down the stairs and witnessed it when it happened. I was seen.

I was told to keep my mouth shut or the same thing would happen to me. Fearing for the life of my unborn child, I complied, but my cooperation is no longer protecting me. I found out that the man's name was Tillman Turner, the local sheriff..."

William's face grew pale. Tillman was a young man... Not much older than himself, and one of his good friends. He choked back the bile that rose in his throat.

"... And that he was questioning Bill's methods with his darkies. I was told this information by one of the slaves here, named Lilly. She was beaten to death for disclosing that information and I was forced to witness it."

The anger that had begun to fester deep inside of him, began to burn. Lilly was just a child! No more than thirteen years old when he had left! No. This could not be true...

"... Bill demanded me to leave this morning at breakfast, but said I must leave my child behind..."

A perplexed look crossed William's features. Why would his father demand her to leave a bastard behind with him? William's heart rate increased exponentially as he considered the implications of this. He was nauseous again. That child wasn't a bastard...It was *his*. Guilt and condemnation consumed him. He had had them right there within his reach, and he had turned his back on them! Broken, he read on.

"... When I refused, he said that I would regret that decision and that little William would never know I existed after today. PLEASE! I am writing this in desperation. I am leaving and I don't know where I'll go, but I have no choice. I have no money and after today, no identity. If I die, I want someone to know the truth of what has happened and bring this man to justice, and make sure that my son grows up knowing and loving the Lord Jesus.

Truly,

Caroline Conner"

William sat back, hard, in the chair in stunned disbelief. Could it be possible? Was his father really capable of the things he had been accused of in this letter? He recalled the horrible things Martha had told him, and the sinking feeling in his gut grew heavier. She had said that Caroline had disappeared. This letter explained why, but could he trust this woman? The woman who, according to his father, had been so deceitful and unfaithful?

He stood to his feet and paced the floor as memories flooded his brain. Everything made sense now. The frantic terror he had seen all over Caroline's face, and the wild way she had protected her child. He choked back guilty tears. *His child...* The untouched state of their bedroom, the sand and the papers scattered on the desk... The missing bedclothes... She had been running for her life! William snuffed out the lamp and waited for his eyes to adjust. Then he crossed the room and rushed quietly back to his bedroom.

After he had closed the door behind him, he lit the lamp by his bed and began searching through his belongings until he found the tin in which he had stored all of his letters from home. He shuffled through them until he found the one that was worn the most. How many times had he read and reread this letter, trying to convince himself that it couldn't be true? It read:

"My dear William,

Son, it pains me greatly to tell you that our dear Caroline has returned North to her family. It pains me even more to tell you that she won't be returning, as she has found a new beau there in New York. I just received her letter today.

Please don't take this news too hard, son. It was expected that she would not stay with us. She spoke of leaving often, after you left us. Caroline had a hard time adjusting to the southern way of life, and I feel that it is better for all that she's removed herself from our family. With God's help, we will all move on the best we know how.

Be safe, my son, and return home to us soon.

With love,

Your Pa"

Now, as he read this letter for the 100th time, he wanted to vomit. He rummaged through the tin again and pulled out the first and only letter that he had received from his wife after his departure for northern Georgia.

"William,

Words simply cannot express to you how much I miss you being here with me. Things are not the same without you here."

Tears formed in his eyes as he continued to read, now having a better understanding of what she meant.

"I never thought I would be afraid to be alone. I'm sorry to complain, my love, I'm just lonely, I guess... I count the days until I will be in your arms again. My heart is fearful that you will not return and, maybe I shouldn't speak such things, but I don't know how I would live without you. Please come home to me? Keep yourself safe. I know I am being selfish, but there is only one you and I love you. I pray for you hourly... every minute, even...

On a happy note, I have a surprise for you when you return! I pray you will be as happy as I am. God has truly blessed us. I must end my letter now. I hear your father in the hall. I must straighten this room so as not to get little Lilly in trouble. She is so dear to me. I have been teaching her to read and she's doing well!

Always know that I love you.

    Yours forever,

    Caroline

PS. Jefferson and Thomas send their love.

PSS. Martha sends her love as well."

William pinched his eyes and tried to stop the flow of grief from consuming him. How much had he lost?

He felt strangled. He rose and stumbled to the door leading from his room onto a private balcony and burst out into the crisp night air. Taking in the air in great gulps, William struggled to control himself. He couldn't wake the house. He knew that to face his father tonight would mean a second Connor guilty of murder. Sinking to his knees, the forlorn and broken man sobbed silently into his hands over the loss of his wife, his son, his friends, his face... his father...*God why?*

The invasive crowing of a rooster roused William from his drunken slumber. He raised his splitting head slowly, and growled at the unforgiving brightness of the morning, allowing his head to fall back against the arm of the pale green, embroidered couch.

Sometime after he had regained control of his emotions last night, William had made his way to his father's study and had helped himself to the good brandy. Drinking himself into a stupor had been the only thing that had numbed the pain tearing through his heart with every breath he took. Now, as he cracked an eye and peered around the study, he tried to remember where he was and how he had gotten there. Gingerly, he raised himself onto one elbow and immediately his free hand flew to his throbbing head. It hurt so bad he couldn't even think straight.

Carefully he stood, wobbling for a moment, and then slowly, gingerly made his way to the kitchen. Martha would know how to fix this...

"Land sakes!" Exclaimed Martha and William winced, "You looks like death, Massah Will!"

She wiped her hands on her apron and hurried from her station at the table, where she had been chopping okra, to help him sit.

"ShooooWEE!" She scrunched up her plump face, "You been in The Massah's bandy wine…"

"Oughtta be 'shamed," she mumbled under her breath, "Ain't been raised ta be no drunk… Serves you right…Don't know iffn I's even gwan ta hep you…fool chile…" she helped him sit at the table and turned to pour him a cup of black coffee, fussing all the while.

"What kinda trubble gots you all in a twist?" Martha set the tin cup in front of him. He looked at it uncertainly.

"You best drink it!" she fussed, "I ain't havin' no wretchin' in my kitchen!"

He winced again and took a sip of some of the strongest coffee he had ever tasted.

"There, now..." Martha crooned as he drank it, "That'll take the edge off'n thet ole poundin' in yo head..."

She went back to chopping.

"Tell Ole Martha what's ailin' you, chile?"

Williams squinted at her in the brightness of the kitchen and asked, "Martha?"

"Yes, baby..."

"Tell me about the baby?"

She looked at him and a broad smile lit up her round face, "Ohhhh, Massah Will!" she breathed, "He's a fine boy! A mighty fine boy! Look jess like his deddy..." She grinned and poked at him playfully, oblivious to the sick look on his face.

"Missy Carrie, she was so proud! She done real good too, bein' her first time birthin'. I's real prouda her. I sho was..." Her face clouded, "It was hard on her though, you bein' gone. She sho cried a lot. 'Specially after yo crazy pa tole her you was dead..." She shook her head sadly.

William remembered Little Wolf remarking that Caroline called out for him as if he were dead...

"Never did undastands why he did thet...But she sho was heppy thet day the baby came! I sho misses her. I wonders if she okay, you know..." Martha jumped to her feet, "Well, Massah William?!"

William was scrambling to the screen door. She rushed after him and stood behind him, fussing, as he emptied his stomach on the grass outside of the kitchen. "You best be glad thet didn't come out in my kitchen!"

Later that afternoon, washed and mostly sober, William stood in front of the looking glass over the wash basin in his bedroom, staring at his disfigured reflection. Would she want him like this? He raised a hand and ran his fingers down the length of the purplish scar. The doc had told him it would fade with time, but could she ever see past the monster he had become and remember the man she had married? Could she love him like this? He had to take the chance. It hadn't been that long since he had left Little Wolf in the woods, a couple miles from the clearing where he had first seen her. Maybe they would still be there. He hoped but couldn't bring himself to pray yet. But there was some business he needed to take care of before he brought his family back into this house...*his family...*

Excited anticipation gave him strength as he stepped away from the looking glass and out of the door. He knew Caroline. He knew her beautiful heart, and he believed that she would not only accept him as he was now but love him in spite of it. It gave him purpose as he strode down the hall, with a confidence that he hadn't felt in months as he jogged down the stairs, and a hope that he thought he would never feel again, as he entered the study where his father sat looking over some papers at his desk.

Bill looked up at his son as he entered the room, "Well, well, well... The hermit emerges..."

William said nothing at first, trying to figure out how to confront the man in front of him.

The older gentleman looked him up and down critically, "Where you goin' all dressed up?"

This was his opening...

"To get my wife... And my son."

"Heh!" Bill laughed sarcastically as he turned his eyes back to the papers on his desk. "Good luck, there, son..."

William swallowed the nasty comment that almost activated his tongue.

"What makes you think that *you* have a son?" Bill snorted without looking.

William retrieved Caroline's letter from the inner pocket of his jacket and dropped it on the desk in front of his father.

"What's this?" Bill looked up at William over his wire rimmed spectacles.

"I was hoping you could tell me."

There was an intensity in William's ice blue eyes that made Bill uneasy. He ignored the tingling in his left arm as he leaned forward and took the letter from the front of the desk and opened it. Readjusting his specs, he began reading.

William watched as his father's face paled and light perspiration glistened on his forehead. Bill finished reading and the hand that laid the letter down was trembling. He pulled a handkerchief from his front pocket and dabbed his forehead and face before looking at his son.

"Well?" William demanded, "What is the meaning of this?"

Bill swallowed visibly, "I...I'm sure I don't know. I told you this woman was weak minded...." His mind raced for what to say next. "She obviously was worse off than we thought. It's a good thing she left when she did! This trash is proof she was crazy."

He picked the letter back up and tossed toward the front of the desk in an attempt to hide the fear and guilt creeping into his heart and written all over his face. The older man looked back at the papers on his desk, absently shuffling through them, "Now, if you don't mind, I have things to do other than deal with the ramblin's of a crazy woman."

William leaned forward menacingly and slammed both hands down on his father's desk, "Don't lie to me..."

Bill composed himself quickly and pointed his finger in William's face, "Don't you threaten me, boy." He gritted his teeth, "You best remember who you're talkin' to."

William continued to lean on the desk, glaring into his father's eyes, "I'm not a boy anymore and you owe me an explanation." The words came through clenched teeth.

Bill was incensed, "You best respect me, William!"

William straightened and turned, laughing incredulously, "Respect?..." He whirled around, "Respect?!..."

Bill nodded angrily, "Boy, I didn't stutter."

William pressed his lips together as he thought of how to respond to the ridiculousness of his father's statement, "You know, Pa? I'm standing here trying to imagine how you could possibly think that I would respect you after what you have done..."

Bill stood to his feet in confrontation, "What *I* have done?! Don't you mean what that lying *wench* has done?" The tingling in his arm grew more painful and spread into his chest.

William clinched and unclenched his teeth, the full force of his fury blazing in his eyes.

"This is an outrage!" Bill sputtered as he snatched the letter from his desk and held it up in the air, "You believe this trash?!"

The younger man's silence spoke louder than his words would have, and he pinned his father with an icy stare.

"William!"

"Tell me something, Pa?" William's voice was low and dangerous, "Where is Lilly?"

"Lilly?" Bill feigned ignorance, but his paling face belied the truth.

William knew his father had purchased Lilly as a six-year-old child to help tend to his ailing mother. He knew his father knew exactly who he was talking about.

"Have you forgotten who Jefferson and Thomas are, as well?... Or are you *trying* to forget them... The looks on their faces when you murdered them?"

Bill's chest felt tight, and his breathing became slightly ragged as he sat down heavily in his chair. "Don't you lecture me about how I deal with my darkies…"

William stepped closer, "Answer a question for me. How long ago did Caroline leave this house?" He watched his father's eyes closely.

Eyes darting away from William, he answered, "...a good seven-eight months.."

"That's a lie, Pa!" William interrupted heatedly.

Bill looked pained and startled.

"I saw her in the clearing the day the tornado came through... And that was just over a month ago! What was she doing here?" He demanded heatedly.

"I...I..."

"And whose baby was that she had with her, Pa?"

"I'm sure I don't know what you're railin' about, William... I don't know anything about no baby..."

"NO MORE LIES!" William roared, "I know all about it! I know about the lies you told Caroline... and you lied to me..." His voice broke, "I was devastated, Pa... And it never even *happened!*"

Bill looked away silently.

"Why would you lie to me like that?" Williams vivid eyes held an agony that pierced the thickness of the tension in the air. "I'm your *son*!"

"She wasn't one of us!" Bill struggled for breath as the pain in his chest magnified, "She caused nothin' but trouble... Interfering with the darkies... Teaching 'em to read..." He said in disgust, "and it seems that her *Yankee* nonsense has gotten into your head, too! She didn't belong here! I say good riddance!" He gasped for air.

"She is my *wife!*" William noticed the deathly pallor of his father's face, but he ignored it.

"*Was* your wife...You should be thanking me..." Bill struggled to breathe, and he grabbed at his chest.

"I'm leaving to find her tonight... You had better pray that I do..." he ground out through clenched teeth as he placed his hands on the desk and leaned forward until their noses were almost touching.

"I only want to know one more thing, Pa..." William let the fullness of his father's betrayal and his agony reflect in his eyes as he spoke. "Would you really have killed the mother of my child?"

Bill opened and closed his mouth and William stood in disgust. "Your silence encourages me."

He turned on his heel and stalked out of the room.

Bill sat in his chair, sweaty and ashen white, struggling to breathe. Red hot pain tore through his chest, and as his son stepped out of the room and into his future, Bill Connor stepped out of his earthly life and into the presence of God Almighty at the Judgment Seat.

CHAPTER FIFTEEN

"Okay!" Summer clapped her hands once, "It's as simple as that!" The smell of freshly cut roses was almost as sweet as the hope that she saw on her new employee's face.

Jill smiled radiantly at her new employer; she had always liked Summer. She just never dreamed that she would be in a position to have to ask her for a job. The nursing home paid so well, and she was on her way to catching up... but, David.

Jill put the thought out of her mind and grinned excitedly, "Thank you SO much! You'll never know how much I appreciate this!" She put the last of the fire and ice, long stem roses in a vase and carefully tied a red ribbon around it before she put them to bed in the cooler.

"No prob!" Summer smiled, wiping the cut stems off of the counter into a trash bin that she had slid under the edge of the counter. "But if you don't mind me asking... Why did Sunny Birch let you go?"

Jill sighed and her expression clouded, "I hate to say it, but it was because of David..."

Summer frowned and dropped the cloth onto the countertop, "What? That doesn't make sense!"

"It does if you know my son..." Jill sighed and shook her head as she made her way to the supply closet to retrieve a broom.

"One of the coordinators made him mad, I guess, said something about his blue hair and me not being a good mother...and...being a rebellious 14-year-old boy...He slit the guy's tires, keyed his car, and tagged the building in front of his parking space with profanity..."

Summer felt sorry for you the young mother, but she had to laugh, "Wow. When he does it, he goes all out, huh?"

"Yes... He does..." Jill smiled wearily as she swept up the pieces of stems that had fallen in the floor, "Yes, he does."

"I'll understand if you don't want him to hang around up here... It's just been really hard on him... The move and all... And he still asks about his dad." Jill turned sad eyes to Summer, "How do you tell a kid who idolizes someone that they don't care that he even exists...?"

Summer was thoughtful for a moment. "I think I kinda know how he feels... Kinda..." She smiled sweetly at Jill, "How about this? If David wants to, I'll hire him to feed and rotate the cut flowers?"

Jill smiled broadly, but was doubtful, "I...don't...know if that's up his alley or not, but I'll ask him." Then a thought occurred to her, and she stopped sweeping and tapped her forefinger on her chin playfully, "You know…he *has* been after me for a pro-board... Maybe it would be good for him to work for it...?"

"Sounds like a plan!" Summer laughed and agreed.

Jill laughed too and Summer decided that she really did like her a lot.

"Hey, Sugar!" Summer blushed as she recognized the buttery voice on the other end of the line.

"Hey, yourself." She responded shyly. *Where did this shyness come from??*

"When are you coming back to Pickinsville? I miss my Sunshine..." Chris drawled.

"I'm almost done here," she grinned into the phone, "I took care of the shop and, oh! The owner of the building said that if the price was right he would consider selling... I wasn't sure what the right price might be... Or what to say, for that matter... So I told him I would get back to him."

"Good girl!" He toyed with the pen lying across his legal pad, "How's the packing going?"

"Almost done..." Summer sighed lightly, "I had no idea that I had so much crap hidden in that apartment... I've only been there a month!" She laughed, "Mow was glad to see me, though…"

"Mow?"

"Oh! That's right! I haven't told you about him." A smile danced across her face as she wondered how her fat cat would respond to another man in her life... "He's my cat."

Chris almost sneezed just at the thought of it. He was highly allergic to cats... Not to mention the fact that he pretty much hated them.

"Can't wait to meet him…" he lied.

"So…" He changed the subject, "I've got some great news! I hired some help for the estate!"

Summer frowned and dismissed the red flag that she felt down inside, "Chris...? I thought we discussed this already? I want to keep the help that's already there..."

"Oh, I haven't fired anyone... Just added a few more." He lied. She would never have to know that he had only kept on the extremely aged or stupid ones... No one that would pose a threat to his objective.

Summer was silent for a second, "…Okay, I guess…" But something didn't feel right about this. Maybe it was just that he had done it without checking with her first … That had to be it. She *was* incredibly independent.

"So…When are you going to be back in my arms again?"

The bold question surprised and excited her, "Um..." she stumbled to find words, "Um...ha-ha! In a few days, I guess?"

Chris smiled into the phone. He could visualize that charming blush creeping up her graceful neck and covering her innocent... no... *naive* face. He lowered his voice instinctively, "I don't know if I can wait that long..."

Summer did not miss the innuendo in his tone, and she gulped. She was so incredibly glad that he couldn't see her right now!

"Wellll..." She made an attempt at being coy, "You're just gonna have to..."

Chris' throaty chuckle sent chills down her spine in a good way, "Well, we'll just have to see about that, won't we, Miss Dalton?"

"SUMMER! HEY, SUMMER!"

Summer whipped around as she looked for the juvenile voice that had hailed her. She waved as she spotted a skinny ninth grader, named Rusty, whom she had clobbered in a one-on-one basketball game last week at the church.

"Hey Chris, I need to scoot. I just ran into a friend... I'll call you back, okay?" She motioned for Rusty to come over.

"Sure, sweets!" Chris forced his voice to sound light,

"Who's this 'friend'?" A foreign feeling made his pulse quicken... Was this what jealousy felt like?

"Oh, just a basketball buddy that I TOTALLY annihilated last week!" She laughed as she punched Rusty in the arm.

"No way, Sunny! You TOTALLY cheated!" Rusty defended.

She laughed, "Chris, I need to go..."

"Okay, Don't forget to call me later... I want to tell you what I have planned for you when you get back home."

"Okay...Bye..." Summer was bothered as she ended the call. 'Home'. This was the only *home* she had ever known... But he was right. After next week, she would be gone and the estate in Pickinsville would be her home.

Dismissing the dark mood, Summer slapped Rusty in the back of the head playfully and bounced out of his reach.

"Ready for a rematch, pup?"

"Honest, Ma! I didn't do it!" A very upset, 14-year-old David exclaimed as he, his mother, Chad, and Pastor Jim stood in the vandalized office.

"I didn't say that you did... I just asked you to tell me what you were doing during that time... If you weren't with Chad, then you had to be somewhere... Where were you?"

He rolled his eyes and crossed his arms over his chest, his jaw set stubbornly.

"David... Please don't do this..." Jill pleaded, "I just need an answer..."

Chad and Jim kept silent as they watched the interaction between the boy and his mother.

"Why?... You won't believe me." He turned his head away from her and stared out the open window where the blinds hung crookedly.

Jill sighed deeply, fighting back frustrated tears, "I want to believe you, but it makes it hard when you won't tell me where you were or what you were doing? David, what am I supposed to think?"

He shrugged without looking, "I don't know..."

"Do you understand how serious this is?" She pointed at the profanity on the wall, "Honey, this is the same color paint that you used at Sunny Birch and, David! It's all over you!" She spread her hands out in petition.

He shoved his hands deep into his pockets to hide the scarlet evidence.

"Just tell me where you were, David, and I'll believe you!"

David sniffed back a tear and looked at Chad and then back at his mother. Chad's heart was breaking. He didn't want to believe that David had done this, but the evidence was not looking good... Chad knew David well enough to know that he was hiding something.

"David?" Jill asked again.

"I can't..." he began.

"Can't what?"

"I can't tell you, okay?!" He shouted.

"Why?!" She shouted back.

Chad could tell this was getting them nowhere.

"Hey... Jill. Why don't you head on home and let David hang out a while..." He looked at David, "Sound good to you?"

David smirked and shrugged; Code language: "Yes."

Jill sighed and wiped a frustrated tear with the back of her hand and let Chad escort her to the front door, leaving David with Pastor Jim.

"Chad, I just don't know what to do anymore..." She started to cry.

At a loss, he put an arm around her shoulders and squeezed her. "Trust God, Jill... and trust David."

She wearily laid her head on his shoulder, "I'm trying,

Chad... But I don't know how much more of this I can take..."

Summer pulled her suburban into the church parking lot and found a space close to the building. She had sworn that she would never darken the doors of this place again, but it was the only decent blacktop in town. *Leave it to God to use a lanky kid to get me back on the premises.*

Rusty was hot on her tail, having followed her the four blocks, on his bike, from the shop to the church. Hopping out of her behemoth oven, she slammed the door and jogged to the sidewalk holding up one finger to Rusty, "Be right back!" she called, "Get ready to cry like a little baby girl!" she teased, as she bounced backward playfully.

"Yeah, right!" he called after her.

Summer nearly slammed into Chad and Jill as she rounded the corner. He had his arm around the pretty brunette and she was leaning on him. Summer couldn't explain the feeling she experienced, but she didn't like it... at all.

"Whoa!" Chad exclaimed, "Hey, Summer!"

He released Jill and reached forward to prevent Summer

from running over them both.

Summer looked from one to the other, "Hey... Just here to grab a ball." She explained as she pasted on a fake smile that fooled Jill, but not Chad. "Rusty's begging for another whipping..." She motioned toward the parking lot as she noticed the redness of Jill's eyes...

"Everything okay?" Her gaze passed from Jill to Chad and back to Jill again...*Lover's quarrel?* Why did she even care? She had Chris... *But still...*

Jill looked at Chad, uncertainly, and then back at Summer, "Um...There was an incident while I was at the shop today..." she began nervously, "Someone has accused David of vandalizing your dad's office..."

Summer was shocked. Her dad's office had been vandalized? Wow.

"This has nothing to do with my ability to work for you though, does it?" Jill was desperate. She needed this job so bad... "Please, I..."

Summer looked at her in confusion for a moment. Then, the light bulb clicked on.

"OH!....No!" She reached out and took Jill's hand, "Jill! The job is yours... and David's, too... If he wants it." Summer was sincere.

Chad watched in amazement as she proceeded to minister to Jill's confidence, his attraction to her deepening. And the beautiful thing was, Summer didn't even realize she was doing it...It was just who she was...Caring, kind...and so very beautiful.

"SUMMER!" Rusty's voice squeaked as he yelled her name, "YOU CHICKEN, OR WHAT?"

She grinned at Chad, "That's my cue, folks!" To Jill she smiled and said, "Just make sure you're there by 8:30 on Monday, okay?"

Grateful tears filled Jill's eyes as she startled Summer with a spontaneous embrace.

"Thank you! Oh, Summer, thank you so much!"

Summer scrunched her nose at Chad as she patted Jill's back awkwardly, inwardly hoping the other woman would release her death hold on her. When Jill finally released her, Summer smiled a goodbye to both of them as she bellowed over her shoulder, "GIMME A SEC, BRAT!"

Turning her eyes to the office door, Summer bounded up the steps and entered the room where she had declared she would never forgive one of the only men in her life that she had ever trusted. As she left the couple behind, she tried to understand the feeling that seeing the two of them together had caused, and why she even cared, for that matter.

Chad chuckled when Summer hollered at Rusty, and watched with longing as she bounded up the cement steps and snatched open the jingling front door.

"She really is amazing..." Jill said.

Chad jumped slightly. He had forgotten she was there. "Yes... She is..." His gaze lingered on the closed door.

Jill noticed with a smile, "Have you asked her out yet?"

Startled, Chad jerked his attention back to Jill's knowing smile, "What are you talking about?"

"Walk me to my car, silly man."

Chad blushed and complied, "It's that obvious?" He ducked his head and cut his eyes at her shyly.

"Just a lot..." she laughed, "So...You didn't answer my question."

"Hmm?" Chad was lost again, thinking about how much he loved the way Summer interacted so naturally with the teens, "Oh! Yeah..."

"Well...?"

"I don't see how that's any of your business..." He laughed.

"Turned you down, huh?"

Chad laughed and nodded, "Flat."

He chuckled, but it faded as he thought about their

conversation at Ruth's Diner... Just friends...*Chris Morgan*...

"Hey... Earth to you...?" Jill snapped her fingers as they approached her older Cutlass. "Lost you there for a sec..."

"Sorry... She's got a new life..." He sighed softly and put on a happy face, "and it doesn't include a small-town youth pastor."

Jill frowned sympathetically, "I'm sorry, Chad..." She tapped her slender finger on her pretty chin, "You know..." She stated facetiously, "I think I have a friend that just might be single..."

Chad laughed for real, "No thanks. I've got enough on my plate to deal with without adding a female to the menu... God knows, that's the last thing I need right now..." *But it was the very thing he wanted,* he thought as he closed the car door and turned, heading back into the church to talk with David.

CHAPTER SIXTEEN

"David..." Jim looked at the young man standing silent in his office as he leaned his backside against his disheveled desk. "Can I ask you a question?"

There was no response or movement from David.

"You don't have to answer..."

Good... I wasn't gonna... David rolled his eyes. He wasn't telling nobody nothing about anything. Pastor Jim was the only person, other than Chad, that he trusted, but he just couldn't tell them what they wanted to know. It would hurt his mom too much...

"What are things like at home?"

David's deep brown eyes looked up at him in surprise. This wasn't the question he'd expected not to answer ...

Jim's gaze searched deep into the hurt stare of the boy standing across from him. "Are things okay at home?"

David dropped his head quickly to keep Pastor Jim from seeing the unwanted tears that sprang to his eyes when he thought about the question.

Things sucked. His mom was always crying...He couldn't remember the last time he had heard her laugh...or even seen her smile for that matter. He couldn't do anything right, there was no food in the fridge and there was almost none in the cabinets. The lights got cut off yesterday... His mom had told him that there must have been a tree fall on the power lines... But everyone else in their trailer park had electricity... He hated that his mom was having such a hard time... He hated his dad for taking so long to come back. Nothing was okay at home. Nothing.

Jim sensed the emotion that David was struggling with, "Wanna talk about it?"

"No." David sniffed as he angrily swiped a renegade tear with the back of his hand and kept his eyes on the ground.

"Okay." Jim moved from his place in front of the desk and sat down behind it. He began to restack strewn papers, and when he didn't speak again, David raised his head and looked at the pastor.

"Well aren't you going to ask me where I was?... Or what I was doing?"

Jim kept his eyes on the task at hand. He tapped a stack of papers on the desk to straighten them, "Nope."

Confusion flashed across David's face. He was thoughtful for a minute.

"Why?" he asked.

"Figure it's none of my business..." Jim kept working.

"You're not going to accuse me?" David took a step

toward the desk.

Jim looked up into David's eyes, "Why would I do that?"

The teen shoved his paint covered hands deep into his pockets, "Uh...I don't know...? 'Cuz you think I did it...?"

Jim smiled genuinely, "I would have to actually believe that, to do that."

"Y-You really don't think I did this?" David's eyes traveled around the room and then rested on Jim again.

Jim chuckled, "David, I've seen your work...and this..." he pointed to the profanity tattooed across the wall, "This doesn't do you justice. Absolutely no creativity at all."

David grinned shyly and visibly relaxed as he plopped down in a chair across the desk from Jim. He turned a critical eye to the blazing red tag, "Yeah." He agreed... P.J. was pretty cool. They were both silent for a few minutes, Jim organizing and David watching him

"P.J.?"

Jim looked up at him.

"Can you keep a secret?"

Jim kept his face expressionless as he nodded slowly.

"You know, you asked about home?"

He nodded again.

"It sucks." David looked at his worn-out skate shoes as he kicked at a pen lying in the floor.

"Okay."

David looked up at Jim, "No... I mean it *really* sucks..." As if he didn't think Jim understood how bad he really thought it was.

"So…Wanna talk about it?" Jim asked for the second time.

The teen grew silent and looked down again as a small tear slid out of the corner of his left eye.

"Not really…"

"Okay." Jim went back to organizing his desk.

David grew frustrated and looked at him, "Why don't you, like, ask me why it sucks or why I feel like that…or something??"

Jim smiled and looked into his eyes, "Because, if you don't want to talk about it then, #1-I can't make you and, #2-it's none of my business."

The teen conceded.

They were quiet again.

"It hasn't ever been this bad…" David's soft voice brought Jim's attention to rest on his downcast face. He was quiet, letting David talk it out.

"We've always been able to make it before... But... I don't know..."

Jim's heart was breaking for this kid with the blue faux hawk. That was an adult line of worry.

"Mom said we'll be fine, but..." The eyes that met Jim's were watery and uncertain, "it doesn't look fine to me..." Another tear slid down his cheek.

"…and it's my fault…"

Jim had suspected there were some feelings like this involved and he had been praying for an opportunity to speak into this young man's life. He silently thanked God for this chance and prayed for wisdom.

"How do you figure?" He asked gently.

The strong-willed David crumbled and buried his face into his hands.

"Mom can't keep a job because of me... If we don't eat... It's my fault... If we don't have lights... It's my fault..." he hiccupped, "I'm the reason we have that piece-of-crap car that doesn't work half the time. I stole her car and wrecked it... but she couldn't fix it because she didn't have the money...Again, my fault."

Wow. Talk about a heavy load to bear. Poor kid.

"She would be better off without me..."

A flicker of concern crossed Jim's face, "What does that mean?"

David snorted, "I'm not going to kill myself, if that's what you mean."

Jim handed the boy a tissue, "Well, what *did* you mean by that?"

David took the tissue and wiped his nose that had been dripping,"Just that it wouldn't be so hard for her if she didn't have to worry about me..."

"Where you planning on going?"

David shrugged, "I don't know... Robbie said I could hang with him for a while, but his folks will be home from wherever they went, in a month, and then I would have to go."

"Robbie?" Jim asked.

"He's a guy I met at the skate park..."

"Okay…" Jim fought the urge to grill David about who this guy was and what he knew about him. But he knew that, with a kid like this one, you had to be careful how you approached topics like this.

"No! P.J., for real. He's cool." David assured the pastor as Chad entered the office and plopped down into a chair next to David.

"Who's cool?" Chad asked and looked back and forth between the two, mentally making a note to talk with

Jim, later, about his daughter.

"Robbie." David answered.

"You mean that dude that wears his pants three sizes too small, and black lipstick?" Chad leaned back in the chair and put his hands behind his head, "What about him?"

Jim tried unsuccessfully to hide his surprise.

"He's emo, duh." David smiled at Chad and the youth pastor slapped his blue faux hawk playfully.

"David was thinking about staying with him for a month so his mom could get on her feet," Jim brought Chad up to date on the last couple of statements.

"Is that so?" Chad turned a pointed stare onto David, "What are you running from?"

Chad's 'cut-to-the-chase' methods made Jim nervous at times, but he trusted the young man's instincts. He also knew that Chad spent a lot of time with these kids, giving him the right to speak into their lives that way. It was a relationship that Jim didn't, and never would, have with them. He was too…What did they call it…? 'Fogey'.

"Nothing." David lied.

"If you weren't running, you would stay with Alex…" Chad referred to the kid who had invited him to church and had prayed with David when he received Christ. They were like brothers, so he knew something was up.

David was silent and avoided Chad's eyes.

"Hey!" Jim clapped his hands once, "How 'bout I leave y'all to it? I've got to run on home. Barb will have my goat if I'm late for supper again. Lock up when you leave..." He knew David would never open up completely with him there, so he was removing himself.

Chad smiled his appreciation, and David shrugged.

The door closed securing the office and Chad eyed the teenager sitting next to him, "Fess up."

David's head popped up, "I didn't do it!"

Confusion crossed Chad's chiseled face, "Didn't do what?"

The teens eyes moved around the office.

"Oh!" Chad laughed, "I would be surprised and disappointed if you did... You can do a lot better than this..." He motioned to the red paint on the wall. "I was talking about why you want to stay with this Robbie character... I thought we talked about closing the door to the past?"

David looked at Chad, his brown eyes holding a turmoil that Chad was trying to understand, but this kid still had a lot that was closed off to his youth pastor. He stared down at his shoes and refused to make eye contact.

"Okay." Chad conceded, "I won't push, but you know I'm going to tell you the truth, right?" He looked at David, willing him to look into his eyes.

SKELETON KEY

David looked up. That's one reason why he liked Chad so much. He was honest... brutally... and there was no hidden agenda. He was real. This guy just cared about him.

"Robbie is bad news for you, dude. Jesus loves him and so I have to, too... But I'm going to be honest with you... It ain't easy to love a guy that hangs out at the skate park to scan for runners."

David dropped his eyes again and the Holy Spirit told Chad what the problem was.

"David," he began, "You don't need money that bad."

"What do you know?" David barked with a vehemence he didn't really feel, "You don't know anything about what my life is like! You act like you do...But you don't!"

The seconds on the nearby wall clock ticked loudly in the silence as Chad asked the Lord what to say to this kid...

Tell him your story...

"All right, dude." Chad leaned forward in his chair and grabbed David's chair turning it forcefully to face him, "Here's the deal."

David shifted nervously in his chair as Chad jerk-dragged his chair to face him.

"You're the one who doesn't know what you're talking about. Get comfortable. You're about to hear why Jesus is my superhero..."

Jim let himself out of the church and locked the front door behind him. He was still stunned about the state of his office. How on earth could that have happened? He had just stepped out of his office long enough to hit the bathroom and then make a few copies in the resource room. Who could have done this? He knew that whoever had done it, had intended to pin the deed on the troubled young teenager in his office right now. Jim shoved his hands into the pockets of his slacks and jingled the keys and change in them as he walked around the corner of the church building, and onto the recently paved blacktop parking lot.

The strange thing was that nothing seemed to be missing. It seemed that the perpetrators simply wanted to shake things up, and they had succeeded.

Seeing Summer's truck he immediately scanned the blacktop for his daughter and the sound of scuffling sneakers and playful laughter drew his attention to the area across the parking lot designated for basketball.

The sight of Summer's beautiful smile and her easy manner with Rusty caused Jim's heart to twist painfully. He wanted so badly to intrude and to try to make things right with his daughter, but instead he just watched her from a distance. Somehow, he knew that she wasn't ready yet. Barb had told him about her conversation with Summer and he was hopeful, but he also knew enough about his daughter to know that she was not one that could be persuaded or pressured. So, without interrupting their game, he made his way to his gold, Crown Victoria and opened the door.

The heat almost suffocated him as he sat down in the golden oven and fished the keys out of his pocket. He placed them in the ignition and cranked the car.

Instantly, the air that had been blowing hard and cold when he parked, was now blowing over one hundred degrees. He pushed the buttons, and the front windows came down and would stay that way until the air blowing from the vents cooled off. He glanced at Summer. If she had heard him, she did not acknowledge him.

Lord, I seem to be needing Your help a whole lot these days. Father, I don't know how to fix this mess that I have found myself in... I thought I was doing right by protecting her from the truth, but now... Well, now it just seems like it was the coward's way. I need Your wisdom and guidance...

He put the car in gear and began to back out of his parking place. As he stretched his arm over the back of his seat and turned his head to watch behind him, a faint glimmer near the tree line behind the church caught his eye.

"What is that?" he wondered out loud. Backing out of the space, he then put the car in drive and rode slowly across the parking lot toward the back.

Summer looked up as she saw his car nearing them. *"Great..."* she thought, *"I knew I shouldn't have come here...",* but as he drove closer, she noticed that his attention was on the tree line and not her. She turned her own eyes to the tree line in the direction he was looking, shielding her eyes from the sun, trying to see what he was looking at.

WHOOSH! The basketball swished with ease through the net over her head.

"WHOO HOOO!!" Rusty threw his fists into the air and hooted victoriously, "14-12!! You LOSE! Loos-uh-herrrr!" He threw an 'L' shape onto his forehead.

"Hey!" She protested, "SO not fair!"

"Who's the little baby girl, now? Huh?" The teen laughed as he retrieved the ball and dribbled it easily.

"Yeah, yeah..." Summer flashed a confident grin at Rusty, "You had to cheat to beat me, Turkey..."

"Whatever, Summer!" He laughed as he noticed for the first time, the car pulling up to the edge of the pavement close to them. He waved as he recognized their pastor getting out of the car.

"Hey, P.J.!" He shouted, even though Jim was only feet away.

"Hey there, Rusty." Jim stated not taking his eyes off of the place where the glimmer had been, as he stepped out of the car and shut the door.

Summer watched with interest, from a distance, as her dad made his way across the grass and stooped down at the tree line. Rusty trotted over to Jim as he squatted there, contemplating on whether to pick it up or to leave it there and call the police.

"Whoa, P.J.! What's that?" he asked.

An uncommon fear gripped Jimmy's stomach, "Interesting, Rusty... Interesting, is what it is."

CHAPTER SEVENTEEN

Three Months Later...

Soft, snowy lace gently drifted downward from the grey sky over the encampment for the third time in two days. Snows were unusual for this part of the South. Little Wolf made his way to the hut he had constructed for Caroline. He smiled to himself as he recalled the day that he had built it. He had had quite a time keeping her out of the way. She kept insisting that she could do it. He allowed himself a chuckle as he remembered how she had landed soundly on her back side with the weight of a small felled tree before she had finally given in and let him do it alone. She was a strong woman...and a stubborn one.

The smile on his face faded as he thought about the man that she believed to be dead. His honor had checked him on many different occasions as his heart, and his persistent squaw, had nudged him to tell the lonely and grieving woman about her man. He simply could not break his word no matter how much he regretted giving it.

The hazy smoke drifted upward in spirals from the center of the animal hide-covered tent. He admired his work as he came closer. A prepubescent bark alerted the inhabitant of the tent that there was a visitor. Caroline wearily untied the top of the door flap and peeked out. Seeing her best friend's husband, she grinned and untied the rest, releasing the heavy leather door.

"Hello!" She called to him in Creek.

He smiled his answer as he ducked into her teepee. The puppy he had given her was growing quickly. Obviously excited, it danced and hopped around his knees and stole a few licks as Little Wolf entered the tent.

"Come…in…?" She laughed softly as she struggled with the new language.

"Thank you." He stopped to scratch the pup's soft ears.

"How…are…" Carolyn began in her new language. She searched for the right word…*What had Kalana said it was, again?*…"Oh!" She heaved a frustrated sigh and fanned her hands, "How are you and Kalana?" She gave up and picked up her native English as she quieted the puppy and shewed him away to his bed next to the fire.

Little Wolf laughed. It was a deep, rich sound that made Caroline happy on the inside every time she heard it.

"We are good. I came to check your wood supply. It grows colder and I think the snow is here for the night."

Caroline shivered involuntarily. She was so thankful for Little Wolf and Kalana. *If it wasn't for them…* She didn't even want to think about that. She closed her eyes briefly.

"Thank you so much, Little Wolf. My stack *is* a little

low... I would get more by myself, but..."

Little Wolf shook his head, "You don't have a man... Your little one is too small, yet, for the cold." He turned and restacked the small amount of wood inside the teepee, not seeing the cloud pass over her face.

You don't have a man...

The simple, matter-of-fact statement caused her heart to wrench inside her chest. Would she ever get over the loss of William? Would she ever move past this ache?

She had been with the tribe for coming on four months now, and there had been several of the young men who had expressed an interest in her, but she just wasn't ready... Kalana had laughed once and said that it was probably her hair that had them following her around.

Her hair...

The trip to the winter site was a fear-filled one because of that very thing. She recalled how Kalana had braided her hair tightly and covered her head with a deer hide and a woven blanket to keep watching eyes from seeing its golden color...

Little Wolf stood and watched her as she turned slowly to retrieve her fussing baby, waking from a nap.

"You think of William...?"

Sad eyes looked at him and she nodded. "I don't think I will ever heal..." Tears threatened as she knelt, unwrapped her son and began the diapering process. At a little more than four months old, Willie was a bundle of smiles and flapping arms and legs. He grinned at his mother and squealed his excitement and Caroline nearly fell into tears. His smile was so much like his father's.

"You will heal," he stated matter-of-factly as he squatted and checked the remainder of her supplies, "Heart wounds heal just like flesh wounds. It is a deep wound. It will take longer… but it will heal." Little Wolf stood and made his way to the door.

Caroline looked into his kind eyes.

"It is good to grieve your loss. It is not good to live there." And with that, he ducked out and left Caroline with her thoughts.

Had she been living in her grief? She tried to remember her life over the last few months. There were certain things that she remembered, but on the whole it was a mystery to her. How could one live their life and not remember the details about it? Caroline frowned as she fastened the diaper cloth around little Willie's bottom. Maybe Little Wolf was right...

Baby Willie kicked and gurgled to regain his mama's attention and she delighted him with a nose rub and a tickle as she picked him up, nestled him in her arms and prepared to nurse him. He flapped his arms in excitement and Caroline laughed lovingly at his enthusiasm as he turned his head, mouth wide and tongue smacking before she could even get him latched on. He was such a joy.

"Lord, Jesus," she prayed as she relaxed her shoulders, "Please help me to move on... I loved him so much... But he's not here anymore." Tears formed in her golden eyes and slowly made their way down her cheeks. "I can't keep wishing for him to come home to me... He's gone and I have to accept that and let him go..."

She looked down at the beginning of downy curls on her infant son's little head. With her free hand, she caressed the back of his soft head, "I don't want to forget him... I never will forget him... But I'm willing for You to help me close my heart to the past ...." she leaned forward and pressed a kiss onto her baby's head and inhaled his smoky sweetness, "...and open my heart to the future..."

"Hey there, hot stuff!" Summer trotted up to her grandmother's wheelchair as the nurse wheeled her to the curbing to await pick up.

"Summer!" Surprised, Naomi grinned happily and reached her arms out for a hug from her favorite granddaughter... Her only granddaughter...

The two shared a big squeeze.

"Oh! I was SO worried about you!" Naomi scolded.

Summer smiled sheepishly, "I know, Nanna... I'm sorry about that... I kinda had a meltdown..." She took a few of Naomi's things and loaded him into the back of her brand new, silver Toyota Sequoia.

"Whose car is this?!" Naomi exclaimed.

"It's mine!" Summer grinned as she went back to the curb to retrieve the rest of Naomi's belongings.

Concern flashed across Naomi's face, "Can you afford this...?"

Summer popped her head out of the back where she was loading bags and smiled mysteriously, "I have a lot to tell you, Nanna..."

Naomi put a hand over her eyes and the other playfully over her heart, "Lord Jesus! Don't let them put my Sunny in jail!"

Laughing loudly, Summer played along. She hurriedly threw the remaining items in the back and slammed the hatch loudly as she hopped to the curbing, locked the wheels on the wheelchair and rushed to load her Nana carefully into the passenger seat.

"C'mon, old lady! They're hot on my tail!"

"Oh, psssh!" Naomi giggled, but her smile faded at Summer's seriously distressed face. "Summer?! Are you playing?... Please tell me you are!" Naomi's eyes were wide, and the nurse was hiding her amusement.

"NO! GET IN! HURRY!!" Summer gently grabbed her arm and helped her sit down in the vehicle. She quickly buckled her in and slammed the door. Winking and waving at the laughing nurse, she trotted around to the driver's side and hopped in.

"Summer??" Naomi gripped the door handle as her granddaughter punched the gas and the vehicle jumped forward. "Dear Lord!", she gasped as she placed a hand over her heart.

No longer able to keep a straight face, Summer pulled her foot out of the carburetor and cracked up as Naomi fussed, "Summer Dalton, I am not a young woman! You almost gave me a heart attack!... Thinkin' you were actually serious..."

Summer grinned at her grandmother widely, "I know...and I'm sorry." She giggled, "I just couldn't resist. I just left the dealership." Summer reached over and squeezed Naomi's hand. "...And no, I didn't steal it."

Naomi returned the squeeze and chuckled in spite of herself. "You did have me goin', there..." She relaxed into the soft, grey, leather seat and rub her hands along the cushion next to her legs, "How are you affording this though?"

Summer smiled, "Well, it turns out that I'm rich."

Naomi nodded, "Rich in love, I know, honey. But seriously?" She quoted the saying that she had drilled into Summer's brain as a child growing up on a small-town pastor's salary.

Summer shook her head and laughed as she flicked on

her turn signal and braked at the red light. "I *am* serious, Nanna...I'm rich...like...*money* rich. As in...*35 million plus,* kind of rich." Her golden eyes shimmered with the excitement of it as her smile widened.

Naomi's mouth fell open, "You can't be serious?!"

"Oh... But I am..." Summer was so tickled.

"But...?"

"That attorney that called? He wanted to get with me because my grandfather was rich, and I was his closest relative! Isn't that amazing?!... I mean about the money... Not that the guy died... Well, you know what I mean!"

"Oh, honey! I'm so happy for you!" Naomi patted the car seat with a happy smile, "That explains a lot!... Have you told your dad?" she wanted to know.

Summer shook her head and, when she saw Naomi's expression and then the head shake, she wanted to explain and make an excuse... but what would she say? That she was at the church, but she was too chicken to talk to her dad who was only 20 feet away? SO! She just ignored the look on her Nanna's face and changed the subject.

"Guess what else?" She began. Naomi smiled knowingly and looked out the window of the Sequoia at the familiar houses whizzing by as they neared her home of thirty-six years.

"I can't imagine?" Her aging eyes returned to Summer,

"Tell me dear. I'm dreadfully short on good gossip!"

Summer laughed and obliged her, "Remember that attorney?"

Naomi nodded.

"Well…" Summer paused for effect and eyed her Nanna out of the corner of her eye, "We're dating!"

This news disturbed Naomi for some reason. She had assumed that the glow that she had noticed as soon as she had seen Summer, had been put there by that sweet handsome youth pastor. This was news indeed…She skillfully masked her concern as she fiddled with the button on her blouse.

"Hmm…Must be a good one for you to approve… When do I get to make my decision on this fella?" She wanted a chance to let her discernment and the Holy Spirit tell her what kind of man was courting her Sunny.

"Soon, Nanna…" Summer grinned and reached over and squeezed Naomi's hand again, "Soon."

Naomi caught sight of her house through the windshield and clapped her hands happily as they pulled into her driveway and Summer put the vehicle in park.

"I've missed being home, so much!" She leaned forward to grab her purse and felt the door to find the release handle. After a few seconds, she located it and was getting out as Summer rounded the back of the vehicle.

"NANNA!" Summer scolded, "You sit down right now!

I'll help you."

"Poppycock! I'm just fine..." She stood and retrieved her cane from the front seat and began walking up the sidewalk to her front door. "See?"

"I see you being stubborn, is what I see..." Summer grumbled as she went to get Naomi's bags out of the back.

"I heard that."

"And what experience do you have Mr....?"

"Uh, Billings...Edward Billings..." the older gentleman shifted nervously in his seat. Lawyers made him nervous. Especially since he had just gotten out on parole. He didn't recognize this one though, so that was a good thing.

"Right! Right." Chris smiled at Edward.

"I, uh...well...before...well, you know..." he stammered, referring to his incarceration, "...I was a handyman at this old lady's house..." Ed still wasn't sure why this lawyer was even talking to him.

"What kind of handyman?"

"Well...I guess I did pretty much everything that needed to be done. You know, keep the lawn cut, hedges trimmed, leaves raked. I fixed anything that needed fixin' too. That was a while ago, though..."

Chris smiled. This guy was perfect. Not too bright, with a record... "Great!" He scribbled some numbers down on a piece of paper, "This is the address and my cell phone numbers. Be there at 7:00 AM. I'll let you in and give you a key to the sheds."

Ed was stunned, "Just like that?"

Chris smiled again, "Just like that."

Relief flooded Ed's wrinkled face as he clasped Chris' outstretched hand in his own. "You don't know how much I appreciate this!"

"No, Mr. Billings," the handsome attorney smiled knowingly, "I'm the one who is grateful to you."

"I won't let you down, Mr. Morgan." He said earnestly, "You can count on me."

"I'm sure I can, Mr. Billings, I'm sure I can..."

"Are you sure this is what you want, honey?" Summer's mother asked as she wrapped another plate in newspaper and placed it in a box. She had been at her daughter's apartment all afternoon helping her pack up the last of her belongings. Barb was still unsure about this move. Something just didn't feel right. But, she had dutifully put her mind and efforts into helping Summer and had dismissed the misgivings... sort of.

Summer nodded, "Yes ma'am. I'm sure. I've never fit in here... and now I know why." She shrugged and finished taping a box closed and wrote 'BATHROOM' in big letters across it.

"I can't help but feel like this is a mistake, Summer..." Barb paused in her packing and looked into her daughter's eyes.

"Why is what I want to do always a mistake?" Summer sighed. She knew that wasn't a true statement. Her mom had always supported her decisions, even when she didn't agree with them, but Summer didn't care. "Am I incapable of making good decisions on my own?"

Barb sensed the steel in her daughter's tone, "Absolutely not... I just think that there is always wisdom in seeking wise counsel..." She wrapped another plate, "I always did... in big decisions like this one..."

"Well, I'm not *you* and I did seek counsel…from my attorney." She carried the box across the room to the door and stacked it on top of two more boxes, "… and he advised me to make a clean break and clear my head. And that's the best advice I've heard lately."

"Honey, why would you ask him about this and not me?

Do you even know where he stands on issues that are important to you? What kind of moral code he has?" Barb shook her head as she placed the wrapped plate securely into the box and reached for another. "… And I don't think that encouraging someone to run away from their problems is ever good advice."

Summer stopped and stared at her mom. She clenched and unclenched her teeth. How had she known that the conversation would come to this? It frustrated and angered her.

"I didn't agree to your help here so I could get a sermon. I've heard enough sermons to last me the rest of my *life*. I'm trying to move on with my life. The last thing I need is for you to be preaching at me about running away. I'm *not* running away. Let's just get that straight. I'm simply removing myself from where I have never belonged."

Tears formed in Barb's eyes and Summer felt like a heel, but she refused to take any of it back. It was true...wasn't it? Of course it was! Her gut told her so...and Chris had confirmed it. That was enough for her.

"Is that really how you feel, Summer?" Barb asked, her heart hurting over the words her daughter had just shot at her, so carelessly. To Barb, it was like Summer was declaring that she had not only never belonged but had never been loved. All of the years of nurturing and kisses on booboo's, mother-daughter play dates, softball games, basketball games...years of sacrifices...Was her daughter really saying that it meant nothing?

Summer ignored the gentle voice in her heart cautioning her to tread carefully, "Yes, *Mother*, that's how I really feel. No one has ever accepted me here and I'm going to find a place where I can be myself, and not worry about what so-and-so thinks about what I did or didn't do right. I'm sick of trying to make everyone happy." She stalked into the kitchen to close the lid on the box.

Barb finished wrapping the last plate and placed it in the box on the counter. She turned to the sink, squeezed some dish soap onto her hands, and washed the ink off of them. Summer watched as her mom quietly dried her hands on the scarlet dish towel on the counter and turned to pick up her purse off of the counter.

"Uh!" Summer huffed, "What? So now you're leaving?...C'mon, Mom… You can't be serious?"

Barb couldn't look at her daughter as she retrieved her keys from her purse and walked to the door. In all of the years that she had raised and loved Summer; she had never been so hurt. Summer watched in irritated surprise as her mother reached for the doorknob and wordlessly let herself out of the apartment.

What in the actual world? Was everyone in this God-forsaken town going crazy? Well, *fine*! If that's how it was going to be, then *fine*! Summer angrily finished loading the box she had started and snatched the tape dispenser up vehemently. She slapped the tape across the flaps, snapped the tape and rubbed her hand across it to seal it.

This was the very reason she was getting out of this worthless place. She snatched up the box, marched across the room and slammed it down on the floor by the door. She couldn't please anybody! Not even her own mother!

She's not your mother...She never really loved you...You remind her of your father's infidelity...and always will.

Summer's heart and face twisted as the vicious words flitted across her mind. Who was she kidding? Well, as soon as she could get all of her stuff loaded, she was out of here.

Awakened by the noise, Mow stretched lazily and slowly hefted his massive body off of the blanket Summer had thrown in the floor for him earlier. He moseyed into the kitchenette, checked his bowl, and complained loudly when he found it empty.

Summer stomped back to the kitchen and the sheer force of her entry into the small kitchen area, sent his fat body scampering and skidding to get out of her way. Green eyes wide, he hid under the table and chairs, staring out at his crazed mistress.

"Why am I even doing this?" Summer shouted into the emptiness as she threw her hands in the air, "I'm freaking rich! I can pay someone to do this!"

She stormed to the back of the apartment and retrieved Mow's travel kennel from the empty closet in her relatively empty bedroom, and marched back into the living room. She plopped it noisily onto the table and sent Mow streaking back to the bedroom.

"MOW!" she bellowed, "Get in here!"

He was all too willing *not* to comply with the wild woman in the other room.

When he didn't come running...like she knew he wouldn't...Summer marched into the bedroom and snatched the closet door open for the second time. He hunkered down and scanned for an escape route.

Summer looked at his huge eyes and immediately felt awful. She calmed herself and squatted slowly, reaching for him. He squinted his eyes shut and shrank from her as she took hold of him, pulled him to her, and gathered his fat body into her arms. Burying her face in his neck, Summer apologized to her frightened pet and struggled to heft them both up off of the floor.

"Oh…Mow-Mow…I'm sorry…I'ms not mad at dat fat kittehn…" she sing-songed as she kissed his fluffy neck. Gradually he began to purr as he decided to forgive her... until she pushed him into his kennel. He maneuvered his hefty frame until he was staring at her out of the kennel door.

"Don't look at me like that."

CHAPTER EIGHTEEN

Two Years Later...

Lucas Waters galloped across the clearing toward the encampment he had been ministering at for the past year. A smile played about his rugged face as he thought of the woman he had grown to love. It had been such a surprise to find her there... a beautiful and solemn white woman living among the people he had come to know as his own. His thoughts of her rare smile and long golden hair warmed his heart, even as the dropping temperature chilled his bones. He recalled how she had been so distant and how protective the people had been of her. Now, almost a year later, he was nervous and excited about his plan to meet with her this evening. He prayed that he wouldn't make a mess of what he intended to say...

"Caroline!" Kalana's surprised laughter filled the warm tent.

"What?" Caroline giggled uncomfortably beside her.

"What is this?!" Kalana held up a soft, creamy butter-white, leather ceremonial dress decorated with deer teeth, intricate beading, and a few hawk feathers.

"I made it for you..." She blushed, no longer struggling with the language of her adopted people.

Kalana smiled widely through happy tears, "I've never seen anything so beautiful..." She draped it over her swollen abdomen, "it's a little small, though..."

Caroline laughed, "Silly! It's for after the baby comes..." She looked down at her hands, "for when you dedicate her to the Lord."

"Oh!" Kalana wrapped her in her arms and held her for a moment and the two women shared a meaningful embrace. "Thank you, Sister!" She released Caroline and sat back, giving the baby in her very full womb as much room as possible. She looked down and lovingly caressed her belly, "Her?"

Caroline nodded matter-of-factly as she shifted to her knees and reached for the other gift that was waiting in her woven bag, "Yes, 'her'...Which reminds me..." she pulled out a small package carefully wrapped in tanned deer hide and tied with twine. She smiled tenderly at her friend as she laid it in what was left of Kalana's lap.

Kalana looked from the gift to Caroline in question.

"This one is for the baby." Carolyn smiled and sat down excitedly, and when Kalana hesitated, she exclaimed, "Well, open it!"

The beautiful, bronzed woman grinned at her friend's

excitement and untied the twine. Unwrapping the leather, she found a delicate, handmade rag doll unlike any she had ever seen. The doll was made of cloth and had a white face with perfectly stitched features... including bright red lips, neatly braided fabric hair, and as she lifted the precious gift, it jingled brightly with a tinkling sound!

Surprise illuminated her face and joy lit her friend's.

"How is this accomplished?!" she asked as she shook the doll, and the sweet tinkling filled the air.

Caroline clapped her hands excitedly, "Do you like it?"

Kalana nodded happily, "How does it make that sound?"

"I put a little Jingle Bell in its head before I stitched it closed!" She laughed, "Doesn't it make a lovely sound?"

"Oh, yes!" Kalana shook it again. "Sister...thank you!"

The sound of hoof beats interrupted their private party and when male voices could be heard, Caroline blushed deeply. Kalana watched her with pleasure. She had been praying for a long time that the day would come when her friend would allow herself to love again.

They could hear the men outside and Caroline hurriedly gathered her belongings and started toward the tied door.

"Where are you going in such a rush?" Kalana laughed as she watched her suddenly flustered friend.

"Hmm? Oh! I, er, I need to go get Willie. Grandmother

will have put him in her stew by now, I'm sure!" She untied the leather strap, "Hope you like them! I'll see you later!" She ducked out and smiled a hurried goodbye to Little Wolf and to the handsome man standing there with him.

Phew! That was close!

Something inside her heart leapt whenever she saw that man, lately, and it was *not* something she wanted to happen. In fact, she had willed herself not to even look at the man, but every time he was near, she found herself daydreaming about what it would feel like to be held by him...kissed by him...protected by him...loved and cherished by him...

She thought it even now! What was happening to her?! She didn't want this! Or did she? Caroline shook her head to clear it as she hurried away, so engrossed in her own thoughts that she didn't hear the footfalls behind her. Caroline startled and turned as she felt a strong hand on her arm. She found herself face to face with the very object of her thoughts.

"Caroline," his warm breath was puffing visibly in the chilly evening air.

She swallowed, blushing furiously.

"Could we talk?" He spoke to her in her native English.

What to say? Yes, yes, YES!...No, no, NO! She had to get away... She could use Willie as an excuse.

"I'm really in a rush, Lucas..." She purposely spoke to him in Creek and took a few steps to distance herself from this enigma of a man, "... need to get my son..."

The image of Caroline's vivacious toddler danced across his mind, and he smiled. "I'll walk with you," he stated as he fell easily into the language and into step beside her.

Heat filled her downcast face and she pulled the blanket tighter around her head and shoulders.

"It's a pretty night." He mentally kicked himself at the stupidity of the statement.

Caroline nodded noncommittally, wishing that Grandmother's tent was not the furthest one away...

Lucas tried again. "How is Willie?"

Caroline knew she shouldn't be rude...but it was definitely safer. "He's good." She turned her eyes to the worn path.

This was not going how he had envisioned it. He started again.

"I was in town today, and picked up a few books you might like..."

Caroline stopped and looked into his eyes for the first time that evening. Such gentle eyes... She mentally shook herself. Lucas made it sound like 'town' was just around the corner, not the half day's ride that it really was. She cocked her head to the right and scrutinized the man standing beside her.

"I have too many books..." She lied and resumed her fast-paced walk.

Lucas smiled broadly, knowing he had piqued her interest. He had visited her teepee many times with Little Wolf delivering firewood and picking up the beautiful hides that Caroline tanned and chewed for the purpose of trading in town. He had seen the rudimentary library of scholastic books that she had been teaching the children from. There were very few pleasure reading books…

"Oh, I don't know..." he quipped, "Not sure that one could ever have too many books…" He trotted to catch up to her, amused at how much ground such a small woman could cover.

Caroline remained silent, not trusting herself at this moment with him so near.

This was not going well at all. Lucas took a deep breath and reached for the hand that had fallen to her side as she hurried to reach her destination. There was a chemistry between them, and he knew it. She had to feel it too. He could see it in her eyes and in the way she blushed when they would talk. He could see it in the way that she avoided spending excessive time alone with him. Surely, he wasn't dreaming it..?

He had prayed many nights about Caroline and his feelings for her and, instead of subsiding, they grew only stronger. He couldn't continue to pretend that he wanted nothing more than a casual friendship with her.

Her breath caught in her throat as electricity flew from his fingers into her hand and up her arm, shocking her heart.

"Caroline..." His strong hand held her tightly and the momentum of the brisk pace she had taken forced her to stop suddenly and turn to face him, almost causing her to stumble.

His hands reached out and took hold of the sides of her arms to steady her. The feeling of his large hands on her arms electrified her heart again and she stared up at him, wide eyed.

Lucas wasn't sure if he understood her reaction, but he pressed on. She had to know how he felt and if she wouldn't allow him a private moment, he would just lay it out there for all of the woods to see and hear.

"Caroline, I..." he began haltingly... where had all that courage from a moment before just gone? She continued to stare at him, not sure if she could even speak if he were to ask her a question.

"I..." his green eyes earnestly searched the depths of her golden ones as if seeking a kindred feeling there, "You need to know that my intentions towards you are to court you."

He gulped and squeezed his eyes shut as he released her arms. Embarrassed, he shoved a hand in his pocket and slowly ran the other down his face in humiliation.

Nothing romantic about that.

No wooing, no meaningful oratory. Seconds ticked by and shame colored his face a deeper shade of red with every silent second that passed. Lucas couldn't bring himself to look at the woman in front of him. He shifted his weight from one foot to the other.

Caroline was shocked... Kalana had hinted that Lucas had feelings for her, but she had dared not believe it. Could it be? Could this man really be standing here before her, laying his heart out at her feet? Immediately she felt guilt and remorse for how she had run away from him, and literally forced the man to declare his intentions to anyone who had happened upon the path. What was more surprising, though, was what was going on in her own heart. She stared at Lucas, looking very boyish and vulnerable, and suddenly there was a glimmer of hope. Was it possible?

He was turning to walk away when she slowly reached her small hand toward him and touched his arm. He looked at her hand there on the sleeve of his jacket and then into her large, doe-like eyes. For a moment the two stared at each other, not sure what to say. And then Caroline broke the silence in English.

"I loved him." Tears formed in her eyes, "I will always love him..." her voice cracked with emotion as she searched for words.

Lucas looked into her eyes and listened quietly, inwardly preparing himself to be rejected. His heart began to race as she stepped closer to him, leaving her hand on his arm.

"And..." a tear escaped from her left eye and traced its way down her tanned cheek, "...for a long time I thought my heart would never beat again."

The rhythm of his pulse quickened in anticipation of her next words.

"But then you came to our camp..." She sniffed as another tear followed suit and her voice began to tremble, "You were a friend to me, and it was good to hear my language...speak my language again. It was good to speak of the Lord with you..."

Timidly, she slid her hand down his sleeve to grasp his strong hand. She placed her other hand over her heart as she willed herself to put into words what she had been running from for months. "I found myself looking forward to our time together... The deep spiritual conversations we had... But it suddenly scared me to realize that it wasn't the conversation that I longed for anymore... It was..." a shy smile and a deep blush colored her small face, "it was time spent with you."

Lucas thought he would shout to the sky. He fought the urge to pull her close to him and kiss her soundly. Instead, he reached for the other hand. She gave it to him willingly and he marveled at how right it felt.

"I didn't want this to happen... I loved William so much. I felt that I was betraying his memory by feeling this way... But I just couldn't stop it..." She allowed Lucas to pull her gently into his arms. She laid her head against his broad chest marveling at how good it felt to be held again… Realizing how very much she had missed it and needed it. "I found myself thinking less and less about how much I had lost, and more and more about how I would keep myself from loving you…"

Lucas 's heart leapt at her words. She loved him. He pressed his lips against the part in her hair inhaling the smoky, woody scent, "How did that work out for you?" He chuckled softly.

She smiled into his coat as she nestled her face closer to his heart. It felt so good to be held like this... "Not so well, I'm afraid."

The two stood that way for what seemed like forever, each enjoying the nearness of the other.

"Thank you…" Caroline whispered into his coat.

Lucas smiled softly into her hair, "What for?"

"The books…"

CHAPTER NINETEEN

"Welcome home, Mees Dalton…Meester Morgan…" a pretty Latina brunette in her mid-twenties smiled sweetly at Summer as she opened the heavy mahogany front door and stepped aside for her mistress to enter.

Summer smiled back, hiding the frustration she felt. It had not been a good day so far. Why was it that every man in her life seemed to think that she was incapable of making her own decisions? It was infuriating! She stepped into the front hallway for the first time as the resident mistress of the Connor estate, and what should have been a defining moment, was forgotten in the conversation that was replaying itself in her mind. She set her keys down on the elaborate sofa table as she stepped into the ornate colonial library. The plush olive-green carpet invited her to remove her uncomfortable heels and squish her toes through the thick softness.

Chris followed her into the room and closed the sliding wooden doors behind him.

"How could you do that?!" Summer fired at him as soon as he turned around.

"I was acting in your best interest, Summer…" Chris sighed impatiently.

"In my best interest? Are you actually serious?!"

She threw her hand in the air and moved over to one of the four large bookshelves that covered the walls of the room. It really was an impressive collection of first editions and confederate historical documents. *Calm down, Sunny Girl... Keep your cool...*

Chris walked around the chocolate, suede couch in the center of the room and sat down. "Yes, Summer, I acted in your best interest. You needed some clear perspective on the matter, and I simply did what I thought was best for you... my client..."

"Whoa, whoa, whoa..." Summer waved her hands incredulously, "...Your *client*?"

Chris immediately checked himself. He was going to have to be careful how he handled this. She was so beautiful... And he was having trouble keeping himself distant from her. He found himself doubting the original plan and trying to figure out a new one... one that did not include hurting her. No matter which plan, Summer Dalton was smarter than he had imagined, and he didn't need her catching on before he wanted her to. He had to stay a step ahead of her.

"Darling," he crooned, "There are some matters that I'm sure you don't want just anyone handling... You need someone close to you... who knows you... someone like me, to take care of unsightly things like this..."

"Unslightly? Chris, my mother is not an unsightly problem, and the way you just brushed her off..." Summer sputtered, "Like...Like...Like I don't even care about her! That was uncalled for and unacceptable!"

"Aw, Honey…" he drawled as he poured himself two fingers of aged brandy.

"You threatened her with a *restraining* order, Chris!" Summer put one hand on her hip and the other she ran through her hair in agitation, "I mean, honestly! What could you have *possibly* been thinking?!... She's my *mother* for Christ's sake!"

He took a sip of the strong beverage, "Technically, she's not your mother... And sweetheart! You're trying to make a new start here, right?"

Summer glared at him, but she listened.

"The last thing you need is to have the past coming back to bring you down over, and over again..." he took another sip and swallowed as he continued, "…reminding you of who you used to be. You need a clean break. I'm simply helping you with that... Honest, Sunny. If I had known it would upset you like this, I wouldn't have done it. I mean..." he looked into his tumbler and swirled the caramel-colored liquid around and around. He smiled inwardly, "I thought I was doing you a favor…to hear *you* talk..."

His statement hit its mark with the deadly accuracy he was counting on. Summer felt nauseous as she recalled the last time she had seen her mom. That night in the apartment... How she had ranted to him about her entire family being a bunch of religious freaks that she couldn't wait to get away from.

Chris was right... He had simply acted upon what she had led him to believe.

It's your fault... The voice in her head accused her.

She turned her back on Chris and faced the bookshelves. She let her fingers trace the age-old volumes lining the shelf where she was standing. Chris had only said to Barb what she, herself, had been thinking.

"Don't be so hard on yourself, sweetheart..." Chris reassured her, "... I kicked my folks to the curb when I was eighteen years old, and it was the best decision I ever made."

Summer looked at him. Is that what she was doing? He was so handsome sitting there on the couch, arms draped over the back of the cushion. He did seem to have it all together. Maybe he was right?

Chris patted the seat behind him, and she reluctantly moved to sit there. She leaned against his body and allowed her own body to relax, but her thoughts were far from peaceful.

Call your mom...No. I can't...*She'll understand*...No, she won't...*Trust Me*...I already did.

Chris smiled smugly as she settled in beside him. He wasn't called the best defense attorney in the South for nothing. He could convince any jury that the worst criminal was a saint, if he was paid enough, so convincing Summer that a saint was a criminal shouldn't be too hard for him. It was already proving to be much simpler than he had thought...and the payoff was definitely worth it.

"What do you think, Jatory?" Jim asked the officer as they walked back across the parking lot headed to his recently restored office. As soon as the investigators had taken pictures and dusted, the grounds committee had not wasted any time in covering the obscenity that tainted the wall in the pastor's office.

"I can't quite figure it out, but I'm sure that cell phone that the investigator found this afternoon will give us a few answers." He jotted a few notes down in his small notepad before stuffing it back into his shirt pocket. "I'm glad you called me. I have to be honest, Pastor Jim, I don't have a good feeling about that pistol you found."

"Zero Ten, What's your status?" A voice crackled over his radio.

Jatory leaned his head to the side and pressed the call button on the radio on his shoulder, "Zero Ten, Dispatch, I'm 10-8."

"10-4," came the crackled reply.

"Can you think of anyone who has a problem with you?" Jatory asked his pastor. He loved this man's heart and his passion. His respect for the man had quadrupled after he had witnessed how Jim had handled himself in the face of the shocking revelation brought forth by the head of the deacon board.

Jim could think of several lately, and he said as much.

"What about Tom Davies?" Jatory asked.

"What about him?"

"Do you think he could be behind this?"

"Who? Tom?" Jim thought for a moment, "I don't think so...?"

"I don't know, Jim. He seemed pretty heated the other night..."

Jim shook his head, "Tom's a bully, but I don't think he would actually do something as crazy as this..."

"Well, who else can you think of that would want to get a message across to you?" Jatory asked as he opened the front door for Jim to enter. The phone was ringing, and Jim stepped over to the reception desk to pick it up

"First Baptist, Watson. Pastor Jim speaking..."

"Your days are numbered..." an alien sounding voice drawled over the line.

"Excuse me?" Adrenaline shot through his veins, and he motioned for Jatory to come near. Quietly, he put the phone on speaker in time for both of them to hear the caller say:

"Your days are numbered. Do the right thing…or else..."

"Who is this??" He demanded, but the line went dead.

Visibly shaken, Jim returned the receiver to the base and looked at a wide-eyed Jatory.

"Better think about who else could be behind this," the younger man stated, "and for your own safety, Pastor Jim, I would suggest that you not be here alone until we get this hammered out."

Brrring! Brrring!

The phone in Tom Davies' kitchen rang loudly.

"I'm comin', I'm a-comin'!" He reached for the phone, "Yello!"

"*Idiot!!*" A woman's voice accused him the instant she heard his deep bass voice.

"Whoa, now! Just where do you get off calling me an idiot?" he snapped back.

"What kind of stunt was that?" she demanded.

"What are you talking about?" he barked, heatedly.

"Don't play stupid with me, Tom Davies! That little

fiasco of a scare tactic you tried to pull…"

Tom glared at the wall in silence. He turned his faded blue eyes toward the kitchen window where his wife's favorite blue gingham curtain swayed in the early autumn breeze.

"I told you to let *me* do the thinking!" she hissed, "You are just as useless as my late husband told me you were!"

"Now, you wait just a cotton-pickin' minute!" he huffed, "There ain't no…"

"No, *YOU*, wait!" She interrupted, "I have worked too hard to get this far, and I won't let you blow it for me. If you get caught, I'm washing my hands of you. You'll go down all by yourself, you hear me?" she snarled.

"Now don't get your knickers in a twist!" he retorted nervously. He could feel his blood pressure rising. "There's nothing that can tie either one of us to anything, in fact, the kid I hired to do it made it look like the blue-haired kid did it."

"Fool!", she barked, "You *hired* someone?? What if he rats you out?"

There was silence on the line.

"You didn't think about that did you, you imbecile?" The disdain in her voice was unmistakable.

"I paid him plenty…" His head began to ache as his stomach began to churn. He remembered the call he had gotten this morning from that kid. It hadn't been a good conversation. The gun wasn't as much of a problem as that cell phone. Every conversation Tom had had with that kid had been to that cell phone number.

"...Besides," Tom continued, "he ain't from around here." He was still trying to figure out how to go about finding that phone.

More silence.

"You better hope, for your own sake, that this doesn't come back and bite you..."

"Don't you mean *us*...?" Tom growled.

"No, Tom, I mean you." The woman snapped. "*You* are the fool who decided to take matters into his own hands, and *you* are the fool who will take the fall for it... not me."

"Nothing's going to happen, Betty."

"We'll see."

Click.

The hands that hung up the receiver were sweaty. Tom stood and stared at the wall, his mind racing. Running his fingers through his white hair, he decided he had to get in touch with that Robbie kid again and talk to him. Maybe, just maybe, if he paid him enough he could keep him quiet...

Chad smiled as he trotted down the porch steps of Jill and David's trailer. Jesus was so amazing! When Chad had shared the story of his own troubles... Split home, living on the streets at the age of 13, drug addiction, a few minutes in heaven after an overdose, God's forgiveness and freedom, and most importantly, the restoration of everything that Satan had stolen from him... David had opened up completely, without hesitation, about everything. Chad recalled with pleasure the look on the young teen's face when he had told David that Summer wanted him to work for her.

Lifting the handle, Chad pulled open the door of his truck. Plopping into the driver's seat, he recalled David's promises of hard work and extra hours. Laughing to himself, he started the ignition. He absolutely loved being the hands and feet of Jesus. What an honor...He was still humbled every time God chose to use him like that. It brought tears of gratitude to his eyes.

Chad knew that he had been the worst of sinners, and to know that the God of all creation loved him, even in the middle of everything he was doing wrong, saved his life, and forgave him for all of it? Let alone gave him precious people like David and his mother to shepherd... It was almost too much to take in.

The radio in his truck was singing about how beautiful the Lord was and he closed his eyes and leaned his head on the steering wheel. Tears fell from his closed eyes as he sang, "And I'm left in awe of You...and I'm left in awe of You..."

Thank You, Dad... Thank You, thank You, thank You... I can't think of anything else to say that expresses how my heart feels, right now, in this moment. Thank You for seeing past who the world told me I was, to who You created me to be. Help me to be that person... I love You... I love You for what You have done in me... You found me in my brokenness then You put me back together again. I love You for what You are still doing. I love You for what You are doing in David and Julie's lives. Oh, how I love You, Jesus. My King... Thank You... Thank You... Thank You.

David watched through the window with a new respect for Chad, as the youth pastor jogged down the porch stairs. He had no idea that Chad had been through some of the very same struggles that he was going through, now. It felt good to know that there was someone who actually *understood*.

Curiously, he watched Chad get into his truck and lean forward onto the steering wheel. David moved the curtain so he could see better. Was Chad crying? Intrigued, he watched Chad praise God in a way that he wanted to, but he didn't know if he could. Watching his beloved youth pastor blatantly love on God like that, David prayed for the first time since his salvation.

"Jesus... I want that... But I don't know how." A tear slid unnoticed down his slender cheek. "I don't want the old me anymore. It hurts... And please make it better for mom... She can't take much more."

"Caroline!"

Caroline sat straight up on her mat. The urgency in Little Wolf's distressed voice frightened her. He was always so calm. She struggled with the ties on her door as she scrambled outside, the look on his face chilled her to the bone.

"Little Wolf!" She gasped in the cold night air, "What's happened?"

His voice trembled, "Kalana…"

She had never seen Little Wolf so visibly upset. Carolyn sprang into action. She ducked back into the tent, grabbed Willie up from his warm pallet and wrapped the sleepy-eyed toddler in blankets. She hurriedly ducked back out and looked intently at the obviously disturbed man.

"Where is she?" she demanded.

"She left to have the child, but she came back... She could hardly walk..."

"Is Grandmother with her?" Grandmother was a capable midwife, but she was slow in coming sometimes.

"Yes, but..." His desperation made her nauseous.

"Where is Running Deer?" She asked, referring to their toddler son, and Willie's playmate.

"He is with my sister."

She passed Willie to him and ran to their teepee. She could hear her sister long before she arrived there. She rushed into the tent and dropped to her knees beside Kalana. Her bronze face was ashen and pale with pain, and her large brown eyes were black with fear when she turned them desperately to her best friend.

Caroline looked at Grandmother.

"It has been too long..." Grandmother clucked her tongue and worried quietly, "There is a problem. I must check the baby."

She handed Caroline a blanket and motioned toward Kalana. Caroline looked at the blanket in confusion and then back at the older woman.

"Roll it. Let her bite it." She stated matter-of-factly.

"Oh! Yes!" Caroline hurriedly did as she was told.

"Sister..." she crooned, "Grandmother needs you to bite down on this...It will help with the pain..." *Lord Jesus, PLEASE?! She needs You! Help her!*

Kalana nodded and obeyed. Caroline kept her eyes on the beautiful young woman as Grandmother proceeded to check the baby internally. Caroline fought tears as Kalana writhed and moaned in pain. The rolled blanket she was biting on muffled a scream as another contraction seized her, and her exhausted body contracted with it. Caroline coached her through it, as Grandmother had trained her to do.

"The baby will not come." Grandmother stated worriedly.

Kalana groaned and let her head fall back as the pain subsided, her face and hair wet with perspiration.

"What do you mean?" Caroline asked fearfully trying not to let Kalana hear the concern in her voice.

Grandmother motioned for her young assistant, who was there rubbing Kalana's back, to take Caroline's place at her side, and ducked out of the tent motioning for Caroline to follow. Caroline struggled with leaving her friend, but Grandmother's determined insistence propelled her out of the warmth of the tent, into the cold night air.

Little Wolf must have deposited Willie at another teepee, because he met them as they exited, and Willie was nowhere in sight.

"What did you mean in there?" Caroline demanded respectfully.

"The baby cannot come. It is in the wrong position."

Little Wolf looked sick.

"What does that mean?!" Caroline insisted.

"It means they will both die if it is not cut out." Grandmother stated.

"Can't you turn it?" Caroline nearly shrieked in desperation. She had seen Grandmother perform this technique a few times and that sounded safer than cutting this baby out!

"It will not turn, and it's too late. Kalana grows weaker with every pain."

Caroline felt faint and Little Wolf appeared to feel the same. *Cut out?* In the two years that she had lived with this tribe, there had been no births like this one. She wondered if Kalana would survive a surgery like that! *Lord Jesus!*

"It must be done." Little Wolf's voice held a confidence that he did not feel.

"What?!" Caroline spun around to look incredulously at this man who had obviously lost his mind, "She could die!"

"She will die if it is not done." he said quietly, and Grandmother nodded. Inside the tent, Kalana screamed again.

"Have you done this before?" Caroline demanded in an urgently hushed tone and Grandmother was silent. The ebony eyes that stared back at her were dark and somber.

SKELETON KEY

"NO!" Caroline shouted in a whisper, "No, no, NO!"

The sound of galloping hoof beats approaching interrupted the desperate huddle and as the riders came into view, they could hear angry shouts. there was a heavy thud and a cloud of dust as two men tumbled into the middle of the little group. The women jumped back, and Little Wolf jumped into the tussle.

"Luke!" Caroline gasped as she recognized one of the men. She had never seen him be violent.

"Doc Reid, you don't have a choice! If you don't…(grunt)…help that poor woman…(grunt)...so help me…(ooof!)…*I'll hang for shooting you…(grunt)…myself!*" Lucas bellowed as he muscled the middle-aged doctor to the ground. Little Wolf pounced on Lucas and pried his hands loose, releasing the vice-like grip on the indignant doctor.

"*Lucas! This…is…not(grunt)…the…way!*" Little Wolf yelled as he struggled to restrain his friend.

Doc Reid picked himself up off of the ground and dusted himself off self-righteously. He looked for his hat, lost somewhere between the fall and the impromptu wrestling match. *Hmph! Some preacher!*

"If you'da been upfront with me, then I'da told ya back at my cabin that I don't doctor no Injuns." He looked with disdain at Little Wolf, "… and I ain't starting tonight!" He turned away from the men and all but ran into Caroline.

"Please, Doctor Reid?!" She pleaded with him, "They could both die if surgery isn't done!" As if on cue, another agonized scream came from the tent.

Unconvinced, he snorted heartlessly, "Two less Injuns to worry about!"

"You can't mean that!" Caroline was shocked as she watched the man turn away. "Can't you hear how much pain she is in?" She grabbed his sleeve in desperation, "We *need* you! We don't know how to do it! We could *kill* her!...*PLEASE?!*"

"Not my problem! Now help me find my horse!" He snatched away from Caroline.

The click of a gun hammer going back halted the entire scene. Lucas had wrestled away from Little Wolf and had drawn his gun. Caroline gasped, golden eyes huge, and threw her hands to her mouth.

"Take another step, Doc. See if I'm toyin' with ya."

Doc stopped in his tracks. Slowly he turned to face Lucas.

"Is that a threat, Lucas Waters?"

"No, Sir. That would be a statement of fact." He spit and wiped blood from his dirty, busted lip with the back of his sleeve, "I ain't always been a preacher."

Doc gulped visibly and looked from the startled faces of the other people standing there, to the stone set face of the man aiming a pearl handled six shooter at his chest.

"Well, now…" he chuckled nervously, "Won't do the lady any good to shoot the Doc, now would it?" He looked at Caroline, "Where is she?"

Caroline looked at Doc incredulously and wondered if he was really asking that silly question. There was only one tent howling like a coyote in this camp.

Doc Reid looked back at Lucas with a resigned consternation as he followed the women to the tent, "Fetch my bag…Since you knocked it to Kingdom come…"

Lucas grinned as he carefully released the hammer on his gun and replaced it in his holster, "Sure thing, Doc."

After retrieving the bag from the brush ten feet away and depositing it in the teepee, he moseyed over to the fire to comfort and encourage his friend. Sitting down on the earth beside Little Wolf, he grinned and shoved himplayfully on the shoulder.

"Scared ya, didn't I?"

CHAPTER TWENTY

The golden sun warmed her face as she rolled over toward the large, sheer-curtained windows. She could hear the birds chirping in the great oak tree beside her open window, beyond the balcony. She slid her hands under the deliciously soft pillow and squeezed it, burying her face deep into its comfort. Summer smiled to herself as she sleepily squinted in the bright morning light and watched with contented pleasure as the morning breeze gently coaxed the sheer, white curtains into a lazy slow dance. She released the pillow and reached lazily across the bed to scratch the belly of the snoozing fat cat on the bed beside her.

"This is better than that old hard mattress we're used to, huh, Fat Cat?"

He purred his agreement.

"Am I forgiven?"

She smiled as Mow yawned hugely and stretched his front legs forward, arching his back and spreading his feline toes wide, until she was almost certain she heard the cracking of his joints. He leaned forward and repeated the process for his hind legs and then waddled heavily over to his mistress and laid down almost on top of her face.

"Pfft! I'll take that as a 'yes'..." She chuckled as she

pushed him over. "If you're looking for your butt, it's in my face, sir."

Summer rolled onto her back, stretching lazily, letting her arms fall lifelessly onto the bed. Mow cracked a green eye and peered at her sleepily. She filled her lungs with a contented sigh and tried to remember the last time she had felt this much satisfaction.

Her smile broadened as she stared up at the high, white ceiling and the ornate molding that accented the pale, yellow walls. She wondered if the house had changed much in the last one hundred fifty years... Besides the addition of ceiling fans and central heat and air, of course. Stretching one last time, she threw the goose down comforter back. Mow jerked his head up as the comforter landed close to his face.

"Time to greet the day!" Summer chirped and slid off the high, antique sleigh bed onto a plush white oriental rug decorated with blue roses, that covered the beautiful hardwood floor. Her bare feet sank into the softness and Summer squished her toes around in it. She smiled at herself. Mow purred deep in his throat as he yawned and stretched again.

Stepping off of the softness of the rug and onto the hard floor, she crossed the threshold of the sitting room attached to her bedroom. It was one of the reasons she had chosen this room to be hers. As Summer walked into the room, she was struck, again, with how lovely the furniture was. Simple, yet elegant. There was a loveseat that had a high scrolled back, and the cushion of it was deep, navy-blue velveteen. There were two matching chairs; one on either side of it; and an armoire in the corner. All were situated so that whoever was sitting there had a full view of the lovely landscape just behind the lacey curtains that covered pane glass double doors.

She smiled when a muffled thud and an irritated "churrrrp" alerted her to Mow's exit off of the high bed. She walked over to the doors leading to the balcony and opened them both, letting in the semi-cool morning breeze. As she turned, Mow was poking an uncertain head into the sitting room.

"Oh, come on, fraidy cat..." She encouraged the uncertain kitty. His large, green eyes peered at her from around the thick door frame, "Better get used to it. This is home now..."

Home...

Somehow, she felt like she was trying to convince herself of that more than her reluctant feline. Summer shook her head. *I'm not going down that road right now.*

Her eyes fell on her favorite piece of furniture in the room: an old cherry roll top desk. She smiled as she let her curiosity lead her to sit in the smooth, wooden chair and lift the rolltop. Summer was surprised by how smoothly the lid rolled up. This thing had to be as old as the house! As her fingers ran over the top of the desk she wondered what kind of letters had been pinned at this desk. Who had they been writing to? What had they been writing about? Her imagination led her in a thousand different directions. There was a drawer in the center, and she pulled it out, imagining what secrets it might hold...but she was disappointed to find it empty other than a tiny little skeleton key.

"I wonder what this goes to..." Her voice sounded strangely loud in the quiet of the morning. "Hmm..." Thoughtfully, Summer picked it up and carried it into the bedroom with her.

Mow, who had just gotten the courage to enter the room that she had just exited, chirped at her from the floor in front of the velvet love seat.

"Well, you shouldn't take so long, chicken..." She fussed lightheartedly as she placed the tiny key on her dresser.

He waddled quickly out of the sitting room and placed his front paws on the side of the bed. He looked at the top of the bed and then at Summer. When she paid him no mind, he chirped again.

"What? You can't heave your chubba-tub up there?"

He purred with pleasure as his mistress scooped him up and deposited him on the softness of the goose down comforter. He circled twice and puffed pawed a few times before settling in.

Summer chuckled and shook her head, "Lazy cat..."

She turned to get something to wear out of her suitcase... But it was missing.

"What in the?" She grunted.

Sunny Girl, you are going crazy! I know I put that thing on this chair!

She clearly remembered heaving that huge beast over the arm of the Victorian looking sitting chair next to the windows...and she knew that something that huge couldn't just walk off! She walked over to the intercom next to the closed door leading into the hallway.

"How does this thingy work again?" she wondered out loud.

Summer tried to remember what Chris had said. "Why did he even have these things installed?" she grunted.

With a frustrated sigh, she jabbed the white button... As opposed to the red one.

"Um...Hello?...Anybody there?" *Wow, that was intelligent.*

The intercom popped lightly, "Sí, Señorita. How can I halp choo?" A sweet, Latina voice chirped.

"Um...I'm looking for my clothes...? Have you seen them?" This was ridiculous. She should have just gone downstairs.

"Sartainly, Meess. Dey are in jor room."

Summer frowned, "Where?... I don't see them...?"

"Dey arr put away, Meess."

"Ohhhh…" Summer didn't know how she felt about that.

Then she thought of something. "When did you do that?"

"Maria, she put dem away while choo and el señor were eating anoche…er…ah…last…night…?"

"Oh!" Summer was relieved, "I didn't notice…"

How could she not have noticed that the hulking suitcase wasn't on the chair when she had come in last night? How distracted she had been last night during dinner and the rest of the evening could have something to do with it… She took her finger off of the button and started to turn away. Her manners chastised her, and she quickly pressed the button again.

"Thank you…er…What's your name?"

"My name es Rosa, and choo arr welcome, Meess."

Summer walked to the dresser and opened the top drawer. There, she found all of her underclothes and socks, neatly organized. The next drawer revealed sleepwear. She continued down the dresser finding all of her folded clothing.

This is weird. They put away my underwear? Summer shook her head. *Nuh uh. We need to discuss some boundaries, here… Obviously.*

Chris's long fingers tapped the steering wheel of his silver Porsche as he waited for the light to change. His mind ran over the events of the evening before… The phone call from Summer's adoptive mother, the following heated argument, the too quiet dinner. Why did this bother him so much? How was this any different from any other 'job'?

Could it be the insane amount of money at stake? His gut told him that it had more to do with the woman at stake.

This is not the time to be developing a conscience…

Chris didn't want to admit that it had nothing to do with an issue of conscience at this point. He was falling in love with her.

Exasperated with himself, he slammed the car into gear when the light changed, and squealed the tires as he stomped on the accelerator. How could he have let this happen? It had barely been a month! Changing gears as quickly as he was accelerating, Chris sped out of the city. This was not a happy development…and unfortunately, not one that he could do anything about.

She had unknowingly taken his breath yesterday afternoon when she turned her blazing, golden eyes on him. She had been irate and completely right…and *completely* stunning. It was rotten, what he had done, and for the first time in a very long time, he had felt remorse for his actions…but being the incredible actor that he was, had hidden it impeccably.

Strangely, the last thing he wanted to ever see was that look on her face again, knowing that he had been the one to put it there. Chris sighed in frustration. He wanted Summer. Wanted her more than he had ever wanted anything. It was a foreign and slightly terrifying feeling for the cocky young attorney.

A deep longing filled him as he remembered the innocence in her beautiful eyes the first time he held her in his arms. She believed him to be what he said he was, and somehow Summer made him want to be that man. He ran his fingers through his dark curls and propped his elbow on the door as he sped down the road stretching out in front of him.

In that moment, Chris made a decision. He would put a new plan into action. Forget forty percent. The only woman he wanted to share that fortune with was Summer...But he would have to be careful. He had thought this new plan out in detail as he had lain awake in his bed, last night. He wanted the money...Bad...But there was no reason why he had to lose Summer in the taking of it. There were just a few minor details to take care of, and where he had an issue with getting rid of Summer, he certainly had no problem at all with taking care of a certain *other* thorn in his flesh.

He smiled in satisfaction as the issue settled itself in his mind.

"Who said you can't have your cake and eat it too?"

KNOCK! KNOCK! KNOCK!

"Pastor Jim?" An urgent voice called.

Barb walked to the front screen door of the pastorium and smiled through it at the young woman standing on her small front porch. She recognized her as the mother of one of the church's teens, and Naomi's favorite nurse at Sunny Birch.

"Oh…Hi, Barb…" the young woman looked down momentarily. She looked back up and there was concern in her eyes, "is Pastor Jim around?"

Barb opened the screen door wide and stepped aside with a smile, "Yes, he is. Won't you come in?"

"Thank you…" Jill nervously returned her smile.

"Have a seat, love. I'll go get him." Barb motioned toward the couch in the modest living room.

Jill nodded and walked across the creaky hardwood floor, sat down on the pillowy, blue sofa and waited. She didn't know who else to go to. She had tried to contact Summer, but her phone went straight to voicemail. The clock on the mantle ticked the seconds loudly as she waited, rather impatiently, for the pastor to enter the room.

"Hey, Jill!" Jim walked into the small living room,

"What's up?" He asked as he took the wing chair opposite the sofa.

"Pastor Jim, I didn't know where else to go..." her large eyes were pleading and scared.

Jim leaned forward in the chair, "What's happened? Is David okay?"

Jill shook her dark head hard enough to make her ponytail swish and waved her hand slightly, "No, no. For once, it's not David. It's the shop."

Jim cocked his head in confusion, "The shop?"

"Someone broke in."

Jim sat straight up, "Broke in?? To Summer's shop?!"

Distraught, Jill nodded, "Yes, and it's destroyed!" She melted into tears.

"What do you mean?" Barb asked as she sat down next to Jill and wrapped her arms around the young woman to comfort her. She shot a concerned look at her husband.

"All the windows are busted out; the coolers are busted...They...they trashed the place!" She sobbed, "I...I don't understand..."

"Shh, now…" Barb patted her shoulder, "You did right, honey..."

"Agitated, Jim stood to his feet, "I'm calling Jatory."

"Oh, good idea, dear." The older woman agreed as Jim started into the kitchen to grab the phone.

"There, there...Are you all right, hon?" She asked the younger woman.

Jill sniffed and sat back, nodding as she wiped her face with the tissue that Barb handed her, "I'm fine...Just a little shaken up...I...I think I walked in on them..."

Jim was walking back into the room as he dialed the number for the Watson Police Department.

"Did I hear you right?" He asked her.

"Uh-huh," Jill nodded and sniffed, "I heard a crash in the back of the store as I opened the front door... Which now that I think about it, was kind of silly... I could have just stepped through the window..." she stated ruefully. "I was so startled that I jumped back into my car and left... I didn't know what to do..." Tears began to fall again.

"Watson Police Department," came the voice on the other end of the line.

"Jatory Goodman, please. This is Jim Dalton."

"You want to hold while I patch you through to his cell phone?"

"Sure."

"Hold, please."

On the other end a recorded voice bragged about the

improvements to the crime rate and other accomplishments of the Watson City Police Department since Bob Townsend had been made Chief of Police. Jim rolled his eyes. He knew the guy was egotistical, but this was ridiculous.

"I'm just glad nothing happened to you, Jill." he stated as he waited for Jatory's voice.

The line began ringing again.

"Officer Goodman." Jatory answered the call.

"Jatory."

"Pastor, I was just fixin' to call you."

"Really? Why?"

"I think you better come see what I'm looking at…

CHAPTER TWENTY-ONE

Jim, Barb, and Jill were speechless when they pulled up at the scene. Flames licked the sky maliciously as Summer's precious flower shop blazed ferociously in the early autumn evening. The local volunteer firefighters were doing everything they could to control it until the firefighters from the next town over could get there to help. The water they were spraying only seemed to feed and heighten the angry flames as they threatened the neighboring buildings.

"Dear God..." Barb covered her mouth in horror as her eyes filled with tears. She looked at her stunned husband and reached for his hand, "J...Jim...! Summer's shop!"

Jim drew her into his arms helplessly as Jill stood beside the car watching her dreams for a new start literally go up in smoke. Her hands fell from her head, where they had flown, and hung lifelessly by her side. This was it. She was officially going to lose everything...even David. There had been hope, even with the shambles left after the break in, but now...Now...?

It was gone...

The weight of the realization of it slammed her to her knees on the asphalt. *Why God?!...Why?!*

The scene touched Jatory's heart as he made his way to the civilians that had just arrived there. He had noticed her as she stepped out of the back of the passenger door of Pastor Jim's Crown Vic.

She was tall and slender...maybe a little too slender...with very simple clothing and smooth dark hair, swept up into a ponytail. She had a natural olive complexion and wore very little, if any, makeup. There was just something about her simplicity that appealed to him. When she hit her knees, it was as if an unseen force had pushed her there. If he didn't know better he would have thought that this was her building and business instead of Summer Dalton's.

Her shoulders shook as she rocked back and forth, holding herself tightly, as if there was no one else to comfort her. The image spoke to the protector inside of him and he instinctively made his way to the distraught young woman and knelt beside her.

"Why, God?!" he heard her moan, "Why?!"

Oblivious to the man kneeling beside her, Jill mourned her life and every bad decision she had ever made. She nearly jumped out of her skin when she felt a warm hand on her shoulder. Assuming that it was her pastor or his wife, she leaned into the strong embrace of the young officer there beside her. Jatory cradled her thin shoulders and held her tight as she cried.

"What am I going to do now?" she moaned to no one in particular, "How am I going to make it?...(sob)...My rent is 3 months past due and the only reason I'm not on the street is because I told my landlord about my new job..." The arms encircling her tightened compassionately.

"My lights have been off for almost a month... I've been borrowing electricity from my neighbor..."

Jatory decided to ignore that revelation.

"... And water, too... (hiccup) If it wasn't for the church, there wouldn't be food in my cabinets and my car is on empty." She sobbed, "I have nothing! And Family Services is coming out in a week for a review..."

Jatory stiffened slightly...Family Services?

"I was going to have good news for them, this time...but now..." Jill hiccupped a sob, "Now..." Her voice was warbly and uncontrollably loud, "I'm going to lose David!"

"Oh, Jill!" Barb cried, "Don't say that!" as she rushed to Jill's side.

Jatory loosened his hold on her as the pastor's wife knelt beside her and wrapped her own arms around the obviously devastated young woman.

"Hey, Jatory." Jim's face was pale and grim as he rounded the front of the car.

Jill's head snapped up when she heard Jim's voice, and her puffy hazel eyes were huge as she turned her head slowly to see a very attractive African American officer stand and shake the pastor's hand. Humiliation colored her face and she felt like puking. She had just aired all of her dirty laundry to a complete stranger...And then realization hit, and fear almost stole her life force. She had openly admitted to stealing electricity and water! A slender hand covered her gaping mouth.

Barb noticed Jill's face grow pale and her expression startled the pastor's wife. "Jill! What is it?!"

Jatory and Jim looked down at the wide-eyed young woman and the officer smiled knowingly.

Jill's eyes were wide, and her hand shook violently as she pointed a slender finger at the handsome officer, "A...Are you g...going to a...arrest...m...me?" she snubbed and hiccupped, mentally cursing her lack of control over her own voice.

"What?!" Barb cried, "Jill! Why on earth would he do such a thing? You had nothing to do with this!"

She shot a 'Say Something!' look at Jim.

He frowned in complete confusion and Jatory chuckled.

"Jill...I..." Jim began as he scratched his graying head.

"No." Jatory stated, professionally.

Jill didn't believe him, and her lovely hazel eyes told him so, quite plainly.

"W...why n...not?" she hiccupped suspiciously.

"Because, it sounds to me like you have enough to worry about..." His light brown eyes searched her large fearful ones and what he saw in them erased his earlier misgivings.

Barb looked back and forth between the two of them, "What in the world is this about?"

Jatory shrugged his shoulders, "I have no idea." He winked directly at Jill and walked away with Jim.

"You poor thing..." Barb, having missed the wink, shook her head and nestled Jill into her motherly arms. This poor girl had obviously had too much trauma for one day. She adopted the young woman, right then and there, and purposed that she was going to personally see that this girl...and her rebellious son...were well taken care of.

From the safety and the warmth of Barb's embrace, Jill watched the young officer suspiciously as he walked away. Why would he do that? He could one hundred precent arrest her...She decided that she would steer clear of him at all costs. *No one* was that nice. *No one*. He must want something...And she had been down that road one too many times. David was a product of one of those trips. No. She certainly wasn't about to go *there* again. No matter how handsome he was.

It had been a tough couple of weeks for their family,

Caroline recalled. After the baby's birth, Kalana had recovered surprisingly fast, but the baby just wasn't thriving. Kalana was becoming more and more discouraged, as days passed, and the baby continued to refuse to nurse and was sickly. The teepees could be drafty at times and Little Wolf had done everything he could to keep out the bitter cold, but they just couldn't seem to keep the baby warm enough. Caroline and Kalana had spent many hours praying, and Caroline had fasted earnestly for the child's healing. She smiled warmly as she remembered the turning point.

Little Wolf, Running Deer, and Willie had been staying with Grandmother while Caroline stayed with Kalana. On one of Little Wolf's visits, he had brought the boys with him. At first, Caroline was nervous about having the rambunctious toddlers that close to the fragile baby, but Kalana had been delighted to see her son, and Willie as well. Kalana held her tiny new baby and allowed each small boy to have a turn looking her over and touching her tiny fingers and toes.

When Running Deer touched the baby, an almost audible voice spoke to Caroline. It said, *'Willie shall lay hands on the child, and she shall be healed'* It was so real that she looked for the person speaking. She realized, suddenly, that it was the Lord.

"But," she argued internally, *"he can't even talk plainly, Lord...How can he pray for the baby to be healed?"*

There was no reply.

Caroline had struggled with her faith at that point. Would they think she was insane if she declared what the Lord had told her to do?... Or rather, her *toddler* to do? She sat on it, teetering back and forth between sides for what seemed like forever.

It was Willie's turn to see and touch the baby, and his chubby little fingers reached out and caressed her soft baby skin. His sweet lips formed a pretty 'O' as he marveled at the infant, and his precious, little cherub face beamed with sudden excitement. Caroline watched in amazement as her son kissed the little one on her head and grinned up at his 'Kali'.

"No more boo-boo, Kali!" he declared in his toddler-ish language.

Caroline couldn't believe her ears. Her mouth fell open and Kalana laughed out loud. With her free hand, Kalana lovingly ran her fingers through Willie's soft blonde curls, and she pulled him gently into a one-armed embrace, placing a soft kiss on top of his little head.

"I know, Willie," she squeezed him softly, "Thank you for touching her…"

Willie beamed with toddler pride and clapped his hands. Only then did he notice his mother sitting across the tent.

"Ma-Ma!" He scrambled joyfully over to her and climbed into her open arms, "Ma-Ma! No more boo-boo!"

Tears filled her eyes as she hugged her little one tightly, "Yes, I know... Jesus made her all better didn't he?"

His blonde curls bounced as he nodded his head happily, "Mhmm! And ME!"

Caroline snuggled him and laughed, "Yes! And YOU!"

Satisfied, he wriggled out of her arms and darted back out of the tent to find his friend.

The sister-friends' tearful eyes met, and Caroline laughed, "He told you, too, didn't He?"

Caroline's heart rejoiced for her friends. Kalana was almost back to normal, and the baby was doing so well now. It had been three weeks since the birth and she had never dreamed that she could be so happy, after losing William. Caroline paused in her stitching. This was the first time she had thought of him in a month now. She prepared herself for the guilt that she had become accustomed to, but it never came. There was only joy!

Caroline hummed the tune of Kalana's lullaby as she busied herself happily with the last of the stitches on the last of the cloth diapers that she was sewing for Kalana and her sweetest little, baby girl. The song had intrigued her from the first time she heard her friends rich, alto voice singing softly to the precious miracle that they had been blessed with. Caroline smiled and softly sang the words in the haunting melody:

"Winter moon, Coldest night

Came my small one, Love's Delight

Dreams of peace and blessing sweet

All for you my baby...

Wind come soft, sing your song

Rock gently, small one all night long

Owl's cry high above

All for you my White Dove

Oooo, Oooo

All for you, my baby

Oooo, Oooo

All for you my White Dove"

"White Dove..." She mused aloud, "What a beautiful name..."

The crunch of frozen grass outside of her teepee sent excited adrenaline pulsing through her veins. He was here! The footfalls belonged to a man that had, quite unexpectedly, revived her lifeless heart.

He's late.

He had promised to come by and walk with her and Willie to visit Kalana and her family. She would scold him later, she chuckled to herself...*gently.*

Excitedly, she hurried to tie the last knot. She cut the thread with her teeth and placed the diaper neatly on top of the others. She felt of her hair and pinched her cheeks to make them rosier, and as quickly as it had come into her thoughts, William's memory fell to the back of her mind as she anxiously awaited for Lucas to enter.

Seconds passed by and no Lucas. She furrowed her brow.

"Hmm…" Caroline quickly tied the diapers in a piece of gingham that she had purchased on a rare trip to the trading post. "What is he *doing* out there?" She fussed mentally.

Leaving the gift on her pallet, she threw on a deer hide and stepped to the door flap. Stooping, Caroline untied it deftly and stepped out into the bright sunlight. She squinted and shielded her eyes against the brightness of the winter sun in the cloudless sky. When she saw him, her heart melted in spite of the freezing weather.

Lucas stood outside her tent, hat in hand, with the most forlorn looking bouquet of twigs and dry leaves she had ever seen. He was wearing a sheepish grin and his sandy blonde hair was slicked down in a most unnatural way. He looked absolutely pitiful and absolutely dashing all at the same time.

She laughed musically and he loved the sound of it. He was looking forward to many years of being the culprit of that beautiful noise.

"Lucas Waters, are those flowers for me?" She grinned impishly.

He glanced at his pitiful creation and his answering crooked grin thrilled her soul.

She laughed again, pulling the deer hide tighter around her shoulders as a frigid breeze invaded her warmth, "What in heaven's name are you doing standing out here in the freezing cold with no hat on?"

"I…ah…Well…er…" Lucas stumbled over his words. And all of nature seemed to notice. Suddenly the happy woodland chatter seemed, to him, to turn into happy woodland laughter. Hadn't he practiced this a thousand times?

"Oh, pssshh! Come inside before you catch your death." Caroline fussed and turned to duck back into the tent as a scarlet cardinal flitted past.

"I ain't coming in right this second." he argued.

"Well, why not?" she demanded.

"There's something I've been meaning to talk with you about…"

"Well, come inside and we can talk about it while I get my things…" she insisted.

"It ain't like that, Carrie…!" He fidgeted uncomfortably. Why was this woman so hard to deal with? A woodpecker hammered a distant tree.

"Lucas! This is ridiculous!" Caroline raised her voice slightly. This man could be so infuriating sometimes! He was so stubborn!

"What could you possibly have to say to me that couldn't be said in the warmth of my hut?"

"Confound it all, woman! You frustrate the hound out of me!" He slapped his hat on his head, grit his teeth and thrust the scraggly bunch of twigs at her, "Caroline Connor, will you marry me?"

A dry, brown leaf from the sad bouquet drifted silently to the ground.

Her mouth sagged open for a moment as what Lucas had just said sunk into her consciousness. Then, laughing joyously, Caroline threw herself into his arms, causing him to drop his pitiful creation altogether.

"Is that a 'yes' then?" He laughed as he caught her.

In answer, she kissed him like she had dreamed of doing for weeks now, and it left both of them breathless and warmed them to their toes.

He pushed her away abruptly and held her at arm's length, shocked at his reaction to her kiss, "Don't you do that anymore." His voice was husky with emotion and desire.

Innocently confused, Caroline looked at him, "Why?"

Lucas grinned boyishly, "Because, Missy, if you do... I'll have a lot of repenting to do... and I'm the preacher!"

Caroline laughed again, this time softly as she looked deeply into his eyes. How had this happened? This intense feeling? This sense of belonging? She melted into him as he pulled her into his embrace and held her. It felt so good and so right. She inhaled the scent of smoke and leather, fresh air and pine... *his scent*... And she held him with all the strength of her emotion.

As Lucas held her close to his body, he relished the smallness of her. Her strength and her fragility. He marveled that a woman as remarkable as her could ever care for someone like him, yet here she was, holding him desperately, agreeing to be his wife...to be his. He tightened his arms around her slender frame and pressed his nose and lips to the top of her head.

"Lucas...?"

"Yes?" He sat his chin where his lips had been and watched a small, brown rabbit sneak out of a bush.

"Thank you for the lovely flowers."

He looked at the ridiculous sticks and twigs now scattered on the ground and smiled.

"You liked those, huh?"

"Mmhm." She nodded against his chest.

"Oh, and Lucas? One more thing?"

He smiled and laid his cheek on the top of her head as he closed his eyes and held her close to his heart.

"What is it?"

"You're late."

"Just like a woman..." He grunted with a satisfied smile.

Evening was settling in, and the season was changing again. Spring was on its way and the land was slowly awakening from its winter slumber. It had been almost three years since his father had passed into eternity, leaving him with the fortune and the responsibility of the Connor estate. Many times, Will had wondered if it was his father's final revenge to die and prevent him from leaving to find his wife and son.

He knew it was ridiculous, but it was there in the back of his mind with every passing day, month, year. Ironically, one thing he *could* thank his father for was his dealing with the Yanks and the contracts he set in place to guarantee the future for the Connor estate, before he died. Because of that, the destitute fate of neighboring plantations after the War was not theirs, and it also allowed William to free the slaves, deed pieces of land to their families, and give them a fair wage if they chose to stay.

Hope filled his heart as he stood on the balcony looking out over the peaceful front drive, as the golden-orange evening sun sank behind the moss-covered trees, painting the sky with ambers, indigos, and rose.

Next week.

He inhaled deeply.

In six days' time, he would finally be ready to leave the plantation in capable hands and bring his wife and son home.

If she can see past the monster…

William shook the intrusive thought from his head, as he turned and stepped back into the suite adjoining the bedroom they had shared. He walked over to Caroline's rolltop desk and ran his fingers along the smooth wood on the back of the chair, imagining her there.

He knew Caroline. He knew her heart. He knew she would accept him as he was, if she could ever forgive him for how he had abandoned her. Shame and guilt washed over him as he pulled the chair out and sat down at his beloved wife's desk.

He had thought about what he would say to her when he found her.

If she's even alive…

His thoughts lingered there for a moment. He shook his head and shoved the thoughts away. He would know if she was gone. He still felt the light of hope, deep inside, and it would lead him to her…

In six days' time.

For the first time in more than two years, William could

see the light at the end of the tunnel, and it was Caroline. It had always been Caroline, and now, thanks to reports from some trackers he had befriended, he knew where she would be, if she was indeed still living. His search was almost over. He stood with purpose and a hopeful smile flitted across his scarred features as he stepped through the doorway, strode through the bedroom, and entered the hall with a joy he had not felt in years.

CHAPTER TWENTY-TWO

"WHAT?!" The exclamation bounced off of the walls in the elegant dining room of Summer's estate. The young woman placing Summer's dinner in front of her, nearly dropped the plate.

"I'm sorry!" Summer mouthed to her silently as she tried to comprehend what her mother had just told her.

Chris looked at her in question. "Everything Okay?"

"Mom," she spoke into her cell phone, "can you hang on just a minute...?"

Chris rolled his eyes and threw his hands in the air, "Come on! Are you serious? Didn't we just have this conversation?"

Summer glared at him and covered the mouthpiece, "Do you mind? This is kind of important!"

Chris clenched his teeth and his blue eyes snapped as he struggled to maintain his collected facade. These people were really trying his patience.

"Mom, what do you mean 'it's destroyed'? What happened?!" She demanded.

The handsome attorney wondered what tragedy Summer's mother had invented, this time, so she would have an excuse to invade in her life again. He took a bite of the delicious looking lasagna on his plate.

And this evening began with such promise...

He raised his glass of shiraz to take a drink, but the intensity of the look on Summer's face caused him to stop, wine glass midair.

"Summer, what is it?" He set his glass down, keeping his attention on her.

"Well, do they have any leads?" She asked her mom as she raised her forefinger in a 'one minute' gesture.

Leads..? This is surprising...and annoying. Chris mentally ran through possible scenarios.

She sat back, nodded her head, and ran her fingers through her hair.

"I'll be there, probably after lunch, tomorrow..."

Chris sighed in exasperation. He wished he could hear the conversation on the other end of the line. He picked up the folded cloth napkin beside his plate and wiped his mouth, just for something to do, as he waited for Summer to get off the phone.

"Okay... Hey, how is Jill taking it?"

She nodded her head again, "Hey, don't do that. I'll take care of it."

Pause.

"Mom, don't be difficult. You can't afford it...I can."

Chris bristled. So that's what it was. They wanted her money. He tossed his napkin onto the table in contempt.

"Well, I'm at least going to share that expense...Oh, hey! Have you thought about letting them stay in my old room?"

Pause.

"Yes, ma'am. I'm not going to be needing it anymore, so I don't see why they can't stay there until things get better..."

Another pause.

"I'll stay in a hotel, Mom...It's okay. They need it more than I do... Yes, I'm sure."

Chris was confused, but he wouldn't be for long, if he could help it. What he did know was that Summer was planning on going back to Watson. He was thoughtful for a moment. This little imposition could actually work in his favor...

The well-oiled wheels in his mind began turning. His 'little problem' was in Watson. If he went with Summer, then it could be doubly beneficial. He could dispose of a rather unpleasant relationship, while strengthening his own relationship with Summer, and gaining more of her trust. This could actually be a good thing.

"OK, I'll see you tomorrow...No, you don't have to worry about that. He was kidding..." She shot Chris a dirty look.

"What?" He shook his head and shrugged.

Summer closed her eyes and pressed her fingers to the bridge of her nose, "Okay, Mom... Love you, too."

She ended the call and stared at Chris in shock.

"Summer...What happened?"

She shook her head as she laid the phone on the dark, smooth wood of the table, "My flower shop got broken into..."

"Wow."

"Then torched..."

"What?!" Instantly, Chris knew who was behind it and he was livid. *So we're going rogue, now, are we? We shall see about that.*

Summer snorted, "That's exactly what *I* said..."

Immediately, Chris got up from the table and made his way over to her. He squatted next to her chair, "Are you okay?...What happened?"

With her right hand she reached for the comforting hand that was resting on her knee. With the other she massaged her temple and sighed, "Yeah...and no one knows yet, but they are suspecting arson."

"When are we leaving?"

Surprised, Summer looked into his bright blue eyes, "You're coming with me?"

"Of course I am! I can't let you handle this by yourself... I couldn't live with myself." He tenderly pressed her hand to his lips.

Mildly suspicious, she unsuccessfully tried to read him, "I thought you hated my family..."

"I never said 'hate', per say..." he tilted his head innocently, "I just don't think you should be alone..."

Summer sighed in relief and smiled gratefully, "Chris, thank you so much."

She allowed him to help her out of the chair and she leaned against him as he led her out into the garden, through the open French doors at the end of the room. They sat down on the white, wicker loveseat under a huge, ancient, moss-covered oak tree and he pulled her body closer to him. Summer allowed herself to rest against his strong body and closed her eyes momentarily as a cool evening breeze ran invisible fingers through their hair and toyed sensuously with the moss overhead.

"Do they have any leads?"

Summer sighed and opened her eyes, "Nothing really other than arson. It's hard to tell if anything was stolen because the fire destroyed pretty much everything. Thank God, the neighboring buildings weren't damaged too badly..."

Chris carefully worded his next thoughts, "What were you saying about 'you can't afford it... but I can'...?"

Summer played with a button on his baby blue polo, "Remember the chick I hired to manage the shop?"

"The single mother?...Yes." He stroked her arm as he held her at his side.

"She really needed that job, or she was going to lose her house and her kid."

"Okay?"

"Well, her landlord heard about the fire and kicked her out, so my mom took her in."

"I'm still not following you..."

Placing her slender hand on his muscular chest for leverage, Summer sat up so she could look at him. She loved the way his chest felt under her fingers.

"Jill...That's the chick...she had her lights cut off and owed the power company like six or seven hundred dollars...give or take. My mom and dad were going to pay it for her." She looked up at Chris, "They really don't have that kind of money...I do."

Chris raised a suspicious eyebrow and looked into Summer's golden eyes, "Didn't you tell me she lived in a trailer? That seems like a bit much for an overdue electric bill...And why bail out some woman that is obviously a drag on society? Her kid would probably be better off in the system where he can learn how to fend for himself instead of mooching off of naive people..."

Happy thoughts about his muscular chest disappeared immediately. Summer was incredulous! She removed her hand as quickly as if she had been burned. How could he say something like that about someone he had never even met? She stiffened beside him, shook her head, and looked at him through offended and confused eyes.

"You're serious...?" Her suspicious questioning eyes found his.

Chris defended himself from his relaxed position, "Yes, I'm serious! There are too many people like this 'Jill' that abuse good hearted people like yourself, until they bleed them dry...They 'reform'," he quoted with his fingers, "and then they move on to the next sucker whom they will, yet again, woo with their well-rehearsed sob story..."

She had to agree that there were people like that out there, more and more every day, but his disdain and judgmental attitude astounded and sickened her.

"You have no idea who she is or what she's been through...and you have no right to sit in the judgment seat."

Chris turned his head slightly, keeping his eyes on her. Why was it that he could manipulate and control any jury...any *person* for that matter...but he just couldn't seem to gain an inch with this woman? She was an enigma. It was maddening and invigorating.

"She's a *good* woman, Chris," Summer continued righteously, "and one of my friends." She raised a defensive finger, "She has done *everything* she could to provide for herself and her son...and by herself, I might add."

He smirked knowingly, "Just like so many others who work so hard to *stay* unemployed..."

Summer couldn't believe what she was hearing. How could he be so self-righteous and callous? He had absolutely no idea what he was talking about.

"Jill had nothing to do with what happened at the shop!"

Chris cut his eyes at her, "Didn't you tell me that you gave her the job, in the first place, because she had *lost* her other job?"

"Her son lost that job for her...Thank you very much." she huffed indignantly.

"Then it sounds like Family and Children Services would be doing her a favor."

"You know what?" furious, Summer stood to her feet stiffly, "If this is the way it's going to be, then stay here. You have no idea what you're even talking about, and this conversation is *over*."

Chris smiled up at her sweetly from the loveseat and chuckled softly, his perfect white smile inviting her to cool her jets.

Why is he smiling like that? Oh! It's infuriating!

Summer's emotions duked it out with her attraction to this maddening man. The pale blue polo he wore made those unnaturally blue eyes even more blue, and the dark eyelashes that were feathered around them made them nearly irresistible...

Okay, so they're totally irresistible...

How could she be so disgusted and so involved all at the same time? It drove her crazy!

"And just what is so funny about anything I've just said to you?" she demanded, her golden eyes crackling, "I fail to find the humor in any of this! You are making assump..."

"Hey, hey, *heyyy*!" he interrupted, as he stood and reached for her. Pulling her stubbornly stiff body into himself, Chris took her chin and turned the face that she had petulantly turned away, to look at him. He searched for her golden eyes and when she gave in and allowed him to look into them, Chris gently ran the back of his fingers across the softness of her cheek.

Summer winced inwardly as the softness of his touch awakened that same longing that she had battled so many times. He always did this. Whenever they disagreed...which was more often than not...he would pull her into his arms and electrify her with his touch and his kiss, causing her to forget the reason they were even fighting. Thinking logically was out of the question whenever he was that close to her. Summer disliked that he held that much power over her...the power to change her with a simple touch. A still small voice whispered that she was heading into dangerous waters, but as she allowed Chris to pull her body close to his, as he so often did, Summer told herself that something that felt so right, couldn't be wrong...could it?

"Easy, Killer..." He chuckled softly and dropped a kiss on her nose, "I didn't mean to upset you."

"Hmph!" She pulled her chin out of his hand and turned her face away from him, once again, with more pluck than she felt.

Think, think, THINK, Summer! Think about anything but how close he is...

"You're right. I *don't* know what I'm talking about..." Chris conceded.

Summer cut her eyes at him suspiciously. This was new...What was he up to?

"...but I'd like to. That's why I want to come with."

He loosened his grip enough to lean back and look her in the face, "And we should stay for a while...until we see what kind of repairs need done and the investigation is complete. It would be best for you to be on hand to make decisions, and you're crazy if you think I'm letting my best girl out of my sight for longer than a few hours." He smiled, "Besides, I want to get to know these people that are your family...Who knows? Maybe one day, they'll be mine too."

Chris' vivid and perceptive eyes watched closely for response to the bait that he had just thrown out.

Summer couldn't believe what she had just heard. This was very much unlike Chris...in a major way. He couldn't stand her family, even though he had technically never met them, and that was a pretty quick change of heart... Like, seconds fast. What happened to 'restraining order' and 'they're taking advantage of you'?...And was that a hint? Well, more like a blatant statement, really...

Her resolve began to crumble and her heart thrilled while her mind tried to process what was happening. What kind of jerk makes an assumption like that?...Especially after being so rude? But, on the other hand...Did he really mean it? Could he really be serious? Was he really implying that he might want to marry her? A million questions and scenarios filled her mind.

The gentle voice in her spirit warned her against it. Something just didn't feel right about any of this, but she couldn't quite put her finger on it. Chris was a 'slick cricket', as her Paw Paw used to say, and she had seen the way this guy dealt with *everyone*...Not just his courtroom. Summer had gotten to know him well enough to know that he was very shrewd, and there was *always* an ulterior motive and agenda. She just didn't want to believe it, in this case.

Chris smiled victoriously.

Jackpot! Every idealistic woman, no matter how independent, wanted a wedding and that obviously included this very stubborn woman. Things were going along very efficiently, indeed.

Now that he had started Summer thinking along those lines, he could focus on the real issue once he got to Watson: Clearing his plate of a distasteful and unwanted side.

Unsure of what to say or how to respond, Summer eyed him suspiciously, "We'll see."

CHAPTER TWENTY-THREE

In the cover of darkness, Jim sat in the pastor's chair on the stage in the spacious emptiness of the sanctuary. It was where he had come many times when he needed peace and answers. He leaned forward placing his elbows on his knees and stared into the dark stillness of the sanctuary at night. Moon light illuminated the stained-glass windows and gave the room an ethereal, sleepy glow.

How many times over the past few months had he questioned God's hand in all of this? How many times had he cried out to a seemingly silent heaven? Why was all of this happening? Was he out of God's will? Was that why he was being pummeled like a light weight in a heavy weight match? A million more questions lead his weary thoughts down the road of doubt.

His thoughts screamed at him: *"It's your fault! You're the reason Summer is gone! You're a liar! You're a failure as a father and a pastor! Your people think you're a joke! You ARE a joke! Where is God? Even HE thinks you're a joke....He knows your heart, right?*

A frustrated, discouraged tear slid down his cheek, "GOD!" His cry echoed in the empty stillness, "WHERE ARE YOU?!"

"I thought you would be happy that I'm visiting you, my dear...?" Sarcasm dripped off of every word as Chris pictured the enraged face of his soon to be ex-partner.

"This was never in the deal, Chris..." she hissed through gritted teeth.

"The deal's changed, sweetheart."

"What do you mean 'the deal's changed'? I'm the one who came up with 'the deal' in the first place!"

"Did you now? That's good to know..." He sneered into the phone, "Need I remind you of your Miranda rights? Everything you say can and *will* be used against you in a court of law..."

"What is that supposed to mean?" She barked uncertainly, a prickle of fear racing through her veins.

Chris allowed himself a self-satisfied chuckle. He was so good at being devious, "Take it how you want it, but I warn you. Do not push me. I let you flex your pathetic little muscles for a while, but I've grown tired of your little game." His voice turned to cold steel, "If you try to interfere or incriminate me in any way, you will regret it...I promise you that. Do not forget that I have connections...Everywhere..."

"Are you *threatening* me?" She snarled.

"No, my dear. That is most definitely a promise." He ended the call and erased any evidence that he had ever had any contact with that woman.

On the other end of the line, in Watson, a very scorned woman seethed and sputtered.

"Just who does he think he is?! I'll show him...I don't need him to get my money..." Her mind raced as she formulated a new plan of her own...One that would not only make her very wealthy, but would also satisfy her need for revenge...

Jatory Goodman sat in his patrol car in the dark corner of the church parking lot, pondering the events of the past week. He still couldn't get over the feeling that the incident at the church and the fire at Summer's place were connected in some way, but he just couldn't put a finger on it. The case had been turned over to investigation, so technically he was off of it, but he had personal reasons for making sure the culprit was caught.

Jim had told him that he didn't believe Tom Davies was capable of something like this, and granted, it could be a stretch. But Jatory remembered vividly how angry Tom had been and he remembered, also, the way the deacon had stormed out of the church declaring that Jim would be sorry.

"Mental note to self..." he stated out loud as he jotted some things down on a legal pad, "Question Tom Davies."

He could get written up for poking around like he intended to do, but it was a chance he was willing to take.

He leaned his head back onto the headrest and stared at the dark blue headliner of the car. Why on earth did a man as faithful as Pastor Jim have to go through so much? It just didn't make sense.

"Oh well," he thought, "what doesn't kill us makes us stronger..."

He reached up and switched off the dome light and instantly he was in darkness. He scanned the parking lot, allowing his eyes to adjust before getting out to walk the perimeter of the church and the grounds. Checking his gun, he opened the car door and stepped out into the cool night and took a deep, appreciative breath. It was finally cooling off at night, somewhat.

As he stretched his back, Jatory scanned the grounds and prayed, "Lord, Jesus, keep us all safe tonight...especially my pastor, Lord. He's a good man and I'm sure he's pretty discouraged right about now. Give me wisdom, Lord. I need it...We all do."

Jatory loved the graveyard shift. It was so peaceful, most times, especially in a little town like Watson, and it gave him plenty of time to spend in conversation with Jesus. He slowed as he approached the outside corner of the main building. A scuffling caused him to halt completely. It had been very slight, but loud enough to rouse his suspicions.

Placing his hand on his gun, the young officer eased quietly up to the outer wall and pressed himself against it, waiting, and listening. In a few seconds, he heard it again. Adrenaline pumping, Jatory eased his head around just far enough to get a visual and when he saw the culprit, he almost laughed out loud.

The neighborhood mutt was obviously wanting to be let into the building. He chuckled and started toward the animal when he noticed that the dog was looking in the large window on the side door. Hearing Jatory's soft chuckle, the dog glanced in his direction and then turned his attention back to the door. He whined and scratched at it. When the door handle rattled, Jatory jumped quickly behind one of the large holly bushes, instantly regretting his choice of bushes as the sharp edges and points of the holly bush leaves punished his intrusion.

Someone was in the church!

Quietly, he unholstered his weapon and crouched, waiting for the intruder to exit the building. He tried to catch a glimpse, but the bush was too big and if he moved too much the intruder might hear him, or the mutt would give him away. He held his breath as he heard the door open and then close quietly. He could hear the slight jingle of keys. Every muscle in his lean body was tensed and ready to pounce as the intruder made their way down the walk, every step bringing them closer and closer to the bush behind which Jatory was crouched.

"Just a little closer..." He told himself... *"NOW!"*

Jatory leapt from behind the holly bush, "HOLD IT RIGHT THERE!!"

Jim made his way slowly out of the darkened sanctuary. *What time is it?* He lifted his left arm and pressed a button on the side of his watch to illuminate the ungodly hour. *Wow. 3:00 AM.* He ran a tired hand down the length of his face as he stepped out of the connecting hallway into the office lobby.

"Lord..." his voice sounded like a bullhorn in the thick silence, "I don't have to hear from You to know You're there... but it would be nice."

A scratching sound at the door startled him. Immediately, Jatory's warning about not being at the church alone darted across his mind. Jim crouched and eased over to the office door. He slowly raised his crouched body until his eyes could peep through the door's large window. With a sigh of relief and a rush of breath that he didn't realize he was holding, he stood shaking his head and laughing softly at himself. 'Booker', the stray that frequented the church, had obviously heard his impromptu prayer and was begging for some attention, and some treats.

"Hold on a sec, buddy." Jim spoke softly through the door. The mutt whined in response.

Why am I whispering?

Jim shook his head again as he walked across the midsized lobby area and grabbed a dog treat from the reception desk. He double checked his and Chad 's offices, and finding them secure, he checked his pockets for his keys and pushed open the door.

He still had an apprehensive feeling as he stooped for a moment, slipped Booker his treat and scratched the grateful dog behind his ears. He started down the walkway that would lead to the parking lot. Reaching his hand into his pocket he was pulling his keys out when...

"HOLD IT RIGHT THERE!!" Jatory leapt from behind a large holly bush next to the walkway and blocked the sidewalk, aiming his gun right at Jim's chest.

On impulse, Jim yelled, and his hands shot straight up into the air and the keys that he had been fishing out of his pocket clattered noisily to the cement sidewalk.

"Pastor Jim?" Jatory cocked his head to the side as he lowered his gun.

Jim nodded, heart racing as he lowered his hands and visibly gulped.

"Pastor Jim..." Jatory started to chuckle.

Jim smiled ruefully as he stooped to pick up his keys, "…You already said that…"

The young officer holstered his weapon. "Sorry about that, Pastor…" he was laughing now.

Jim couldn't help but laugh with him as his heart rate slowly returned to normal, and he returned his keys to his pocket.

"Oh, man…" Jatory jested, "You shoulda seen your face!"

"America's Most Wanted, right?" Jim joked as he slapped Jatory on the back. He started down the walkway toward the parking lot and Jatory fell into step beside him.

"You scared the mess outta me, I gotta tell ya…" Jim chuckled as he placed a hand over his slowing heartbeat.

Jatory laughed and agreed, "That makes two of us!" The two men shared an adrenaline induced laugh.

"Seriously, though…" Jatory continued, "If you don't mind me asking, what brings you up here at this time of the morning?"

The smile fell from Jim's face. He shoved his hands in his pockets and sighed heavily, jingling the keys and change in them, "Searching and seeking…"

Jatory nodded. His heart went out to his pastor. This man was definitely being pressed.

"Anymore leads on what happened at Summer's place?" the pastor asked.

Jatory shook his head and glanced at the parking lot as the stepped onto the blacktop, "Not officially."

"What does that mean?"

He looked at Jim, "It means I have my own ideas and suspects."

"Now, I don't want you getting yourself in trouble at work, Jatory." Jim cautioned, "Didn't you tell me that they had turned the case over to investigations?"

Jastory nodded, "Yes, sir, they did. But there are some things I can still check out and not get into *too* much trouble." He didn't want Pastor Jim to know that he had already been chastised by his sergeant and had received a warning that he would be written up if he didn't let it go. This case was personal, and investigations had ruled out a connection between the arson and the break in at the church. Jatory knew in his spirit that it was more than 'strange coincidence'.

Jim eyed him suspiciously but took him at his word. He had never been in law enforcement, but he was pretty sure that when you were told to back off, it meant just that.

Jatory scanned the parking lot for the pastor's car. Not finding it he asked, "Where's your Crown Vic, Pastor?"

"At home." Jim replied.

"You didn't walk over here, did you?" Jatory was uneasy.

Jim nodded, "Sure did."

"Pastor, it's one thing to be locked in tight in a building, but I just don't think it's wise to put yourself out there like a sitting duck. There's somebody out there who wants to get your attention... in not so nice way."

Jim stopped and looked at Jatory. "Jatory, I can't live my life in fear. Fear is not from God and I won't receive it."

"No offense, Pastor, but that's not fear...That's common sense."

"None taken. And there are a lot of things that have to do with the Spirit that don't make good sense, but that doesn't negate the validity of it. I'm not asking you to understand, but I refuse to be a prisoner in my own home *or* my church simply because I am under attack." He started walking again, "if I allow that to happen, then I am allowing the enemy of my soul to have a foothold in my life. Not only will it cripple this ministry," he waved his hand in the direction of the church, "but it will cripple *me* as well."

Jatory's respect for this crazy man deepened.

Jim stopped as they reached the edge of the black top across the road from the pastorium. "You know, shepherds are pretty much painted as meek, docile fellas. But the truth of it is, in the Word, you had to be a pretty tough guy to be a shepherd. There was no telling what you might encounter on the plains of northern Africa and Arabia. The shepherd had to be watchful and ready to defend his flock against wild dogs...bears...sometimes even lions. Imagine what would have happened to his flock had he allowed fear to keep him within the confines of his comfort zone...fearful of what might lurk in the bushes..." He pierced Jatory with his eyes, "Do you understand what I'm saying to you?"

Jatory smiled, "Yes, sir...You're saying that you're walking yourself home and no amount of discussion is changing that."

Jim chuckled and clapped his hand onto Jatory's shoulder, "Yep...Among other things." He extended other hand and Jatory clasped it in his own. "You have a good night...er...morning...and be safe."

"You do the same, Pastor Jim."

Across the parking lot, in the tree line, two pairs of young eyes strained to see what was going on. The one in charge was waiting for the moment when that nosey cop would get lost. He watched as the preacher and the cop shook hands and then the cop started back across the parking lot, scanning the perimeter. He was confident in their hiding place. They had been extremely careful not to be seen. He glanced at his accomplice who was beginning to look a little sick.

"Don't you wimp out on me, man..." He whispered tersely.

His companion cut his eyes at him but didn't say a word.

He was beginning to think it was a mistake to trust this kid. Oh well. It was too late now. That old man was going to be sorry he ever messed with him. All he had to do was plant some evidence and then he would be out of state and out of the picture...and that stupid old man would be left holding the bag.

The cop scanned the perimeter one last time and then got in his car.

Will this jerk ever leave?

Finally, the car slipped into gear and pulled out of the parking lot slowly, shining its spotlight into the tree line. The intruders dropped silently to their stomachs as the light passed over them slowly and then disappeared. As the car accelerated down the road, the leader stood to a crouched position and left his hiding place. The other remained.

"What are you doing? C'mon!" He demanded in a whisper.

His companion shook his head, "I can't do this..."

"What? You suddenly got a conscience? Didn't bother you before..." he mocked.

"Hey, I didn't have anything to do with what you did before!"

"Oh really? You better watch your step, kid. You don't know who you're messing with." He threatened.

"Oh yeah?" The boy said, "I'll go to the cops about

everything! You don't know who *you're* messing with!" He stood to his feet with a bravado he didn't feel.

"I've been patient with you, but don't push me, you little *shit*. I ain't attached to nobody... *Nobody*. You walk away now, and I'll find you...and then *NO ONE* will find you."

David's eyes grew wide, and his heart raced. Chad had been right about Robbie...but he was all alone, now...and scared. His mind raced...

God. Jesus. He was a superhero...Chad said to give Him a chance...

Suddenly, a warmth flooded his soul and filled him with a resolve and a strength that he had never known.

"Well, I'll be easy to find cuz I won't be hiding. The Bible says that no weapon that comes at me will prosper..."

Robbie interrupted and teased him in a sing-song way, "The Bible says, the Bible says...HA! Are you serious?" He shoved David to the ground, "Your precious Bible didn't keep that from 'prospering', did it?" He kicked the boy in the ribs, "...or that!"

David wrapped his arms around himself and sucked in sharply from the force of the blow. It was hard to breathe. "I believe..." he gasped desperately, "...in God...not the Bible to protect me..."

"We'll just see how much your *GOD* actually cares

about a stupid piece of shit like you..." Robbie snarled as he reached down and snatched David to his feet, ignoring the cry of pain that escaped the younger boy. He reared back and formed a fist to pummel this stupid, ungrateful kid.

Davis squeezed his eyes shut and held his head high. If this jerk was gonna hit him, he was going to give him a good target. Seemed to David that he deserved a good beating, anyway, for how stupid he had been.

"I believe You, God...I believe You..." he gasped in between ragged, painful breaths.

"SHUT UP!" Robbie roared.

He was disgusted. Christians were so weak-minded. He determined to put every ounce of hatred and disdain he had for the 'so-called' Christian faith into this beating. If that wouldn't prove to this kid that his 'god' wasn't real, then he would personally pummel him until he regretted ever admitting that he was a 'Christian', and he didn't care if he was breathing after.

Robbie decided that he was going to enjoy this...a lot.

He swung with every memory of hatred and judgment and abandonment that he had experienced from this stupid religion...every ounce of disgust and rage that he had in his body.

Then something happened.

For the first time in his life, David felt the warmth and

love of an unseen force physically wrap itself around his body and embrace him. He remained like that...eyes squeezed shut, chin jutted out...waiting for the blows to come...but the blows never came.

Robbie couldn't believe his eyes....Didn't *want* to believe his eyes...

First there was David...and then instantly, there was a blindingly bright light surrounding the kid. As if the light wasn't spooky enough, when the glowing man standing behind the stupid little punk grabbed his fist and stopped him...

Robbie fled, a million questions screaming through his mind.

David risked cracking one eye open...and then the other, as he watched Robbie hightailing it across the parking lot away from the church.

In pain and amazed, oblivious to what had actually happened, David only knew that Jesus had been there. He had felt Him. He grinned into the night sky, "Thanks, Big Guy."

Across the road, Jim made his way up the back steps of the pastorium. The back door was much quieter than the front and he didn't want to wake Barb.

He prayed as he reached for the handle on the back porch screen door, "Lord...If You could just point us in the right direction…"

"SHUT UP!"

The sound echoed through the otherwise silent night.

Jim's head shot up and he made his way back around to the front of the house. That was at the church! He picked up his pace and started to jog. As he rounded the corner, he stopped as he saw three figures in the back of the parking lot…and one of them was glowing! The hair stood up all over his body and he broke into a dead run. As fast as the glowing figure had appeared, it vanished and one of the figures bolted. He picked up speed and as he grew nearer he recognized David.

"David!" He gasped as he approached, out of breath from the run. He reached for the boy.

David gasped in pain as Jim grabbed him and he turned the teen to face him.

"What happened?" Jim huffed.

David looked into Jim's eyes and when their eyes met, Jim Dalton knew that *GOD. HAD. HEARD.*

SKELETON KEY

EPILOGUE

Excerpt from Book #2: Redemption Key

Caroline breathed a grateful and contented sigh as she turned and gazed upon the object of her praise. His tousled sandy-blonde hair fell across his chiseled features and the rhythmic breathing and soft snores brought her so much happiness. Her heart exploded with emotion as she turned carefully onto her side and watched him sleeping there, beside her in the light of the dying fire.

Caroline Waters.

She had expected to feel a deep sorrow as she said a final goodbye to her beloved William, but oddly, she felt joy and she felt complete and utter fulfillment.

Their wedding had been so different than her first one…a stately oak beside a babbling creek rather than a church with pews…Grandmother and the tribal chief blessing them rather than a preacher in a suit…but it was every bit as sacred and joyous.

Tenderly, she traced the strong line of his jaw with her fingers, relishing the knowledge that this man belonged to her alone. This man, that had revived her dead heart. This man that had been so patient with her pain…Tears sprang to her eyes, and she leaned over and gently brushed a tender kiss across his sleeping lips as she carefully moved to get up. She chuckled to herself when he didn't even move.

This man sleeps like a felled tree.

Quietly, Caroline slipped her dress over her head and tied the leather belt around her waist. Her hands lingered for a moment on her abdomen. She blushed as she wondered about the possibility of a child. Would God bless her again? She prayed that He would.

Smoothing her long honey colored hair into a single braid, she bent to untie the tent door. The morning sun caressed her face and skin deliciously and the sweet aroma of new life greeted her as she stepped out, straightened and stretched blissfully.

The slight breeze carried with it the muffled sound of voices and Caroline turned her head to see who the wind was tattling on. Unable to make out the voices, she sighed happily and dismissed them as she made her way to Little Wolf and Kalana's tent to gather Willie. They had offered to let him stay a few nights so the newlyweds could have some privacy. A shy blush crept up her neck and she smiled to herself as she toyed with a loose tendril of hair. Her heart sighed as she remembered the wonder and preciousness of their first night together.

As she grew nearer, the voices became more pronounced. There was something oddly familiar about one of them, and she stopped in her tracks. She had heard that voice a thousand times in her dreams…She would know it anywhere…

Caroline's heart jumped in her chest and her hands flew to her throat....*WILLIAM*...

ABOUT THE AUTHOR

Nicki Harris is an author, musician, singer-songwriter, and filmmaker from Jackson, GA. A busy wife and mom of six, she has a passion for living authentically even when it lands her solidly in the black sheep category. A self-proclaimed gypsy soul, she loves traveling, making music, and spending time with her family on the lake, where they live.

Made in the USA
Columbia, SC
06 June 2025